Duets™

Two brand-new stories in every volume... twice a month!

Duets Vol. #69

Popular Barbara Daly serves up a delightful Double Duets this month featuring the smart, sexy, sassy Sumner sisters, Faith and Charity. The *Telegraph Herald* says this about Barbara's books. Look for "...a delicious blend of humor, seduction and romance as refreshing as a day in New England."

Duets Vol. #70

Cheryl Anne Porter returns with the second book in her humorous miniseries A FUNNY THING HAPPENED ON THE WAY TO THE DELIVERY ROOM. This talented writer always delivers "a funny ride— a roller coaster of fun and adventure." Joining her is Silhouette author Kate Thomas with a neat premise. What does an overburdened working woman need these days? A stay-at-home "wife!"— in the form of the sexy, ever helpful hero!

Be sure to pick up both Duets volumes today!

You Call *This* Romance!?

"I'm under a good bit of stress," *Faith confessed.*

It occurred to her that she could talk about her stress to Cabot and at the same time take the first step toward her goal of seduction.

He nodded, a font of wisdom in a navy blazer. "You've lost so many jobs, you expect to lose this one. But don't worry. I'm going to give you great references."

She was touched. "Even after all the mistakes I've made? That's sweet."

"Downright noble, I'd say." A smile twitched at his lips, then disappeared. "You're good at this job. You need a little self-confidence, that's all."

"And brake shoes." Self-confidence was all very well, but it didn't pay the rent.

His brow furrowed. "What?"

"And tires." But the job, the brake shoes and the tires were putting less stress on her at the present time than Cabot himself. She needed to get him into a loverly mood. Arouse him. Steer the conversation in a different direction...if she could just figure out where the oars were.

For more, turn to page 9

Are You for Real?

What was Charity's fantasy?

Jason wondered. Would she return to bed in black lace that he could peel off, or naked with a couple of fans strategically placed...?

At last he heard the soft pad of bare feet, and felt her slide down beside him. He put a hand on her shoulder, expecting silky skin and finding... flannel. He ran his hand down her arm, down her side. Flannel. Head-to-toe flannel.

"I hope you don't mind," she whispered. "I'm a little self-conscious about my body." She nuzzled her mouth into his throat in a distinctly unflannel-nightgown way.

He wanted to shout, "Okay! Fine! Whatever!" but he just said, "Mmm," already searching for a point of entry in the seemingly impenetrable fortress of a gown. He wanted to cry out with pure joy when he discovered buttons down the front. Now if only she wasn't—and he wouldn't put it past her—wearing a chastity belt.

At the moment, he was sure he could break the lock with his teeth.

For more, turn to page 197

HARLEQUIN DUETS

ISBN 0-373-44135-5

Copyright in the collection:
Copyright © 2002 by Harlequin Books S.A.

The publisher acknowledges the copyright holder
of the individual works as follows:

YOU CALL *THIS* ROMANCE!?
Copyright © 2002 by Barbara Daly

ARE YOU FOR REAL?
Copyright © 2002 by Barbara Daly

You Call
This Romance!?

BARBARA
DALY

TORONTO • NEW YORK • LONDON
AMSTERDAM • PARIS • SYDNEY • HAMBURG
STOCKHOLM • ATHENS • TOKYO • MILAN • MADRID
PRAGUE • WARSAW • BUDAPEST • AUCKLAND

Dear Reader,

Do you have a sister? I'm so envious if you do!
Growing up an only child, I was always fascinated by
the relationships among sisters. I observed that they
seemed to divide up the personality traits, and the
oldest got first choice. If she chose to be "the smart
one," the next sister was "the pretty one." If a third
sister came along, she might be "the artistic one," or
"the athletic one." Or, of course, "the wild one." I knew
of one sad case in which the older sister was "my sweet
baby" and the younger, "the other one."

Since I couldn't have sisters of my own, I simply had
to invent some. The Sumner sisters, Faith, Hope and
Charity, divvied up the personality traits all right, but
not according to any of the current literature on birth
order! Hope's the middle child, but she's always been
the leader. (For the story of her tumble into love, read
A Long Hot Christmas, Harlequin Temptation, December
2001.) Now, with Valentine's Day approaching, it's
hearts and flowers for Faith and Charity and two
romantic stories from me to you.

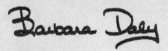

Barbara Daly

Books by Barbara Daly

HARLEQUIN DUETS
13—GREAT GENES!
34—NEVER SAY NEVER!

HARLEQUIN TEMPTATION
859—A LONG HOT CHRISTMAS

To David Ernstmeyer and Kate Carpenter,
my heartfelt thanks for taking care of my kids
when they got too old to listen to me.

1

CABOT DRENNAN STARED at the woman across the wrought-iron table from him. She meant more to him than anyone else in the world at this particular moment in his life. She meant what Charlie McCarthy meant to Edgar Bergen all those long years ago, what Judy Garland meant to the Metro Goldwyn Mayer studio, what Groucho meant to the Marx Brothers, what Larry and Curly meant to Moe.

Tippy Temple—blond, beautiful, angelic, today's supporting actress and with Cabot's expert advice and assistance, tomorrow's biggest box-office hit—was hysterical.

"I'm gonna kill 'im, Cabot," she screamed, her exquisite mouth twisted into something downright ugly. "That..." From that mouth came a string of expletives that sent chills up Cabot's spine—chills of fear that the neighbors might be listening. "He can't do that to me. He promised!" She burst into tears.

Cabot watched in despair. These were not the pretty tears that had run down her pristine face in *A Kiss to Build a Dream On*. They were tears of the purest, most vindictive rage.

One thing you could say about Tippy. She was a damned fine actress.

The tears ceased abruptly as Tippy reached for a cigarette. "I'm gonna call home and get a contract put out on him," she said. "I'm gonna tell 'em to kill him slow, cut off his..."

"Tippy!"

"...toes one at a time and then his... What?" Sulkily she blew a stream of smoke through the nostrils of her perfect nose.

"There's nothing we can do to Josh Barnett," he said, struggling for a calm he himself did not feel. These were his hopes and dreams going up in smoke, as it were. "Josh agreed to marry you for the publicity, and he's backed out on us. It was his right. It's not like money changed hands, or we signed a—" Thinking it over, Cabot decided not to bring up the word *contract* again. "—a legal document."

Tippy's face contorted again. "He did more than back out, that..."

Cabot winced as another string of expletives bristled through the smoke. He'd had no idea there were so many pejorative phrases in the English language. "He eloped with Kathy, that..." Now the adjectives turned on Kathy Simpson, the star who'd beaten Tippy out for the lead in *Kiss* and now, it seemed, had stolen the co-star, Josh, as well. Tippy's scowl deepened. "I'm gonna get her taken out, too, that..."

"Tippy, we must be calm and think this over."

"Oh," she said with a sudden breeziness, "I don't need to think it over. I know exactly how I want it done. I'll have the mob asphyxiate her with hair spray."

Cabot closed his eyes. "That's not what I meant.

What I meant was, we need to think what to do next. I've already scheduled the chapel, the flowers, the reception. All we need is a groom.''

She threw her slender, golden arms up in the air. ''Well, ain't that just great. All we need's a groom. Yeah, sure. So whadda you gonna do? Tour the agencies? Ask 'em, 'Hey, who'll marry Tippy? Anybody'll do.' You think that won't get around in a New York minute?''

Tippy also surprised him occasionally with her intelligence, which was hard to see through the smoke. ''Of course not,'' he said, although that possibility had been going through his mind. ''If Josh leaks the news to anybody, we'll spread the word that you ditched him for...for...somebody else,'' he finished lamely.

''Who?''

''That is the question,'' he admitted.

He was unnerved to see that she was gazing at him speculatively. She stubbed out her cigarette, reached for a stick of gum, chewed it vigorously, pursed her full, sweetly bruised mouth and blew a bubble, all the while gazing at him with those big blue eyes.

''I'll give it some thought,'' he said hurriedly. ''While I'm thinking, I'll move right ahead with the honeymoon plans. You just relax, calm down, don't spend another minute worrying about it. Leave it all up to me.''

She took the gum out of her mouth and deposited it in a tissue. The big blue eyes filled with tears in a way that made her look like the on-screen Tippy again. ''I really had hopes for Josh and me,'' she said in a soft, wistful voice that carried not a hint of Brooklyn in it. "I thought maybe we'd fall in love for real, live happily ever after just like in the fairy tales. But Kathy won, on-screen and off, and my heart is b-b-broken." She burst into the most beautiful sobs he'd ever heard.

FLYING DOWN THE FREEWAY in his powerful sports car, he pondered what he was going to do now. Tippy Temple had talent, looks, a frightening determination, everything it took to succeed. From that point on it was up to him, her publicist, to see that she did succeed. There was *nothing* he wouldn't do to move her toward stardom. And his career would take off along with hers. Just one big star would make him among the most sought-after publicists in the film industry.

He needed that.

So he had a little challenge here. Josh Barnett, Hollywood's latest heartthrob, had backed out, had eloped with an actress who'd already made it, figuring Kathy could do more for his screen career than Tippy could. Or maybe Josh had actually fallen in love with Kathy Simpson during the making of *Kiss*. It happened sometimes. Cabot growled softly. Forget love. He had to be thinking about who was going to marry Tippy.

Did the "who" really matter? Wasn't the wedding what it was all about? Tippy saying her vows while every local television station filmed her, the video of her splashy honeymoon picked up by the national film news programs, Tippy's declarations of happiness alongside the photographs in *Variety*. It was *all* about

Tippy getting married. Who cared who the groom was?

Might as well be…

Aw, no. I don't want to. But who else am I going to get? He thought and thought. In the old days the Hollywood studios took care of arranging marriages, dates, even children for their stars. Now the job was up to publicity agents like him. He chewed his lower lip and thought some more. Tippy was right. He couldn't go after an endless number of groom prospects without the word getting out that her marriage was nothing more than a publicity stunt. This town fed on gossip—a low-fat, low-carb, high-energy diet. That's why everybody was so thin.

There was only one answer, and Tippy had figured it out faster than he had. He'd already compromised his principles by dreaming up this sham marriage as a way of boosting Tippy to stardom. What would one more compromise matter?

A lot, that's what. He wouldn't do it.

Unless he had to.

PALM FRONDS RUSTLED in the gentle breeze, making drowsy whishing sounds. The sand gleamed golden, warming her feet as she stepped dreamily toward an ocean of everchanging green and blue, white tipped, frothy and enticing as a key-lime pie.

"Faith?"

Her loose, lacy white shirt slipped down her tanned shoulders as she neared the shore, and with an impatient gesture she flung it to the sand, longing for the touch of the sun-warmed water against her desire-heated skin. She...

"Faith Sumner!"

...walked straight into the Caribbean and drowned.

"What!" said Faith as the palm trees folded. "Oh, Mr. Wycoff! Was there something you wanted?"

"A travel agent. That's what I wanted, Miss Sumner. Not Sleeping Beauty."

"Why, thank you," Faith said, feeling herself blush a little, "but I was certainly not sleeping. I was concentrating intently on the many details of Mr. and Mrs. Mulden's trip to the Cayman Islands. There are, as you know, *many* details, *numerous, important* details to fill in." *Don't apologize,* her younger sister Hope had told her. *Be assertive.*

"You were obviously daydreaming," said Mr. Wycoff, looking down his stubby nose at her, "and the Muldens are expecting you to have finalized these *many, numerous, important* details by five this afternoon."

"And that's exactly what I will have done," said Faith. Whirling to the computer, she saw the screen saver her youngest sister Charity had custom-designed for her. Words moved across the monitor in waves: *Focus, Faith. Focus, Faith.* She wiggled the mouse and was thrilled to see that it *was* the Muldens' file that appeared on the screen. "Hotel confirmation number," she murmured, stabbing at the keyboard. Mr. Wycoff strode back to his private office. "Bicycle rental confirmation number. Boat trip to..."

He waited for her on the shore, his legs apart and

his arms folded over his chest, his darkly tanned body massive and virile in snug black swim briefs that left no doubt that his desire equaled, even surmounted, hers. She moved toward him slowly, the saltwater sliding off her slickly oiled skin in sheets, and his gaze roamed her shamelessly, bringing a hot flush to her face and a tingling sensation between her thighs that intensified with every step. They were face to face. She reached into the waiting picnic basket and pulled out the cut-glass dish filled with luscious tropical fruit.

Fresh pineapple, dripping golden juice, slippery wedges of deliciously scented mango, long, thin slices of papaya garnished with slivers of fresh lime and mint leaves.

"A bite of pineapple," she murmured, "to cool off those hot eyes of yours."

"Nothing beats a great pineapple, but not now."

Faith shrieked, leaped straight up from her chair and spun to face the man she'd just been fantasizing about on the beach.

Except they weren't on a beach. They were in the bright white environment of Wycoff Worldwide Travel Agency—*"We make your dreams come true"*—in the Westwood area of Los Angeles, surrounded by the hum of telephones, computer beeps and the voices of the four other Wycoff agents and their clients.

There were a few minor differences in the man himself. For one thing, he was wearing a three-piece suit, not a small, tight black swimsuit. For another, she wouldn't exactly describe his gaze as "hot with passion." "Hot with annoyance" was more like it.

"I'm sorry," she said, trying to organize her hair, her skirt, her blue silk sweater set and her mind all at the same time as she collapsed back into her desk chair. "I guess I was, um—" Might as well use the same line on him that had more-or-less worked with Mr. Wycoff. "—was concentrating so hard on my work that I didn't see you come in."

He wasn't buying it. "Annoyance" was no longer sufficient to describe his mood. He looked like a bomb on a short fuse. Except for those things, he was identical to the man on the beach—big, dark haired, tanned, more or less drop-dead gorgeous. Just looking at his scowling face was reawakening the bothersome tingle.

This was no time to tingle. It was time to focus, and focusing on him would not exactly be painful.

"Please sit down. How may I help you?"

He sat down hard in the chair beside her desk, simultaneously handing her a card he'd fished out of the breast pocket of his suit coat. "You can plan a honeymoon for my client," he said as if he would rather be tied to a stake and surrounded by dry firewood than planning a honeymoon.

Faith had to wrench her gaze away from his mouth in order to glance at the card. His lower lip was so full and curved so sensuously he should have been wearing a fig leaf over it. "'Cabot Drennan,'" she murmured, "'Publicist to the Stars.' Oh, my goodness, what an exciting job. Well, Cabot..." Mr. Wycoff said to go straight for first names, unless you were talking to *him*. "There's nothing I enjoy more than planning honeymoons. In fact, honeymoons are my specialty." That wasn't quite the truth, but it was the direction she intended to go in and she'd been doing a lot of research on her own time—and quite a bit more on Mr. Wycoff's. "What sort of location were you thinking of?" Her own dream honeymoon havens began flitting through her mind.

"Someplace with good light and a dependable electrical system."

She blinked. "And an air of romance, I would imagine," she said hopefully. "Have you considered the Cayman Islands?" It would be so efficient to send this client honeymooning right along with the Muldens.

"How's the phone system there?"

Faith slid her gaze down from his close-cropped head of black hair to his chocolate-brown eyes. "Well, I've been online with many of the hotels there this week, but I don't suppose that makes me an authority on the subject. There's Rio de Janeiro," she said, warming to her task. "What could be more romantic?"

"Too far."

"Mexico, then. It's closer to L.A., if your client is concerned about being too far from home, and the coastal towns have some lovely resorts with absolutely private bungalows, perfect for a…"

"Privacy is the last thing she wants."

Odder and odder. "Has she considered a cruise?"

"You're trapped on a cruise." A muscle twitched tensely in his cheek.

"She's already trapped, in a manner of speaking," Faith said earnestly. "Once she promises to have and to hold, in sickness or in…"

His face reddened with impatience. "I didn't come here for a lecture on family values."

"How about the coast of Maine?"

"Too cold. She'll have goose bumps in the photos."

"Oh. Of course. She'll want to take a lot of pictures for her memory book."

He heaved a deep sigh. "She's an up-and-coming young actress." For a moment his eyes shifted left and he seemed uncomfortable. "I'll be taking a crew along to make a video of the honeymoon."

"A video? You're going to film this woman's honeymoon?"

"Yes."

Faith straightened, locked her knees tightly together and pursed her lips. "Well. I'm very sorry," she said, "but we at Wycoff Worldwide wouldn't consider being a party to that kind of film. I'm afraid you will have to look elsewhere for travel assistance."

He half rose from the chair. As big as he was, it scared Faith a little, but she stiffened her backbone. Standards were standards, and she was not going to make the arrangements for a porn flick.

"I don't intend to film *that* part of the honeymoon, for God's sake," he said in a deep growl that thinned out his sexy lower lip until it was nearly normal.

"In that case," she squeaked, "we at Wycoff are happy to assist you."

He sat down again, his lower lip relaxed, and Faith was faced with a whole new issue, most of it going on below the waistband of her flowered silk skirt.

"Look—" He stared at her left breast.

Feel free to touch the display. But he wasn't actually looking at her breast. He was looking at the rectangular silver pin just above her left breast, the one with her name on it.

"—Faith, this is a fairly simple thing I'm asking you to do. I want you to make the arrangements for a honeymoon in an accessible location with top-flight technological services—" he halted for a moment, looking thoughtful "—and dependable beauticians and manicurists—" he paused again "—and it has to be a well-known honeymoon spot." His glower returned.

Faith swiveled her chair a little to face him more fully, just as she'd learned to do in People Skills, the only course in the Travel Agent program she hadn't daydreamed her way through. But the instructor hadn't mentioned what to do if, when her knees brushed the client's, it sent a shot of electricity through her entire body. As though he'd felt it too, his gaze briefly melted over her.

"I'm sure I can make your dreams come true," she murmured. "I mean, her dreams."

He snorted. "But can you make the reservations?"

Faith took a deep breath, gave herself the condensed version of her sister Hope's lecture on presenting herself positively and said, "Of course. First we'll find the location of her dreams. That may take a little research."

"Time is money. You never have enough of either one."

He had a way with words. "Tomorrow," she said. "By tomorrow I'll be able to offer you a choice of desirable locations and we'll proceed from there."

"Today would be better."

Today she had to get the Cayman Islands organized to receive the Muldens. "I'll do my best," she promised.

"I was thinking Reno."

She stared at him blankly. "It's certainly well-known as a spot for quick marriages," she said. "Is this a quick marriage? Oh, dear," she said at once, "I didn't mean that the way it sounded. I was just thinking how many truly romantic places there were and wondering…"

"The hotel is your problem, not the romance." If anything, he looked even grimmer and less romantic than he had before. "The thing about Reno," he went on, "is it's close and it's got all those hokey round beds and pink rooms and AC current."

"It does have those advantages." She felt deeply disappointed in him. A publicist who looked like a romantic fantasy should be able to rise above Reno, or even Niagara Falls. Not that Reno wasn't a lot of fun and the Falls weren't fantastic, but you only got one honeymoon, and it ought to be…

"I sense you don't approve."

Faith jolted in her chair. "My job is to send her where she wants to go," she assured him, "not to approve or disapprove."

"So make it Reno," he said. "Tippy will be crazy about Reno."

"Tippy?" Faith said, and then it hit her. "You're not talking about Tippy Temple."

For a moment he looked uncomfortable. "Yes. You've heard of her?"

"I saw her interview on the Scott Trent Show and liked her so much I rented her movie." Faith felt breathless as she lapsed into a reverie about the romantic film she'd watched last weekend.

"Her first big movie, I think," she said. "*A Kiss to Build a Dream On.* She may not have been the lead, but she was the star as far as I'm concerned." She sighed. "She's beautiful, and so sweet. Oh, the way she gave up Josh Barnett to the heroine, what's-her-name, was the most touching, the most *heroic* act. I'm so happy she's found her true love in real life." She focused her gaze on Cabot. "May I ask, would it be too personal a question, who she's marrying?"

In the silence, she watched a variety of expressions cross Cabot's face. His eyes widened, then narrowed as he chewed on his lower lip, and at last he settled for lines of grim resignation.

"Me," he said.

2

THERE IT WAS. He'd made his decision, sitting across from the cutest little woman he'd ever met, looking into her gray eyes and realizing it was time to fish or cut bait.

Maybe he wasn't so much cutting bait as cutting off the light of sudden attraction he'd seen and recognized in those eyes, and responded to in a big way. Cute little persons weren't on his agenda right now. Little stars who deserved to be big stars were. When he had a stable of successful clients, he'd be free to look for the kind of woman he'd like to spend the rest of his life with, the kind of woman…

The kind of woman who'd lose that light of sudden attraction the second she heard he was already spoken for. That's what Faith Sumner had done. The dreamy quality of her gaze was gone, replaced by a look as severely professional as he guessed a butterfly like Faith could manage.

FAITH DIDN'T REALIZE she'd been daydreaming about honeymooning herself with Cabot Drennan until he hit her with the news that he was the lucky man who was marrying Tippy Temple. That ended the never-fully-realized daydream.

However gorgeous he was, however beautifully he personified the man she would someday love and be cherished by, she had to give up this particular man forever. Even in her dreams. She could never deprive someone as lovely as Tippy Temple of the man of her dreams.

Or the honeymoon of her dreams.

So she relinquished her own happiness. Her heartbreak would be brief, since her daydream hadn't lasted long. She faced Cabot Drennan squarely and said, "Tippy is not going to want to honeymoon in Reno. She'll want to go to the most romantic place in the world. Paris. Venice off-season, or a private villa on the coast of—"

"My cell phone won't work in Europe."

Faith gazed at him for a long, long moment. "An isolated lodge in the Rockies?"

"No."

She leaned toward him a bit. "A tiny bed-and-breakfast in Vermont?"

"No."

"In Napa Valley?"

"No."

Her voice hardened. "A private car on a coast-to-coast train."

"No."

"Williamsburg, Virginia? You can live out your fantasies in Colonial costume."

He gave her a look of scorn. "No."

"Rent San Simeon—you know, the Hearst estate about halfway up the coast? It's a national park, but I think you can rent the bungalows."

He showed his first flicker of interest. "Hmm. Phone, electricity. We could bring in the hairdressers and manicurists and all the other paraphernalia. Rent another bungalow for the crew. Yeah. Find out how much it costs."

Feeling hopeful, Faith spun to her computer. Charity had been one of those kids who taught the rest of the family how to use their first computer. Thanks to her coaching—bullying was more like it—Faith was fairly computer-literate. In a few minutes she had her answer.

"No," Cabot said when he heard the price.

Thoroughly frustrated, Faith collapsed back against her chair. "All right, I'll get to work on accommodations in Reno, but please do this one thing for me?"

His expression said he'd done all he could just by sitting there listening to her ridiculous suggestions.

"Talk to Tippy about this first." Faith was sure the angelic Tippy would have a fit, an angelic fit, of course, about going to Reno, and Cabot would be back, humble and subdued, to take a look at that little bed-and-breakfast in Vermont or the isolated lodge in the Rockies.

"Of course. Then we're through for now?"

Unfortunately. "Yes."

"You'll get right to work on it. You won't wait for Tippy's answer."

"No," Faith lied. Of course she would. And while she waited, she'd finish up the Muldens' arrangements.

"I'll call you early tomorrow morning."

"How early?" Again the look on his face stopped

her. Wordlessly she handed him her business card, which listed her office number, home number, cell phone number, pager number and e-mail address. She was grateful Wycoff printed cards for its agents. She'd never be able to memorize all those numbers.

He took the card, got up and started for the door. Faith watched his every movement, the stride of his long legs, the roll of his broad shoulders, the way his hand wrenched at the door handle. She got up to follow his progress across the street, where he swung smoothly into some sort of small, gleaming silver sports car. He looked terrific in sunglasses.

She stood at the window for a long, long moment, unable to keep herself from resuming her daydream of that tall, dark, domineering man turning into so much custard in her hands. Melting under her touch, while she slyly hid the fact that she was melting too, turning into a river of—

"Faith…" It was Mr. Wycoff right behind her, issuing a warning.

"Yes, sir," Faith said, whirling, "the Muldens. By five."

She'd just reached her desk when the telephone rang. She heard the scratchy static, the fade-in, fade-out sounds of a car phone. "You forgot to ask me when," the voice said.

"Cabot?" She knew it was Cabot because the bottom sort of dropped out of her stomach, and she could feel the flush climbing her cheeks, prickling up into her scalp.

"How can you make reservations when you don't know when the honeymoon is?"

"Well, of course there are the preliminary steps, the general approach, the data-gathering—what are the best hotels and so on and so on." She was gesturing a lot, she noticed, which wasn't going to help make her point over the phone.

"Bull. You forgot to ask. We're getting married on the Fourth of July. Independence Day. You see the irony."

"Yes," Faith said faintly.

"And there's also the fireworks connection. Ought to make good copy." His voice picked up speed. "Less than six months between now and then. I've got a lot to do and I have to know where I'm doing it. So get going."

He hung up. Faith sat still for a moment, feeling stunned. Good copy? Electricity? Lighting? Were these things a man should be thinking about when he was marrying a lovely, sweet-as-she-was-pretty starlet like Tippy Temple? The one thing Faith knew was that Cabot Drennan was in for a hot honeymoon. But that would make good copy, too.

Focus, Faith. Focus, Faith, Focus...

"Okay, okay," she muttered to the screen saver, and with considerable effort, turned her mind toward scuba-diving gear for the Muldens.

FIFTEEN MINUTES LATER, Cabot was back at the house Tippy had rented in the chic Bel Air district, sitting beside her at the pool. At high noon on a perfect Southern California January day, she was turning Nordic-golden before his very eyes while he sweated in his three-piece suit.

"Reno! Awesome! I feel better already," Tippy said, popping her chewing gum at him. "Get us one of those honeymoon suites with a round bed, okay? And a Jacuzzi. I'll look great in a Jacuzzi."

Tippy kept her weight down to nothing by smoking and kept her cigarette count down by chewing bubblegum in between cigarettes. Just now one of her all-time biggest and best bubbles practically obscured her slim, lovely face. Cabot steeled himself for the eventual...

Pop! "The arrangements are underway," he said. "I'll keep you posted."

"Gr-r-eat," Tippy said. Her lower lip began to tremble. "An' I really appreciate you bein' willin' to marry me, after that...that..." Tears welled up.

"Don't cry, Tippy," Cabot said, thinking, *Don't start up with the swearing!* "It's my pleasure. I mean, what's a publicist for?"

One huge droplet slid down her flawless skin as she gazed at him earnestly. "This is going to work for me, isn't it, Cabot? The publicity? Just a little publicity is all I need, right?"

"Jack and I are sure of it," he told her, feeling more kindly toward her. Her agent, Jack Langley, had hired him to promote her to the top ranks and Cabot was determined to do it. She deserved a break, this kid from Brooklyn with no connections. So did he, for that matter, a kid from Hollywood with no connections beyond the ones he'd worked his butt off for. And he wasn't going to let his conscience get in a twist about this thing he'd agreed to do. Whatever

Tippy's private faults, she was, damn it, a good actress.

He felt a smile curving his lips. Good enough to fool that travel agent, Faith Sumner. He'd spotted her from the front door of the agency and had known at once she was the right agent for the job. With her head obviously full of dreams, she'd never figure out that this marriage was made in a publicist's office, not heaven.

She was a pretty little thing. He kept thinking of her as being little. She was about five-five, he'd guess, but with all that curly blond hair floating around her face—hair a lot like Tippy's, actually—and the fluttery way she had about her, she seemed smaller than her size and could easily pass for eighteen.

Her gray eyes were like dark pearls.

Back on track, Drennan. "Tippy," he said gravely, "you do understand we have to keep this quiet."

"Oh, yeah, sure."

He hoped she said "I do" and not "Shoo-uh" when they made their vows. "We can't let anybody figure out this is just a publicity stunt."

"I unnerstan' poifectly, Cabot." Tippy switched from gum to tobacco. "We're in love and we're gonna get married."

Right. Here he was, getting married to a woman he felt sort of protective toward and that was it. And he was doing it entirely to get her name, and his, in the papers. And he figured if the marriage didn't do the trick, the not-so-discreet divorce would.

He fanned the smoke away from his face. "I went to a low-key travel agency in Westwood," he explained. "They'll be less likely to figure it out than one of the agencies around here, and even if they figure it out, less likely to talk."

She turned huge blue eyes on him. No longer wet, now they were calculating. "Low-key? Are you sure they can do it up classy-like?"

"I'll see to it that they do."

"Maybe we ought to do a dry run."

"A what?"

"You know. Rehearse the honeymoon. Go see what this low-key agency set up for us. Take the crew along. Finalize a script for the video. Work on the lighting. Try out the bed. Find me a psychiatrist. See if there's a good pastrami sandwich anywhere. Check out the Chinese restaurants." She stubbed out her cigarette and reached for a fresh pack of bubblegum.

He was startled, as always when Tippy's hardheaded practicality showed itself. "That's a good idea," he said. "It'll be expensive," he warned her, knowing she was rapidly spending the money she'd made from the film Faith had rhapsodized about.

"It'll pay off." She blew a huge bubble.

It had better. On the way to the car, Cabot fiddled with his cell phone, got out Faith's card, started to punch in her office number, then decided not to call her yet. It could wait until morning.

A dry run. Why hadn't he thought of that?

"RENO'S PREMIER HONEYMOON HOTEL. Six spectacular honeymoon suites, featuring water beds, his-and-hers baths with Jacuzzis, his-and-hers dressing rooms…"

Why not his-and-hers beds? Snuggled into her own bed, which was much cozier than a water-filled bed sounded, Faith gazed at the laptop monitor that showed a lurid suite reminiscent of one you'd see in the movies of the fifties. The white-carpeted room was huge. At least, it had been photographed from an angle to make it look huge.

The heart-shaped bed, swathed in pink satin, was the central feature, naturally.

She cuddled a little more deeply into her mound of pillows as the ache of frustrated desire began its climb through her center. She could envision Cabot Drennan, dressed in a paisley silk dressing gown and nothing else, turning down that bed and tossing her, dressed in Passion perfume and nothing else, onto it. Resolutely she substituted a fuzzy image of Tippy Temple for the clear image of herself. If she couldn't allow herself even the briefest, most fleeting thought of sharing that bed with Cabot, at least she was giving him up to a woman who deserved him.

Still, it was disappointing to meet the man of her dreams on the eve, so to speak, of his marriage to another woman.

"...magnificent Olympic pool, saunas, dramatic casino, big-name entertainment, twenty-four-hour room service."

She sighed deeply. Honeymooners would like that—room service at any time of the day or night.

"...European-trained hairstylists and manicurists on the premises, full range of business services..."

This perked her up a little. Cabot would like that, too. He'd need a break from Tippy now and then, surely. While she had her hair and nails done, he could catch up with life at his office. Maybe even call his travel agent to tell her—

—that he'd made a terrible mistake! That he wished he could take it back! Annul the marriage! Come back to Los Angeles to the woman he really...

Yes, this hotel, the Inn of Dreams located right in the heart of downtown Reno, seemed to be exactly what he was looking for.

An e-mail alert popped up in the corner of the screen. Faith opened it. "Hold off on the July reservations until we talk. I'm coming in to your office when it opens. C. Drennan."

Her heart beat a rat-a-tat. Could it be? Were her dreams about to come true?

She leaped out of bed, whirled back to save the data she'd gathered on a diskette to take with her to the office and then darted toward the shower. She had exactly thirty-nine minutes to make herself presentable and beat Cabot to the agency. It was going to be a stretch.

CABOT PACED UP AND DOWN in front of Wycoff's Worldwide wondering why no one was there at two-and-a-half minutes before nine. How could you start working at nine if you didn't get there well beforehand, have your coffee, go through your In box, be ahead of the game before the day actually began? He'd e-mailed his agent that he'd be there at opening time. He'd expected her to be waiting at the door.

He'd wanted her to be waiting at the door.

What was he doing here anyway? Now that he'd

seen who he was working with, now that he'd decided to trust her, why hadn't he just relied on the telephone. He did everything else on the telephone. Well, almost everything else. At this stage in his life, he didn't do much that couldn't be done on the telephone. But it was too late now. He'd said he'd be here and he was here, and where the hell was she?

Exactly at nine, it all happened in a perfectly synchronized fashion. A portly man came to the door and unlocked it at the same time two women and two other men materialized on the sidewalk. Neither of the women was Faith. The group outside forged to the inside, carrying Cabot along with them as they said good-morning to each other and the portly man, then the Wycoff group paused expectantly, waiting.

A minute later Cabot found out what they were waiting for. He heard the squeal of worn tires, the roar of a car engine that needed a new muffler, the grinding of brakes that needed new linings. And in another moment Faith flew through the door, her hair surrounding her face like a golden cloud, her eyes as wild as pearl-gray eyes could get and her silky gray pantsuit in need of a pressing.

A ray of sun shot through the window and straight through her hair, and for a second, Cabot was blinded. He stared at the apparition, trying to still the pounding of his heart.

He strongly felt that he ought to fall to his knees and repent for something or other, and he'd gotten so hard so fast that he actually had something specific to repent.

But the cloud of fire and mist that was Faith Sumner rushed toward him, smoothing her suit with one hand and her hair with another, and gradually reality seeped back.

"Oh, Cabot, sorry you had to wait. Mr. Wycoff—" she turned to the portly man "—sorry to be late. I…"

"Don't waste time apologizing," Cabot interrupted her. He gestured toward her desk. "My plans have changed and I have exactly seventeen minutes to explain the situation."

He observed with satisfaction that the other travel agents immediately began slinking toward their work stations. Wycoff opened his mouth, then closed it and went through a doorway into what was undoubtedly his office, a private one where he would be protected from the hustle and bustle of the actual work.

Faith simply sat down at her desk and gazed at him with a peculiar light in her eyes. So he sat down, too.

"When did you get here?" she asked testily.

"Eight fifty-seven."

"Were they already here?" She gestured around the room at the other agents.

"No, they all sort of appeared at once just as that guy unlocked the door."

"How do they do it?" Her expression pleaded with him to understand. "How do they get here exactly at nine, not a minute early, not a minute late? I swear some alien power beams them to the front door."

"You were only one minute late." He didn't know where his forgiving attitude had come from. He supposed it was coming straight from his groin, which still hadn't stopped acting hopeful.

"When I'm one minute late they're all standing in the center of the waiting area staring at me when I come in." Her shoulders drooped.

She was wearing mascara, but only on one set of blond lashes, and her lipstick, something pale pink and shiny, was crooked. He was fascinated, but he couldn't let on.

"I don't care," he said gruffly. "Here's my problem."

"Oh, yes," she said, "your problem." She whirled and reached down to her computer. After she'd pushed several wrong buttons, she finally got the right one and the monitor began to show signs of life. Next she reached into her handbag, fished around, began hauling things out—a wrench, a sandwich, a paper-clipped bundle of coupons, a tube of stain remover, a romance novel—and eventually pulled out a diskette in an ordinary white envelope. "Got it," she said, waving it at him before she tried to jam it into the CD slot, then into the Zip drive slot and at last, with only the one alternative remaining, slid it smoothly into the A drive.

He waited, tapping one finger on the arm of his chair, trying not to notice the tilt of her perfect little nose, her pale, creamy skin, her small, slender hands as they wreaked their havoc.

She turned back to him, looking triumphant. "Now," she said. "You mentioned a change of plans."

"Yes. Don't make the July reservations yet."

"No? Are you sure?" Her voice softened. So did her face.

"Yes. Make them for the second weekend in February."

Inexplicably, her face fell. "Of course. Certainly. If I can get reservations. You're, ah, moving the wedding back? Oh," she sighed as a calendar mysteriously appeared on the monitor, "that's the weekend before Valentine's Day! Instead of skyrockets, you're going for hearts and fl—"

"No," he interrupted her. "I'm doing a dry run."

"A dry run. Of your honeymoon."

"Anything wrong with that?"

Faith could think of about a million things wrong with that. She considered listing them. Then she considered the new muffler she needed and the funny way her car sounded when she put on the brakes. Her final consideration was the most important. This was her thirteenth job since she'd finished undergraduate school with a degree in languages and no skills beyond French, Spanish and Italian. She had to make this one last.

"Of course not," she said smoothly.

"Okay. So book me a honeymoon suite for the nights of the eighth through the tenth."

She hesitated. "It may not be easy so close to Valentine's Day."

"Don't anticipate trouble." That impatient growl again.

Something about his voice sent her whirling to the screen. "The hotel I've chosen..." she began.

"Just make the reservation."

Silently, feeling oddly sulky, Faith punched at the keyboard, moved the mouse around on a mousepad that had the word *Focus!* printed on it in capital letters. "I'm sorry," she said, "but they're fully booked for... Oops!" Startled, she drew back. "Somebody just broke up." A slot, in fact a deluxe theme suite, had opened up before her very eyes. "Our most popular theme room," they described it on the Web site. She cast a sideways glance at Cabot, feeling he'd somehow done it himself, broken up a couple who had a reservation in his hotel for his room.

"So grab it!" He was half out of his chair, reaching for the mouse.

She grabbed it.

He heaved such a sigh she was sure he was wondering what error in his otherwise impeccable judgment had led him to walk up to her workstation yesterday when all around them automatons were chatting with contented-looking clients while quietly doing everything perfectly, serene, unharried smiles painted on their faces.

With the room safely booked, she asked him, "Shall I reserve a wedding chapel in Reno?"

"No." He growled the word. "I don't intend to be married by Elvis."

"That's more of a Las Vegas thing," Faith explained.

"The answer's still no. The ceremony will be here and we'll fly to Reno. I'll need two limos from the Little Chapel in the Pines to LAX and two waiting at the Reno-Tahoe airport."

"One for each of you?" It came out like a squeak.

Another sigh. "No, one for the crew."

"Oh, yes, the crew." It wasn't her place to tell

Cabot Drennan she thought his honeymoon plans sounded less than romantic. She went to the Web site of her favorite limousine service, the one with plenty of long, long, white, white cars, which they decorated with flowers when they carried a wedding party.

She frowned. Flowers that would freeze if they had to drive over any mountain passes between the airport and Reno. Maybe they used fake in February. Maybe they used fake all the time. How would she know? She'd never ridden in one.

"*What* are you thinking about besides my limos?"

She turned to confront his accusing glare. "Fake flowers," she said before she could stop herself.

"Good idea," he said. "Tell the limo service I want them to cover the lead car in fake flowers."

"No problem." They'd love it.

"Then look up the restaurants in the area and choose five of them."

"Five?" She couldn't help herself.

"Two lunches, three dinners. And limos to take us. No flowers."

"Oh." She turned to him, wondering if she was doing the right thing. "The hotel features twenty-four-hour room service."

"That's very interesting information. Now book the five restaurants."

"Won't you at least want breakfast in bed?" She was feeling sorrier for Tippy Temple's raging hormones by the minute. She knew Tippy Temple's hormones had to be raging at the prospect of being Cabot's bride, because her own hormones were raging just sitting across from him watching him glower at her.

"Okay. Breakfast in the room. After the hairdresser and manicurist leave. Book one of each every morning at seven."

A night with Cabot Drennan could certainly mess a woman up. On the other hand, she couldn't imagine a night with Cabot Drennan would end at seven in the morning.

"Coming right up. How about a massage?"

"Too time-consuming. And I wouldn't want to film it."

"It might relax both of you."

"We're already relaxed," he said tightly. "No massage."

She sighed. "I'll get to work on the restaurants."

"Nothing exotic. Tippy's a salad girl. Meat, potatoes, salad, good wine list. And a bar," he added, sounding glum about the prospect even as he specified it. "We need a smoking section."

"Tippy smokes?" An uneasy feeling slid through her body. She remembered reading something about… When Cabot hesitated, she moved the mouse around and found what she was looking for. Her uneasiness intensified.

"No," he said finally. "I might want an occasional cigar. Or somebody in the film industry might join us for dinner. You know. Just covering all the bases."

"Oh, thank goodness." She expelled a sigh of pure relief. "Because the Inn of Dreams advertises itself as Reno's only no-smoking hotel. I was worried to death there for a minute."

"Stop worrying," Cabot said, his brows drawn together in what Faith would describe as a worried frown. "I'll check in with you tomorrow." He got up.

She really hated to see him leave. She really hated thinking she could get all this together by tomorrow. It would take more focusing than she thought she could manage, especially with the elusive scent of his aftershave lingering around her workstation, the daydreams already appearing on the margins of her mind. Daydreams of her sharing this strange, much-too-organized honeymoon and throwing it at once into spontaneous, passionate chaos.

"O-kay," she said, feeling warm and dreamy.

His frown deepened. "You've got a funny look in your eyes."

"What kind of look?" She locked away the daydreams.

"Never mind. It's gone." And so was he. She didn't even let her gaze follow him to the door. She didn't have to. She'd already memorized every nuance of his body.

3

IN LOS ANGELES ALONE, forget Pasadena and Malibu and all the other contiguous communities, the ratio of travel agents to customers had to be one to ten, and he'd somehow picked the one who made him look at what he did for a living and find it detestable.

Creating an image for a client, a job he was good at, could be described two ways. One was simply bringing out the best in a person.

His father had needed nothing more than some decent promotion. The guy had been a great actor. He'd provided a comfortable living for the family doing bit parts. But he'd never made it to the big time. At last he'd given up trying, ended up teaching drama at a small Midwestern college and acting with the local community theater. He was the reason Cabot had become a publicist in the first place. He'd wanted to do for actors what he wished someone had done for his father.

Nothing detestable about that.

The other way of describing image making was that you were inventing a whole new person out of lies. Tippy was invented.

Cabot realized he was chewing his nails. Twenty-five dollars for the essential executive's manicure these days and he was chewing his nails. He needed to do something with his hands. Of course, he was driving with his hands, but in L.A. that didn't count. He had to call Tippy, but after he'd punched her number into his car phone, he was hands-free again.

"I want to take you to dinner," he said as soon as he'd gotten her on the line.

"Shoo-uh," Tippy said, ending with a big popping sound. "Where? You gonna get a photographer? Get us in *Variety?*"

"That depends," Cabot said mysteriously.

"Well, I got a new dress and I wanna be sure we're going someplace worth wearing it." She sounded cross.

"Wear it. We're going to Spago." The restaurant was always packed with celebrities. Incentive. That's what he needed here. Motivation.

She cheered up right away. Of course, he also heard the ominous sound of a lighter flicking on and the whoosh of breath that meant she'd inhaled a long, satisfying drag from a cigarette.

It would not be an easy evening.

Several hours later he was seated across the table from her. Her streaky blond hair was fluffed out in a cloud that reminded him way too much of Faith's hair and her skin had just the right degree of tan, golden and smooth. Her lipstick was pale. Her fingernails were pale, too, and perfect. She was utterly gorgeous in a dress made of two or three or—well, one too few layers of blue chiffon that made her the focal point of the entire room of beautiful people.

The waiter hovered. Cabot ordered drinks. The second they arrived, Tippy, with extraordinary grace, pulled out a cigarette and held it up expectantly.

"We're in a no-smoking section," Cabot said.

"What the hell were you doing putting us in the no-smoking section?" Her face was sweet. Her tone wasn't.

"You need to get in training," Cabot said.

"What for?" She tapped the cigarette on the table.

"For the dry run. We're booked into a no-smoking hotel."

"So switch hotels."

"Can't. They're all full. It's the weekend before Valentine's Day."

"Well, screw 'em," Tippy said. "Put on the pressure. Pay somebody a little cash under the table." Her face was still sweet. She really was one great actress. Only Cabot could see the tic starting to twitch in the corner of her left eye.

"I'm working with a travel agent," Cabot said. "I don't think she's the put-on-the-pressure, a-little-cash-under-the-table kind of person."

"Screw her too." She punctuated each word with a jab of her swizzle stick, the one that had come with her extra-dry straight-up martini and had once had olives impaled on it.

Cabot felt a hard red flush of anger rising to his face and squelched it by sheer strength of will. "You don't want to do that. She's one of your biggest fans."

"She is?" Sudden interest gleamed in the baby blues.

"Absolutely. She sees you as the saint, the martyr

you played in *Kiss*. Now Tippy,'' he said indulgently, ''a big part of my job is to establish your image in the media minds. Your job is to maintain that image. Have I got this right?''

''Yeah.''

''Well, this travel agent believes in your image. She booked the no-smoking hotel by accident, I think.'' Here Cabot paused for a moment, reflecting that Faith Sumner probably did a good many things by accident. ''She'd be deeply, *deeply* disappointed in you if I told her you couldn't make this one little sacrifice, not smoking for a weekend. You might lose a fan. You can't afford to lose a fan. Not even one.'' This was a subtle reminder that she hadn't made it to the big time yet. There was still room for a little humility, a little accommodation.

She contemplated him coolly, never losing the sweet smile. ''I think you got a little thing for this travel agent,'' she said.

The color rose again to Cabot's face. ''Absolutely—''

''You're not thinkin' about backin' out on me, are you? Like Josh?''

''—not. I've made a commitment…to your career.'' He added after a brief hesitation, ''And I intend to follow through on it.''

''That's a promise.''

''Yes.''

''Scout's honor?''

''Scout's honor.''

She gazed at him. ''Okay, then.''

''Okay what?''

"Okay, keep the friggin' no-smokin' hotel."

"Thanks," Cabot said gratefully. "I promise you we'll have a decent time. I'll stock the room with chocolates and—"

"Whaddya mean 'we'?"

"Pardon?"

"If you think for one minute I'm goin' on that dry run with you you're dumber than I figured. Not smoke for a whole weekend? Fageddaboudit."

"Tippy..." Cabot looked up to see a waiter hovering over them. "Salads," he said, "one Caesar, one Cobb, and bring me the wine list. No, just bring us a bottle of something. I don't suppose you have any hemlock stashed away in the back."

"Is that a California, sir, or a French..."

"He was kidding," Tippy said, melting the waiter with a long, long look, then turning the look on Cabot.

It didn't faze him. He glared at her from across the table. "You expect me to do the dry run alone? Pose for the video by myself?"

"You'd look precious in my going-away suit," Tippy said, "but no, this is the movies, baby. You take a double."

So HERE HE WAS AGAIN, back at Wycoff Worldwide and feeling like a fool. But this time, what he had to do wasn't the kind of thing you could do on the phone.

Just to show himself, and her, that it wasn't anything about her that had brought him back, he gave her a scowl as he walked right past her and straight to the head honcho's office.

He peered in. Wycoff, a portly man with a bulbous nose, sat behind his desk leafing through travel brochures, like a man planning his own vacation. "Harrumph," Cabot said.

Wycoff lifted his head, but he didn't look happy to see Cabot standing there. "May I help you?" he said in an unhelpful tone.

"Yes." Cabot strode in and sat down, refusing to be put off. "Name's Cabot Drennan. Your agent Faith Sumner is working with me on my honeymoon arrangements and I..." He paused, fascinated by the dull-red color suffusing Wycoff's face.

"Say no more. I'll set you up at once with Miss Eldridge. Miss Eldridge has been with me for thirty years, and she—"

"I don't want Miss Eldridge. I want Miss Sumner." Feeling that a dull red flush might be climbing *his* face, he added hastily, "to go on working with me."

"You do? She hasn't somehow booked your cruise on a Russian oil tanker or found you a hotel where an Elderhostel is in session and the food is cafeteria style?"

"Of course not," Cabot snapped. The man was a pig. He disliked him intensely. "She's been terrific," he lied. "Over-the-top. If you had a few more agents like her..."

Now Wycoff blanched and Cabot decided he'd gone too far. He'd only known Faith for two days, but already he could tell he didn't want more than one of her in his life. Although having her in his life would be... *What am I saying? What am I thinking?*

"What I mean is," he said, starting over, "that I have a request that might sound, I mean right at the beginning, until you understand the concept, sort of unusual." Since Wycoff's eyes were darting right and left as if he were looking for help, Cabot barreled right ahead. "I want Ms. Sumner to take the honeymoon with me first."

Wycoff lumbered up out of his chair. "Mr. Brandon, I must—"

"Drennan," said Cabot.

"Mr. Drennan." Wycoff wasn't a whole lot taller standing up than he had been sitting down. That's what Cabot would call short legs. "What you suggest is absolutely out of the question. It's indecent. I could get sued."

For a minute there, Cabot had thought Wycoff actually cared about Faith, in which case, he'd try to forgive the man for being a pig. Now he didn't have to. "What I mean is that I want her there to check out the arrangements in person, on site. It's called 'advancing' the event," he added in case Wycoff needed a buzz word to make things clear. "It would be like standing in for the bride, the way a maid of honor does at the wedding rehearsal. I'd want her to take her complaints to the hotel staff, smooth things out before the actual honeymoon."

Wycoff was thinking about it. It was a good sign.

"My intended is a film star," Cabot threw into the silence. "Wonderful woman, but you know how temperamental actresses can be. I just want things to go well.''

''A movie star?''

Those were magic words in Los Angeles, maybe anywhere. ''Yes. We haven't made the announcement yet, or I'd tell you her name.''

The man's mouth was clearly watering.

''Agent Sumner could do my PR firm a great service,'' Cabot said solemnly. ''But of course I wanted to get your approval first. Then you can talk to her, see how she feels about it.''

''I assure you, Mr. Drennan, that if I'm convinced it's a good idea, Miss Sumner will do as I ask.''

''I thought that might be the case,'' Cabot said, and settled back, satisfied.

FAITH SAT at her desk staring at the *Focus, Faith* screen saver and contemplating the loss of yet another job. It was the only reason Cabot could possibly have for bending Mr. Wycoff's ear.

Once again she'd failed. Where had she gone wrong? Because however well suited she seemed to be for a job, something always went wrong.

Succeeding as a travel agent at Wycoff Worldwide was important to her. The time Hope and Charity had put into coaching her and designing screen savers and mouse pads, that alone was enough to make this job important, to say nothing of the fact that they'd paid for her training.

And she was the oldest. According to the current literature on birth order, she was supposed to be the leader, the competitive one, the…

"Faith!"

...one to carry on the family work ethic, the one most likely to...

"Faith Sumner!"

...walk into Mr. Wycoff's office and get fired. As she staggered forward on leaden feet, she discovered that the feet were wearing unmatched shoes. They were the same color, pearl gray to match her suit. It was the heel height that was different. This meant she'd also taken a mismatched pair to the shoe shop for resoling, which meant that now she'd have to take these two shoes in as well, which would cost twice as much, and the higher-heeled pair hadn't even needed resoling.

Leveling herself by walking on one toe and one heel, she stuck her head through the doorway of Mr. Wycoff's office. "You called?" Her knees buckled under her and her throat closed up. "Sir?" she squeaked.

Cabot Drennan lounged gracefully in one of Mr. Wycoff's visitor chairs, his right ankle crossed over his left knee, looking more serene than she'd ever seen him look. Getting someone sacked must be a real mood-lifter for him. She'd been too agitated earlier to notice how he was dressed, but it had to be Casual Friday at his office because he wasn't in his three-piece suit. He was in khaki shorts, snowy-white running shoes and an even snowier polo shirt. The white gleamed against his all-over tan, and his dark eyes gleamed as he slowly raised his gaze to her face.

But it wasn't Friday. It was Tuesday...no, Wednesday. And his eyes weren't melting over her. She was melting under their steady assault.

"Sit down, Faith," he said. "I have a project to discuss with you."

"I CAN'T DO THAT," Faith protested. "Go on *your* honeymoon? Stay in the honeymoon suite and have all those manicures and go to all those restaurants as if… Well, I can't. It's just too weird." She could hardly breathe. Just sitting there beside Cabot was making her heart pound and generating other unusual symptoms, both pleasurable and distressing. These were not feelings one should have in a gray suit while sitting in one's boss's office. But on a honeymoon…

Going on Cabot's honeymoon was what she wanted to do more than anything, but not like this. Not as a proxy to be coiffed and made up and positioned and photographed, but as a bride, to be loved and cherished. Loved, at least. Frequently and with passion. She was fairly sure that was one task she could focus on without difficulty.

She drew in a sharp breath as he uncrossed his muscled legs and leaned toward her. "Travel agents check out hotels and resorts all the time, don't they?" he said. His look and his tone were persuasive.

"Well, yes."

"I believe you spent a weekend at the Sunny Sands resort on the Gulf Coast during the summer."

Mr. Wycoff's voice startled Faith. It was the first time he'd spoken since he summoned her in, and she'd almost forgotten he was in the room. "Yes," she said, "I did do that. It was an experience I'll never forget.'' It had been a nightmare, free or not. She had no difficulty comprehending why she'd been chosen to receive a complimentary weekend on the Louisiana coast in the searing heat of late August with a hurricane approaching. Her boss had chosen her, hoping she'd blow away in the storm, or be eaten to death by mosquitoes, which dived even faster with a tailwind.

''Same thing,'' Cabot said. His voice pressured her like a firm caress, seeking acquiescence. ''Except I'm comping you, not the hotel. I just want you to go there, go through all the motions. That way I'll know the honeymoon will…will…''

For the first time he seemed to flounder. Faith found him even more charming floundering than being so perfectly self-assured.

''Everything will go just the way a very special person's honeymoon should go,'' he finally concluded.

This brought Faith's mind firmly back to the real bride, the beautiful Tippy Temple. It also stilled her heart a little, cut down on the tingling sensations that made her want to wriggle in her chair. In short, she'd just gotten a shot of reality. If he wanted Tippy to have a perfect honeymoon, maybe he did have a romantic streak.

And it was her job, wasn't it, to make her clients happy?

''Advance work of this sort could come to be an important part of your job.'' Mr. Wycoff's voice carried a cold note of warning. ''Especially as Wycoff Worldwide ceases to be merely a neighborhood standby and becomes a mover and shaker in the film industry travel business. I see this coming, Miss Sumner.'' He cast a significant glance toward Cabot. ''In the very near future.''

One occurrence doesn't equal a trend. That was the thought that went through Faith's mind. It was so alien to the thoughts that usually went through her mind that she couldn't imagine where it had come from. She could hardly say it aloud to Mr. Wycoff in front of the ''occurrence'' in question. What her boss was saying was that if Faith wanted to keep her job she would be his stepping stone to the film industry by taking Cabot Drennan's honeymoon, like it or not, and making him so happy that he'd rush right back to his office to spread the Wycoff name around.

She was suddenly aware that they were both staring at her. Mr. Wycoff's stare was impatient bordering on exasperated, but Cabot's was something else altogether. His dark, winging eyebrows were slightly lifted, his eyes were warm and a smile played around the corners of that suggestive mouth.

He knew he'd get his own way eventually, and it just tickled him to death.

''Well, Faith?'' Mr. Wycoff spoke again, undoubtedly wishing he could get back to his daydream of being ''travel agent to the stars.''

She was cornered. She'd held this job longer than any other, feeling each day that she was poised on the brink of dismissal. Mr. Wycoff did not like her, and she was confident he was just looking for a reason to fire her. She could *not* lose this job. She could not, one more time, call her sisters and then her parents to announce that she was unemployed.

"I don't know why you're making such a big deal out of it," her boss said in a complaining tone.

She didn't intend to tell him, either. She'd better pull herself together and act normal about the whole thing or Cabot would know why she was making such "a big deal" about pretending she was Tippy Temple for a long weekend. So she straightened her shoulders and firmed up her chin.

"Come to think of it, neither do I," she said cheerfully. "Okay, I'll go to Reno on…well, on whatever day we reserved the suite."

"In the limousine with the fake flowers all over it."

She stared at Cabot. "You really want to rehearse the whole thing?"

"Everything but the marriage ceremony." He smiled at her. "We'll start with the going-away-suit part."

"We?"

"Don't forget the second limo for the crew."

"We?"

"Rooms for everybody. And make all those restaurant reservations. We'll start with dinner on—"

"You mean you're going too?"

His eyebrows lowered until they almost met at the bridge of his nose, and he looked at her as though she were truly a dim bulb. "Well, of course. How else can I plan the shots, check the lighting, oil the gears for the real thing?"

"Silly me," she said faintly.

"So now that that's settled…" Mr. Wycoff said.

"I must be going," Cabot said. He rose from his chair and herded Faith out of the office and back to her workstation. She was sorry because now he was behind her and she'd been looking forward to watching him walk again, checking out his height again— six-two, six-three— She wanted to get a closer look at his shoulders and his buns, of course, and while she was at it, the muscle tone of his calves. She hadn't been able to take it all in when he'd had himself covered up in a three-piece suit.

Back at her desk, she called Charity's cell phone and reached her at her new job, then let Charity patch in Hope, who was shopping for office space in New York. She and her new love were going into business together, and Hope was the Real Estate Task Force.

"What's up?" Hope said briskly, while Charity said, "You okay, Faith?"

"Oh, I'm fine," Faith said. "I was just wondering what you wear in Reno in February on your honeymoon."

It really made her crazy when they squealed like that at the same time. She held the phone away from her ear until the squealing faded a little and then said, "Not my honeymoon. Ha. Gotcha."

"You twit," Hope said.

"Whose honeymoon?" Charity said.

"Tippy Temple's."

"Tippy Temple's getting married?" Charity's tone was hushed and reverent.

"You know her?" Faith asked.

"Who's Tippy Temple?" Hope asked.

"Someday you should take time to catch up on pop culture," Charity scolded her. "Tippy Temple's in that movie…"

"…*'A Kiss to Build a Dream on,'*" Faith supplied.

"…and she's fantastic. So sweet…"

"…and I'm going to Reno to fill in for her."

"Wait a minute," Hope said.

"Oh, Hope," Faith said, "not on their *real* honeymoon. This is just a rehearsal."

"A rehearsal for what?" Hope was clearly in a militant feminist mode. Faith had imagined that falling in love would change Hope a little, but apparently she'd been mistaken.

"For the video. I mean…" she halted, realizing she was getting in deeper with every word that came blabbing out of her mouth. "Hope," she said firmly, "it's business. You'll just have to trust my judgment."

"Who's the groom?" Charity said.

Faith couldn't stop herself. "Oh-h-h," she said, sighing, "you mustn't tell a soul, of course, but he's a publicist named Cabot Drennan, and he's everything Tippy deserves, the stuff dreams are made of—tall and tanned, strong and forceful, successful and…"

In the silence, she realized what her sisters already knew, that her judgment was not to be trusted, especially not by her.

4

"I'VE GOT AN ANSWER FOR YOU." Charity sounded abrupt. That meant she was not at her new job, but at one of her remaining modeling sessions and wearing shoes that were too tight.

"Oh, thanks," Faith said. "What was the question?"

"What to wear on a honeymoon in Reno. I was talking to the stylist, and he—"

"It's a moot point now," Faith said, cutting her off. "My trousseau just arrived, courtesy of Cabot Drennan, 'Publicist to the Stars.'"

"Wowie. He's doing it up right," Charity said. "Well, come on, tell me, what'd you get?"

Feeling like Cinderella, Faith unzipped one bag after another. "There's a pale-blue silk suit. With a matching straw hat. And clutch bag."

"Your going-away suit," Charity said, sounding dreamy for once.

"Tippy's going-away suit," Faith corrected her. "And here," she said, unzipping another bag, "is a...oh, I see, it's a layer of crumply silk over a layer of satin. The color of vanilla ice cream. And a cashmere shawl that matches." She pulled the shawl around her shoulders and snuggled into it, relishing the softness of the wool.

"A dinner dress for your wedding night."

Faith took a breath. "A dinner dress for *Tippy's* wedding night."

"Oh. Right. I keep forgetting."

"Tippy won't wear this same dress, of course," Faith said. "She'll wear something similar." She paused. "Probably a size smaller," she concluded grimly.

"Oh, Faith, stop it. If you were any thinner you'd disappear. Hurry up and unpack some more. They're going to call me soon. At least I hope so. My feet are killing me."

Faith unzipped and reported, unzipped and reported. Another fantastic dress, a white silk pantsuit. Bikinis and cover-ups. "You ought to see this," she said finally. "It's a pale-blue satin dressing gown just like the one Lauren Bacall wore in that forties movie, the one about—"

"No underwear?"

Neither Charity nor Hope shared her passion for the romantic old movies and were quick to cut her off when she launched into the plot of one of them. Too used to the maneuver to be offended, Faith riffled through the stack that was piling up on her bed. "No."

"No tempting teddies, black lace bikinis?"

"No. Of course not," she said a moment later. "They won't be photographing Tippy in her underwear."

"Bummer. I'll send you some money," Charity

said at once. "Go out and buy yourself some luscious—"

"Absolutely not," Faith said. "I have plenty of underwear. Just not the kind…" She caught herself. She'd almost said, *Just not the kind I'd like Cabot to see me in.* It was fortunate Charity couldn't see her blushing. "Not the kind Tippy will take on her honeymoon."

"But you'd feel more romantic if you were wearing sexy underwear under those slinky clothes."

This time when Faith took her deep, stress-reducing breath, she also counted to three. "I don't need to feel romantic. I don't *want* to feel romantic, because it's *not my honeymoon.*"

Her impatience faded at once when she was distracted by the note that was attached to one of the handbags in the pile. "Make an appointment at Ricardo's on Rodeo Drive to be fitted for shoes."

"Isn't that thoughtful?" she said to Charity after explaining that her silence was not, in fact, an indication of rage. "My shoes are going to fit."

"Lucky you," Charity groaned. "Oops, my turn. Gotta run."

AT THE SAME TIME he imagined Faith would be trying on her travel wardrobe, Cabot was having an argument with the stylist who would accompany his camera crew to Reno.

"No," he said. "Absolutely not. That's going too far."

"It's no different from putting a wig on a double."

The stylist, a young man with a roosterlike haircut

and a diamond stud in one ear, sounded waspish. His shrunken black T-shirt rode up to show his navel, which brandished a ring set with a matching diamond. But he was good. He had to be good to afford diamonds that big. He had to be good for Cabot to hire him. Look what he'd done for Tippy already, the way he'd groomed her for those television interviews. Made her look like an angel. But Cabot wasn't backing down on this one.

"We're talking about her *eyes,* Joey," he said firmly. "I don't want you messing with her eyes."

"A pair of blue contacts isn't 'messing with her eyes,'" Joey said, rolling his own, which were a suspiciously unnatural shade of turquoise. "Blue contacts and she'll be a perfect double for Tippy."

"She doesn't need to be that perfect."

"What? What? This is Mr. Has-to-be-Perfect I'm hearing? If you want a good take on the lighting she needs blue eyes. Period."

"She's not getting them. Period." Cabot figured he weighed twice what Joey did. When it came to a showdown, the guy didn't have a chance. He'd sulk for a day or two, and the whole time in Reno he'd be saying, "*Well,* if her *eyes* were the right color..." But Cabot had gotten to be an expert at handling sulky people.

He didn't want Faith to lose those pearly-gray eyes. That was where he was coming from. When the truth was, it might be a good idea for her to lose them. He was pretty sure he needed to know her better, but that was an indulgence he'd have to postpone until after the dry run, after the wedding, after the honeymoon, after the divorce....

After the confession.

"Well," Joey said, putting a fist on his hip. "I refuse to back down on the hair. You *promised* you'd send her to Tippy's hairdresser."

"I promised and I'll send her. If she's agreeable." Faith's hair was already enough like Tippy's that... *There I go again.*

Joey tossed his head, but the crisis was over. Cabot went back to scripting the video, plotting potential shots, glancing from time to time at his one-year calendar. October, November. It might be that long before he could even ask Faith to go to a movie with him. The time loomed ahead of him, tedious and lonely.

A FEW THINGS WERE MISSING from the picture. Her mother and sisters should be with her, fluttering around her, making sure she'd remembered everything. While her body zinged with anticipation, what she was anticipating was a weekend of top-level frustration. Her groom had ignored her from the moment she agreed to go on the honeymoon. But she *looked* uncontrovertibly bridal, even if she didn't feel that way.

She was dressed in her blue going-away suit; the rest of her clothes were packed in the three-piece set of tapestry luggage with golden leather trim that Cabot had had delivered the day before. The limo she'd hired to take them to the airport would be along soon. Everything was fine, at least as fine as it could be under the circumstances. So why did she have this niggling feeling she'd forgotten something?

Of course she'd forgotten something. She always forgot something. Usually it was something replaceable—toothpaste, panty hose, a nail file. Then again, she'd once left for Europe without a passport, and she'd made that wretched trip to the Gulf Coast without her credit card, had gone to a baby shower without the present and on one memorable occasion, had started out for the travel agency without her skirt.

Fortunately, her landlord had been leaving for the office at about the same time and had mentioned the omission to her in the most tactful way someone could mention a thing like that. He'd said, "I see the micro-mini is back in style."

So the question was *what* had she forgotten and could she remember what it was before it was too late to do anything about it.

She stepped swiftly into the kitchen to be sure she'd turned off the coffeepot—she hadn't—and the iron—that was still on, too. Even then the niggle didn't go away. If anything, it gained intensity.

She ought to take a coat. Reno could be warm even in February, but one of the restaurants was in the Sierra Nevadas that surrounded the town. She had a yummy new coat, too, a Christmas present. She got it out, tossed it on her pile of luggage and waited for a feeling of comfort to settle in now that she'd checked that item off her mental list. It didn't.

She lived in this tiny dream cottage behind the Mathiases' large, elegant house in return for keeping an eye on the house during their frequent absences and watering their dozens of houseplants, since their staff traveled with them. She'd watered the plants thoroughly yesterday afternoon and explained to them exactly how long she'd be gone, since the ficus tree, in particular, was prone to anxiety attacks. She'd set the alarm system and notified the neighborhood security watch that she'd be away for the weekend. It was probably just a bad habit to feel nervous before a trip because of the sure and certain knowledge she'd forgotten something important.

She picked up her little blue clutch bag and the folder that held all their travel information, took a quick peek in the mirror at the slant of her blue straw hat and started for the front door just as the doorbell rang.

Her driver. She was ready exactly on time. Pretty good, for her.

A vase of daisies sat on the small round table she used for eating and everything else. Maybe the flowers were responsible for the niggle. She should have thrown them away. The water would smell vile by the time she got back, but there wasn't time to do anything about it now. She hesitated, then plucked one daisy blossom out of the bunch, tossed it up in the air as if it were the bridal bouquet—and caught it herself.

A good omen, even if the contest had been fixed.

She opened the door to a grinning, freckled driver who hoisted her luggage and steered her down the flagstone walkway and around the Mathias' house. In front of the main house, he gestured grandly toward the curb. "Enough flowers for you?" he said.

Stunned, Faith eyed the long white limousine, relieved that the Mathiases were not at home to see what their impoverished renter was using for transportation these days. The car was awash in flowers, old-fashioned English garden flowers mingled randomly with huge tropical blossoms in the most garish colors imaginable. They were arranged in swags strung through wreaths, with the occasional sheaf to add visual interest. "It's a leftover Rose Bowl Parade float," she said at last.

"No way! Parade flowers are real. These are made of the purest virgin plastic."

"I sensed, somehow, that they were."

"Indestructible at the highest speeds, in rain, sleet or snow."

"Are we anticipating any of those things today in Southern California?"

"High speeds, maybe."

Faith gave him a sharp look, but he seemed to be serious and quite proud of his vehicle. "Do the doors still open?" she asked him, and they were on their festive way.

Twenty minutes later they reached the Little Chapel in the Pines, and Faith caught her first glimpse of Cabot. It seemed like centuries since she'd last seen him, and he took her breath away. In his black suit, black shirt and black tie, he stood on the cobblestone pathway that led from the historic chapel to the street. Surrounded like a god among mortals by the camera crew with their equipment, he gave every appearance of a man who was issuing orders.

He shot one arm out in front of him and gestured

behind himself with the other. Then he stuck both arms straight out to the sides and swiveled a little. Every movement was filled with a masculine energy that quickened Faith's pulse. She especially liked the swivel. She hoped the driver didn't notice she was drooling.

And then he caught sight of her. She could tell he'd seen her, could see his expression change, could sense his awareness of her. He took a step toward her, then another, almost like a man sleepwalking.

"If you're having second thoughts, now's the time to run."

"What?" The voice of the driver had broken the spell and Faith hurriedly gathered herself up to get out of the car.

"Just kidding," the driver said as he got out and came around to her door.

Cabot was still behaving like a sleepwalker, taking one slow step and then another, but, Faith observed with disappointment, his focus was not on her but on the limousine. Furthermore, the camera crew had fallen into step behind him, and they all marched toward her like a live version of *Night of the Living Dead.*

He had reached her side. "Don't hurt the driver's feelings," she whispered hurriedly. "I'll be sure you have something a bit more…ah…restrained for your honeymoon."

"This is very…flowery," he said.

"I think it's too…" Faith said.

"It'll really show up on film," the cameraman said. He seemed transfixed.

"Like a zit on your nose," Faith said, "but I can…"

"Speaking very frankly, Raff," drawled a crew member, the one with the rooster haircut and an enviable diamond stud in one ear, "I'll have to insist that we restrict the flowers to moderate zone species or tropicals. Not both." He gazed at the car another moment, his head tilted to one side. "Or to pastels or vivids, but not both."

"Pastels would…" Faith began.

"It could handle sheaves *or* wreaths," said the one female member of the crew.

"But not both," they chorused together, and at this point, Faith simply chimed in.

"So what I think we're saying, Cab," said the cameraman, "what I think we're all in agreement on here—do I have this right, Chelsea, Joey, Miss… whatever?—is that the car…"

"Could be toned down some," Cabot said. "But not much. Tippy will like it. Okay, you guys, let's get to work."

But for a moment he lingered, staring at the garishly decorated car. He had to stare at the car, because if he let himself look at Faith he would risk embarrassing both of them. He hadn't let himself go back to the agency or participate in the fittings and hairdresser visits. Three weeks had gone by, and now he was struck all over again by her sheer loveliness. While Joey the stylist had the ability to make Tippy look like an angel, Faith *was* an angel. In the pale-blue suit, her hair floating out from under the broad-brimmed hat, she was a vision of sweetness and beauty.

Faith was what he wished Tippy could be, or could be turned into.

"Shoo-ah," he could hear Tippy saying.

He could sense the tables turning on him in the worst possible way. He didn't have the slightest problem going on a platonic honeymoon with the real Tippy, while the weekend with Tippy's "double" was going to be a struggle with his conscience from this moment on.

Make that retroactive to the day he met her.

"Talent," barked the cameraman, "get in position outside the chapel door."

"Raff," Cabot called across the churchyard, starting in Raff's direction with Faith in his wake, "we are not 'the talent.' We are a bride and groom—"

"Real groom, fake bride," Faith interrupted.

"—who want a professional-looking wedding and honeymoon video." He turned away from Faith in order to give Raff a hard, meaningful look.

He'd had to tell the crew the truth. They'd worked with him many times before, and unlike Faith, they were way too savvy to buy the idea of a honeymoon video that had to be scripted and rehearsed. They were also professionals, as aware as he was that a slip of the tongue could cost them their careers. No one outside their little circle could know the truth. Jack Langley had even conned that worthless twerp Josh Barnett into believing Tippy had actually fallen for her publicist. But Cabot had a feeling that however innocent Faith was, she was a lot smarter than Josh Barnett. Raff needed to watch his words.

"Sorry, boss," Raff said. "Old habits, y'know. I keep forgetting this job's personal." His grin was unrepentant.

Still, feeling sure that Raff wouldn't let him down, he glanced at Faith to find her beautiful eyes infused with ominous suspicion. Cabot's stomach tightened up.

Faith had started to worry about the bride she was doubling for. The way Cabot had said, "Tippy will like it," *it* being that Celebration of Plastic that was the going-away car, indicated his complete lack of understanding of Tippy Temple's personality, her hopes and dreams. Each example of this insensitivity made Faith more sure that Cabot had not consulted Tippy about the arrangements, but was instead barreling ahead in his forceful fashion toward a glitzy media splash of a honeymoon that would offend the daylights out of his true love.

She didn't intend to let him get away with it, but there was nothing she could do about it now, because Raff had just said, "Okay, let's do a take of the leaving-the-church scene," and Joey had echoed, "I want to see a little snuggle-up moment," and all the stray thoughts that had been going through her head flew out when Cabot put his arm around her shoulders.

"Oh, yummy. So *sweet*. Okay, that's good," Joey was saying. "You got it, Raff? Can you stand a little taller, Miss…whatever…" His diamond stud flashed in the morning sun.

"Her name is Faith Sumner," Cabot said a bit irritably, "and of course she can't stand any taller. Just get on with it."

Get on with *what?* She really didn't want to *get on* with what they were getting on with right this minute, which was Cabot's arm holding her closer and closer, snuggling her into the warmth of his shoulder, turning the warmth into raging heat.

"Tilt your head, honey." Joey again. "Chelsea, get the light right there on her...that's it. If she were just a smidge taller, and if her *eyes* were *blue...*"

Faith fanned herself. Joey rushed forward with a powder puff and plunged it onto her nose. Faith sneezed. Chelsea rushed forward with a tissue. A spotlight rocked on its tripod just behind her, and she tossed the tissue to Faith with one hand and rescued the light with the other.

"Oh, for..." Raff said disgustedly. "Can we just get a shot or two here?"

"The sooner the better," Cabot said, and before Faith had a chance to register his grim tone, he tightened his hold around her shoulders, tilted her chin up, which made her grab for her hat, gave her an intimate smile and settled his mouth over hers.

That was when the real trouble began. At the first touch of Cabot's lips, Faith made a firm, if unilateral, decision that she would go on kissing him for a year or so, continuously, no breaks, maybe win some kind of kissing contest. Her mouth melted into his, velvet against velvet, as her insides bubbled like a hot spring.

Her body relaxed into his, seeking him as if it had its own script, her breasts brushing his chest. She sensed his tongue searching for hers, then retreating, holding back. Why would he be holding back? Tentatively she met him halfway, jolted by the electrifying surge of first contact.

"Hold it!" Raff barked.

Of course she would hold it. Hadn't she already promised herself to hold it forever and ever and ever?

"Cut!" she heard above the pleasant buzzing in her ears, and Cabot dropped her as if she were a hot saucepan.

"I'm sorry," he muttered into her ear. "I don't know what happened there."

"No, it was my fault," Faith murmured back. "I—" *I what?* "I was trying to seem *taller* by, ah, reaching up like that." Murmuring was a good idea anyway, since she was having trouble talking.

"No, I overstepped…"

"No, I overacted…"

"No, I…"

"Help her into the car next," Raff said. "Great job, you two. But next time, Miss…ah…"

"Her *name*," Cabot said through his teeth, "is Faith. Surely you can master one name. This is my final warning, all three of you. Her name is Faith. She is not 'she' or 'her' or 'Miss Whatever.' Faith. Got it?"

And while he issued his ultimatum, Faith thought, *Next time? Omigosh, can I survive a next time?*

5

DAZED FROM KISSING FAITH, which had been the surprise of his life and had shaken him to his jaded core, Cabot wasn't sure what to do next. One thing he did observe was that they got plenty of attention on the way to LAX in the garish limo. Tourists lifted their cameras and snapped pictures when they pulled up to the terminal, and they'd do the same thing in July, not even knowing that Tippy Temple was about to step out of the car. When you were in his line of business, attention was a good thing.

Once he'd gotten his little party settled in first-class, with Faith beside him in the window seat and the video crew scattered out in front of him where he could keep an eye on them, it seemed time for small talk. Any kind of talk would do except talk about that kiss and its impact, and since the kiss was all he could think about, he didn't have a clue how to begin. "Nice suit" wouldn't work, because she hadn't had anything to do with choosing it.

Joey and Tippy had chosen it, had chosen the entire trousseau. Tippy loved shopping with Joey. Cabot wished he'd thought to ask Joey if *he'd* like to marry Tippy, since it was only for show.

Modern Day Pygmalion Story: Stylist Marries His

Creation. Cabot could see the headline in his mind's eye, and wished he could see it on the cover of *Variety*. And *People*. And *Vanity Fair*. If Tippy were marrying Joey, he, Cabot, could spend this weekend profitably, which in his addled state meant kissing Faith numerous additional times. And doing more than kissing, if she wanted to.

He wondered if Faith's mental processes felt like his did right this minute—electrical impulses leaping from right brain to left, from front to back and skittering off on the diagonal. If so, he felt sorry for her.

"...and I'm finally figuring out what my sister Charity has been going through as a model," Faith was saying, "except that her shoes never fit. Maybe that's why she's so determined to be a scientist instead. Comfortable shoes."

Since she'd come to his rescue, effortlessly supplying the small talk he couldn't seem to dredge up, Cabot thought he'd better help. "Let me guess," he said. "You have another sister and her name is Hope."

"Yes. How about you?"

He gave her a sidelong glance to find that she wasn't even smiling, when that lovely, surprisingly wide mouth seemed to smile so easily. She seemed nervous. Fear of flying? *I don't think so. Fear of me is more like it.*

"One sister, which I thought was one too many when I was a kid. She's married, now, with two kids. She's an artist, he's a stockbroker. I don't know what they talk about."

"I told you about Charity," Faith rattled on after her brief interest in Cabot's family. "Hope's a big businesswoman in New York. We're all so different. Hope and Charity got all the brains, though.''

She sounded so glum that Cabot found himself wanting to make her feel better. ''Being brainy doesn't necessarily make you successful,'' he suggested, ''and being successful doesn't mean you're brainy.'' It sounded good, but he wasn't sure he'd said anything meaningful. ''You're a good travel agent, and that's not easy.''

She suddenly whipped an earnest gaze around to him and he felt himself melting under it, or at least some of him was melting and some of him was impersonating a stalagmite.

''Do you really think I could be a good travel agent?'' she asked him.

He shifted uneasily in the upholstered seat that would magically become his life jacket if he needed one.

''Because it's practically my last chance to succeed,'' she said mournfully. Her mouth tilted down at the corners. Cabot wanted to settle his fingers right there and tilt it back up. ''I'm thirty years old and my résumé reads like a terrorist's dossier.''

''Now I can't believe you ever...''

''I haven't caused any actual explosions—well, a fire or two—but disaster strikes on every job I've ever held. First there was the Marrakesh caper.''

''That sounds...''

''Yes. Very exciting, doesn't it? And I thought it would be. A very famous author—you'd recognize his name if I dared to say it aloud even now—hired me right out of college to be his research assistant. He was writing a thriller set in Marrakesh.''

Cabot settled in. It seemed he was going to hear the story of her life, which was better than discussing the fact that he hadn't acted very professional when he kissed her. ''He sent you to Marrakesh?''

''He sent me to the *library*. He wasn't about to let go of enough money to send me to Marrakesh. Unlike you. You've spent a fortune already researching your own wedding! And I think that's wonderful. Tippy deserves that kind of thoughtfulness.''

She was gazing earnestly at him again, but there at the end he thought her gaze slid off to the right a little. ''It's tax deductible,'' he said without thinking, because what he was thinking about was Faith's full pink mouth. *Forget the mouth!* ''I'm charging the dry run to my firm,'' he added, improvising rapidly, ''because I can apply the kind of information we'll be gathering to my other clients.''

''Would have been for him, too,'' Faith said. ''Tax deductible, I mean. Anyway, I was slaving away in the M stacks and files, and then—'' she paused, and a dreamy look came over her face ''—one day when I was doing an online search for 'Moroccan Meteorological Trends', I noticed a book called *Explore Madagascar,* and then another one, *The Romance of Mozambique,* and *Don't Miss Macao.* So of course I had to find out what those places were like.''

''You forgot about Marrakesh.'' How could she forget about Marrakesh when she could remember the names of three books she'd read maybe eight years ago that weren't even about Marrakesh, the topic she was supposed to research. The flight attendant hovered over them, and although Cabot didn't drink martinis, the word just fell out of his mouth, probably because it was alliterative.

"Oh," Faith was saying to the woman, "I'd love some white wine, but I'd better not. I'll have—"

"What about a Mai Tai?" Cabot said. "Or a Manhattan."

"I was about to say tomato juice," Faith said, giving him an odd look. "I'm barely competent stone-cold sober. And this may be vacation time for you, but I'm working."

While the attendant got the drinks, it occurred to Cabot that Faith was spilling out the story of her work history to make a point, and that the point might come as unpleasant news for him and his current enterprise.

"So how did the job end?" he asked as soon as he'd taken a restorative gulp of vodka.

Her mouth turned down again. "I woke up one morning and realized he was expecting me to hand him his Marrakesh background the very next day and I had almost nothing for him but basic geography and a printout of a Web site for tourists. So I checked out every old movie that had been set in Marrakesh and filled in the details from those."

"Uh-oh," Cabot said, "most of those were probably made on an MGM lot."

"But still," she argued, "I figured that somebody at MGM would have done better research than I had. Unfortunately, they'd done that research in 1938 or '39 or '40." She sighed deeply. "He had to set the book in 1941 and make it a World War II espionage story.''

''And it bombed.'' He was getting bombed, too.

''No, the publisher promoted it as his first historical novel and it stayed on the bestseller list for sixty-three weeks.''

''But he'd already fired you.''

''And I'd already taken a job as interpreter for an aide to the ambassador to Argentina. Want to hear about that?''

''Well, I...''

''That was going well—I'm quite fluent in Spanish,'' she murmured modestly, ''until one day I got distracted during one of his conversations with a lobby group—something about beef. I hadn't listened to what he was saying, so when it came time to translate I had to make something up.'' She halted, then turned to him, looking quizzical. ''Do you remember that little civil uprising in Argentina about seven years ago? When the beef producers marched on Buenos Aires?''

The last drops of vodka dribbled down the front of his shirt, but Cabot didn't care. ''You did that?'' he said. He felt as if he were strangling.

It was suddenly crystal clear what the point of Faith's story was. Every job she took ended in disaster. And what she was now was a travel agent, *his* travel agent, Tippy's double.

And she was warning him that she was all too likely to blow it.

The question was how? He could think of many, many ways. That was a big part of his job as a pub-

licist, thinking of all the ways something could back-
fire. So he would spend the next four days creeping
warily through a dark forest, waiting for the ogre to
pop out and eat him alive.

And little did she know, this beautiful, delicate
woman who sat beside him in an obvious state of
performance anxiety, that inside him was an ogre
threatening to pop out at any moment and nibble her
into a passionate frenzy.

HE'D BEEN WRONG. He wasn't going to spend the next
four days creeping through a dark forest. The ogre
manifested itself right there at the reception desk of
the Inn of Dreams in downtown Reno. "What do you
mean you don't have three additional rooms reserved?"

"Um, Cabot..." Faith murmured.

"I mean, we have two rooms for your crew and a
honeymoon suite for you, Mr. Drennan, and you're
pretty darned lucky we had that cancellation, because
this *is* the weekend before Valentine's Day."

Cabot gazed at the man for a long moment. "Excuse us for a second," he said, and pulled Faith over
to the side. She was wearing a stricken expression.

"I forgot to book a room for myself," she whispered.

"You forgot to book a room for *me*," he corrected
her. "And the hotel staff thinks we're really on our
honeymoon, right?"

"Well, of course," Faith said. "If they thought we
were just advancing the honeymoon, they wouldn't

treat us the same way they'll treat you and Tippy in July.''

That, at least, made sense. ''You didn't register in Tippy's name.''

Her eyes were very wide and very gray. ''Of course not. We're registered as Mr. and Mrs. Cabot Drennan.''

Something lurched inside Cabot's stomach, but he stoically ignored it. ''Well, let's see what we can do about this,'' he said gruffly, and herded her back to the desk. ''We really have to have three extra rooms,'' he told the clerk. ''As you can see,'' and he gestured back toward Raff, Joey and Chelsea, who milled about restlessly, sensing a problem, ''I have three crew members of various, um, sexes and persuasions.'' This was merely an excuse. Raff and Joey were rooming together. That third room was for him, and every second he spent with Faith made the need for a room of his own more crucial.

The clerk merely shrugged.

He knew a stone wall when he saw one. ''Excuse us again,'' Cabot said, and withdrew his people into a huddle in the artificial shade of an artificial potted palm.

''Okay,'' he said to his entourage, ''it looks like we have to get along with two extra rooms. I'll share a room with Raff and Joey can bunk in with Chelsea.''

''No!'' Joey shrieked as he stamped his foot.

''Why not?'' Cabot said, aware that Faith's lovely gray eyes were following the conversation anxiously.

"You *promised* me *Raff,*" Joey said, and fell into a pout.

"Hey, hold on a minute," Raff said, scowling. "If Chelsea has to share with somebody, it has to be you."

"That's right, Joey," Cabot said. "I can't share with Chelsea."

"Unless you want Carlos to break your neck," Chelsea said in a soft, gentle voice with an accent that spoke of a Southern upbringing. "He's real rigid about things like that."

"Ah," Cabot said. He'd met Carlos, a wrestler, whose adoration of Chelsea was the only indication that he possessed a brain, and the only indication that inside the quiet Chelsea was a tiger about to escape from the zoo. He sent a meaningful glance around the group, then settled it on Faith.

"We'll have to manage somehow, I guess," he said. "It is a suite, after all. It'll have a living room. With a sofa. I'll sleep on the sofa."

"No, I'll sleep on the sofa. This is all my fault and I'll accept the consequences."

"Don't argue. Tradition decrees that the biggest person sleeps in the smallest space."

She could see the exasperation in the lines around his mouth. "We'll break with tradition. I will definitely—"

He whirled and went back to the desk clerk. They all followed him like baby ducks. "You *must* have an extra single room somewhere," he said.

The desk clerk wore the look of an about-to-be-discovered movie star. "In Carson City, maybe," he drawled.

Cabot gave up. "Okay. Fine. Show us to our rooms."

The look he gave Faith started out as a withering one. He wasn't sure how it turned out.

"SO WE'LL SEE YOU GUYS LATER," Cabot told the crew.

"Nope, you'll see us now," Raff informed him. "We have to work on the 'carry over the threshold' scene."

Faith supposed you couldn't expect a professional video-making crew to put romance into what was, for them, a livelihood. For her, too, she reminded herself swiftly. She'd better be thinking of it as the "carry over the threshold" scene, too.

Cabot's mouth was set in a grim line. She was sure he'd rather drop her over a cliff right this minute than carry her over a threshold.

"Okay, then, follow us up." He went from annoyance to resignation in a split second.

They were pretty noticeable, Faith thought, the five of them trotting along behind a bellhop dressed the way bellhops dressed in the old movies, when they delivered luggage to gorgeous women in blue satin dressing gowns.

Raff the cameraman was loading his gun, so to speak, Joey was making darts and dashes at her with a makeup pencil, trying to correct her eyebrow line on the run without destroying her vision and Chelsea was screwing lights into sockets, while she struggled not to trip over tripods that kept opening of their own accord.

"Here we are, folks," sang the bellhop. "Try to get my left side," he said sotto voce to Raff as he flung open the door of the suite.

"Da-dum! Welcome to the Tahoe Jungle Suite!"

"Ah-h-h," Faith moaned.

"Me Tarzan," Cabot muttered.

The five of them hovered outside the door of the suite. "I can't go in until I've had some food," Joey said.

"I'm not going in without hip waders," Raff said. "The bride and groom can test the waters while we set up for the shoot."

Cabot still didn't move any farther into the room, so neither did Faith. She was *not* Jane, and she was afraid to try it alone. Something might drop down from the ceiling, like an anaconda.

The Tahoe Jungle Suite was the realization of a decorator's worst nightmare. Vines twisted up the walls and across the ceiling to form a canopy over a jungle of large-leaf plants, plants with a shine that said, "Plastic!" The "suite" was really one large room, and in the seating area, hammocks replaced sofas. The hammocks were fitted with pads covered in tiger-print satin fabric. The end tables and the coffee tables resembled sections of tree trunk. Plastic tree trunk. With round Lucite tops.

Faith focused on the bed. Enormous, resting on a platform painted to look like a rock ledge, it was the focal point of the room. The base was made of twisted boughs. Plastic boughs, of course. More animal prints—leopard, zebra, cheetah—covered the duvet, the many pillows. It looked like there'd been a massacre of endangered species.

She looked back to find Cabot staring at a hammock. Imagining himself there, maybe.

"I didn't ask what the room theme was," Faith said limply. "I thought hearts and flowers."

The bellhop gave her a you're-not-from-around-here-are-you look. "This is the weekend before Valentine's Day," he said. "The hearts and flowers were booked fifteen months ago. The rest of the year, this is our most popular suite." He did another sweep with his arm. "You have your visual effects," he said dramatically, "and your audio effects!" He pushed a wall switch and the space resonated with the caws of tropical birds, insect twirps, a distant waterfall and a swishing sound that Faith decided was probably the anaconda waiting patiently to pounce.

"Really gives the place character," the bellhop said. He nodded with satisfaction, and his tall, boxy hat bounced on his head.

"It does do that," Cabot said.

Faith couldn't bring herself to look at him. He had to be dying from sheer disgust. It was too much to hope he might be dying to laugh.

"It's fine," he said.

"No, it's not," Faith said.

"Yes, it is," Cabot said. "Tippy will like the ambiance. You ready out there, guys?"

"Ready as we'll ever be," Raff called back.

"It's show time, folks," Cabot said. "Hold on a

minute. I want to splash some water on my face first.''

The next thing she heard was a roll of thunder, a crackle of lightning and a sound from Cabot that, if his voice weren't so masculine, she might have called a scream. As the waiting crew muttered curses and flung down their equipment to dash to the rescue, the bathroom door opened. Cabot emerged, water dripping from his hair and clothes, clutching a leopard-print towel.

"I guess that wasn't the light switch after all," he said, deadly calm.

"It was your rain-forest effects," Faith said.

He stared at his crew for a long, silent moment. "We'll 'cross the threshold' tomorrow," he said in the same overly calm voice. "When the rainy season has passed." He slammed the door in their startled faces.

He glared at her, then turned his back and opened his suitcase. She gazed at his back, watching the elegant, black, soaking-wet suit crumple up, then opened her own large bag the bellhop had positioned on a luggage rack.

"When's dinner?" Cabot said, pulling things out of his suitcase and depositing them in a zebra-striped dresser.

"We have an eight-o'clock reservation," she said, hoping she'd remembered right.

"We have to stay here until eight?" There was an edge of panic in his voice.

She could understand the panic. She couldn't wait to get out of this place herself.

"It will be eight by the time we've unpacked and freshened up and…" It hit her like brand-new information that she was sharing the Tahoe Jungle Suite with a man she found almost irresistible. "And it will be time for dinner before you know it. Cabot…"

"What?" he said, sounding impatient as he unzipped a leather bag and pulled interesting-looking items out of it. Socks, underwear, turtlenecks…

Faith accepted the sad but true fact that everything about Cabot interested her, even his underwear. "I realize this isn't the mood you want for your honeymoon," she said. "By July the demand for hearts and flowers will slow down, and I'm sure I can—"

"I already said," he answered her, bent over a suitcase, "Tippy will like it just fine."

This time the familiar words didn't annoy her. She felt sympathetic, amused, willing to educate him. He didn't have a clue as to what a woman would like. Except that the woman would like him. What woman could keep herself from liking him. Wanting him. Loving him. Giving herself to him…

"I'll confirm the reservation," she said, and hastily involved herself in her unpacking.

Makeup and toiletries, the beautiful outfits with their matching shoes and handbags, belts, chiffon scarves, pashmina stoles. Jewelry—stunning, fake, and, Cabot had told her, borrowed. The pale-blue dressing gown. With shaking fingers she scrambled through the bags, unzipping pockets and ripping open Velcro cubbyholes before finally giving up the search.

That thing that had been niggling at her as she was leaving town—now she knew what it was. She'd forgotten to bring a stitch of underwear.

6

CABOT PULLED A SWEATER over his head, and just as he'd reached that point of no return, with both arms in the air and his head still trying to push through the turtleneck, he heard Faith say, "I need to do a little shopping."

"Forgot something?" He wanted to say, *something else,* but restrained himself.

"Ah, yes, a thong or two."

Nah, she couldn't have said that. His head popped through the sweater. "What?" He could see her now, and her face was flushed pink.

"A thing or two," she mumbled.

Female stuff probably. All he needed to put the perfect shine on the weekend was a surrogate bride with PMS. For a second he tried to imagine Tippy with PMS, but he didn't have to imagine it. Tippy acted like a woman with PMS all the time. "There are shops in the hotel. Go buy your stuff and I'll…" He would lie down quietly on some animal's skin and try to recover from Faith, from the tackiness of the room, from having to share the tackiest room in the world with Faith, all of those things. He might even experiment with the hammock, find out just how bad the night was going to be.

"Don't forget to confirm the restaurant reservation," he couldn't keep himself from adding. "Let's see, I've got all those written permissions to film. You got a separate table for the crew, right?"

"A sep—yes, of course," she said hastily.

"Because I don't want to treat them like staff. They'll do the filming between courses, and they'll be less obtrusive if they have their own table. Did you get the chart telling you what to wear when?"

"Ah…" She scrambled for a minute through a folder that had little pieces of paper sticking out randomly from three sides. "Yes."

"Be back in time to change."

"Yes, Sir," she said, and saluted smartly.

He had to admit he was being a nag. "Sorry," he said, "it's a bad habit."

"Everything will be fine," she said, and gave him a sunny smile as she tripped out the door, her little blue crocodile sandals not making a sound on the three-inch-thick jungle-green carpeting.

HER SMILE FADED as she raced through the hotel, which seemed to be one endless casino, looking for a private spot. At last she found a small foyer with a marble bench and collapsed onto it. With shaking hands she took the restaurant reservations sheet out of the folder and dialed the number of that night's restaurant—the nicest one in the hotel—on her cell phone.

"Confirming a reservation for two this evening in the name Drennan," she said in her best travel agent's voice.

"Yezz, of courzz," came the purring response. "We're eggspecting you." The voice cooled slightly. "You are the ones who are going to be vilming."

"Yes," Faith said. "We'll also need a nearby table for three, same time," she added, and held her breath.

"That is quite impozzible," the voice intoned at last. "We are vully booked."

"But it's very important," Faith said. What had she thought the crew would do? Stand around their table filming them having dinner all evening? "My job depends on it."

"I'm sorry about your job, but I can't make a table where there izz no table." The purr was rapidly turning into a snarl.

"Oh, but you can," Faith said with enthusiasm. "Just set up an extra table for three next to our table. We don't mind being crowded."

"Miss, zizz is not our style at Arturo's of the Inn of Dreams."

"Would you tell me your name, please?" Faith said, feeling desperate.

"Mario."

"Mario," she said, "maybe I should come into the restaurant and discuss this with you privately." So if necessary, she could slip him fifty dollars of her total liquid assets—one hundred thirty-six dollars and change. "I hesitate to tell you over the phone who will be filmed this evening, but she has strong democratic tendencies and will be appalled if her film crew doesn't have its own table."

"Izz this 'she' you refer to a...famous person?"

"Very."

"In politics?"

"Oh, heavens no."

"In the…film industry?"

There it was again, that sound of reverence. "I'm not at liberty to say," Faith said primly. "Her public is very demanding. She values her privacy."

"Ah-h-h," breathed Mario. He sounded as if he were starting to pant. "Well, let me see, Mizzz…"

"I'm their travel agent," Faith said.

"I think if we juggle here, and stagger there…" He seemed to be plotting it out visually. "Yezz. We will have that zecond table ready for your party, Mizzz…"

The purr was back, intensified. She'd saved herself fifty dollars. She wasn't bad at this stuff, just always a little late. Now she had to do the same thing four more times, the two lunches and the two other dinners. She punched viciously at her cell phone.

AN HOUR LATER she stood in front of the hotel's lingerie shop. Bad news, from the window display of silk and lace in Valentine colors of red and white. But surely they had plain white cotton panties and bras hidden away in the drawers, and she had about enough credit left on her credit card for two sets she could keep washing out.

"I need some underwear," she told the clerk.

"Doesn't everybody?" she simpered. "What sort of thing were you looking for?"

"Panties and bras. I forgot mine."

"Ooh, do I ever have some pretty things for you." She whipped out a white silk thong edged in lace and a bra that neither did nor hid anything, as far as Faith could tell.

"No, no, I was thinking more along the lines of…"

"Something more seductive. Aha." The woman laid out another matched set on the counter. This time the thong was black, covered in embroidered red hearts, and the bra was red with two large black hearts forming the cups. "This has been a hot number the last few days," she said.

"It would be a hot number any old time," Faith said. She felt rushed and flustered, and yet she couldn't keep from imagining herself wearing all those hearts, ambushing Cabot at the door of their own tiny honeymoon cottage.

And visions of that insidious sort were exactly the reason she needed to be buying plain white cotton panties and bras. "I'd prefer something simple," she said, "cotton, preferably."

"Cotton?"

"Cotton," Faith said firmly.

"We only have one cotton line," the woman said, casting a dubious glance at Faith. "But—lucky you, it's on sale."

"Wonderful," Faith said. "I'll take…" She looked down at the counter. They were cotton all right, thin cotton animal prints.

"Mix and match," the clerk said gaily. "Wear the leopard with the zebra, or be conservative and wear tiger top and bottom."

"They'd go well with my room," she murmured.

"Oh! Are you in the jungle suite? Lucky you!"

"Uh-huh," Faith said. The panties were, of course,

thongs. The bras scooped so low that Faith wondered why anyone would bother to wear one of them. "I don't suppose you have a camisole," she said.

"No, I've got a teddy," the clerk said.

"No teddies," Faith said sharply. She was running out of time. "I need something to sleep in, too," she said. She thought about Cabot, and added, "A pair of pajamas, *long*-sleeved pajamas with *long* pants. Neck-to-ankle coverage."

The woman gave her a look of sympathy. "I'll check in the back," she said.

While she looked, Faith peeked at the tags on the animal print underwear. The price didn't scare her too badly, so she held the bra up to herself and then the thong, tilting her head to one side as she tried to imagine herself actually wearing them.

There wasn't room in her budget right now for frivolous underwear, and she supposed there wouldn't be until she found a man she wanted so badly to look sexy for that she'd be willing to go into debt. She'd never had a problem getting dates, but several things had kept her from forming a lasting relationship. In the first place, each of her jobs had ended in a way that made it desirable to leave town. But in the second place...

The truth was that she was holding out for a man who made her feel the way her adoptive parents had felt about each other, a man who could bring that special light into her eyes, a man who...

"Hold it!"

She gasped and spun straight into the lens of Raff's camera and the sudden glare of Chelsea's lights.

They'd caught her in a full frontal shot, pressing the tiny underthings to her breasts and her tummy.

"Terrific," Raff said. "A bride-shops-for-sexy-unmentionables scene." He turned to Joey. "And she thought of it all by herself."

"Cabot's going to lo-ove it," Joey said, licking his lips.

"I did not think of it," Faith snapped, flinging the underwear down to the counter. "I forgot my underwear and came in here hoping to find something simple, but they don't have—"

The clerk came bustling out. "I have just what you asked for! Look!" She proudly displayed a pair of long-sleeved pajamas in black that were so sheer a person would be less noticeable naked. "But this one," she said, "would match your room!" She sealed Faith's fate by holding up in front of her a leopard-print mini-length slip-gown that was, if that were possible, more sheer than the pajamas.

"Got it. Smile!" Raff yelled.

"Aargh," Faith shrieked. She gathered up a random selection of underthings and tried to flee.

"Money," shouted the clerk. "You have to pay me for those things."

"Charge them to the room," Joey said.

Faith whirled and came back to the desk. "Don't you dare charge them to Cabot," she said, tossing her card across the counter. She stood there and fumed while the crew stood back and congratulated themselves on a great candid take.

"Your card was not approved for this sum," the clerk reported. Her mouth pursed disapprovingly.

"What sum will they approve?" Faith said, feeling increasingly helpless.

"Charge them to the room," Raff insisted. "Cab would expect you to. I'll sign the ticket if she won't," he told the clerk.

"You are taking over my life," Faith gasped, clutching the unwrapped undies to her bosom.

"That's showbiz, hon," Raff said.

Joey treated her to a spiteful smile and said, "Let the lady put your pretties in a bag, honey, or would you rather run through the casino with a pair of bloomers dangling down the front of your suit."

Chelsea said, "I got a great backlight on that leopard nightie. This was such fun, wasn't it? So spontaneous."

"JUST COULDN'T RESIST the casino, could you?"

She'd been gone so long he'd begun to worry. He couldn't figure out exactly why she'd want to escape now that they'd come this far. Still, he was so consumed by a need to run away from this bizarre suite, from the twinges of desire he felt for Faith each time he allowed himself to look at her and, above all, from the entire situation, that he could easily imagine someone else feeling the same way.

He was surprised, however, by the cold stare with which she greeted his words. She came to a sharp halt just inside the Jungle Nightmare Suite, sending that cold stare toward the spot where he sat on the edge of a hammock, swinging, trying to get up enough nerve to lie down on the thing.

"I have not been in the casino," she announced.

"I've just been through my own private hell and the last thing I need, the very last thing I need is for you to start picking on me."

"Picking on you? *Picking* on you? What happened?"

"You'll find out soon enough," she said grimly. She paused briefly in her stalk toward the "hers" bathroom. "Did you call Tippy and tell her what this suite was like?"

He shifted his gaze away from her. He had to learn to do things like that, make frequent calls to the woman he supposedly adored, or the sharp-eyed Faith would catch on. Until he learned, he'd have to use evasive tactics. "She'll like it. Don't worry."

Faith stifled a sigh. "Then if you'll excuse me, I need to cut off some price tags."

What did she mean by that? It was the first time he'd seen her in anything close to a bad mood. She'd been displeased about his wanting to come to Reno on this honeymoon of his, but not like this. Not icy.

She was even cute icy, though. Finding he was counting off the months of his commitment to Tippy again, Cabot sighed, rolled carefully off the edge of the hammock and went to make himself appropriately debonair for dinner.

The rehearsal for his wedding night dinner. What a laugh.

THE MAÎTRE D'HÔTEL took one look at Faith in her cream-colored outfit and whispered to Cabot, "Iv you'll give me a minute, zir, I can improve the location of your tables."

Cabot could understand the man's feelings. He'd taken one look at Faith in the dress with the thin layer of stuff floating over it, a dress that matched her hair but somehow made you want to drown yourself in her eyes, and desired nothing more than to improve every aspect of Faith's life, from her location to her marital status.

"Give us a quick little shot here in the bar while we wait," Raff said from somewhere near his left elbow.

"I guess you don't mean a shot of whiskey," Cabot growled, then said, "Okay, okay," put a tense arm around Faith's shoulders, feeling silk and the velvet softness of her shawl brush against his hand, and smiled.

"Oh, c'mon," Raff said, coming out from behind the camera to give him a disgusted look. "Right now you just look hungry."

He was hungry all right, but not for the Northern Italian cuisine in which the restaurant specialized. "All right," he groused, "what do you want?"

"In these shots," Joey said, "you'll want to transmit a sense of splendors to come, if you get my drift. Give her a 'just you wait, sweetheart, the night is only beginning' look, and Faith, honey, you give him a look that says 'oh, yummy, yummy.'"

"Joey," Cabot said, struggling for patience, "save this kind of stuff for Tippy. She's the actress. We're just rehearsing in a general kind of way...."

He trailed off because no one seemed to be listening to him. They were all staring at Faith, who had settled in under his arm as if she belonged there.

"She's got it," Raff said. "She's got the look we want. Now, come on, Cab, loosen up a little."

He loosened up enough to look down at Faith. Whatever look she might have been wearing that pleased Raff so much, now she just looked startled.

Her eyes were very wide, and as he gazed down at her, they softened.

He felt like a robot, the way his mouth just went down to meet hers of its own accord, the way the muted noise of the restaurant faded to a pleasant hum, the way he hardly noticed the whir of the camera, the glare of the lights, Joey's fluttering attentions. Just a robot, doing the thing he'd been designed to do, kissing Faith as if there were no reality and no tomorrow.

Her mouth was so soft, so warm, its heated moistness innocently maddening in its suggestiveness. He wanted to sink himself into it, devour her and be devoured. He felt the heat of her body beneath his hands, and the heat increased the intensity of her light flower scent until it surrounded them like a cloud.

"Cut. Good work."

He heard it, he had a feeling something was expected of him, but he didn't give a damn. He had a mission here, and that mission was to kiss Faith as long as she'd let him. His libido quickened when he realized she was doing more than letting him. She was exploring his mouth with hers, reaching for him, her response even sweeter for its innocence. The sweetness was overwhelming, taking him out of himself, out of his own life and onto a higher plane. His arms tightened around her, he drew her closer, heard her gasp…heard a throat-clearing sound and Raff saying "Cut!" a little more sharply than he'd said it before.

With enormous difficulty, exercising all his will-power, Cabot removed his mouth from Faith's, then removed his arms from around her, still feeling like a robot. His head turned mechanically to see his crew staring at him with peculiar expressions on their various faces.

"Your tables are ready, Mr. Drennan." The maître d' wasn't giving him a peculiar look. He was giving him that look people give lovers. It hit Cabot hard that what he had just done was to kiss Faith, really kiss her, right in front of his crew, the restaurant staff and the crowd at the bar.

"I hope you and Miss Temple enjoy your dinner," the maître d' whispered as the waiter led them away.

"Miss who?" Cabot managed to say. The man answered with an exaggerated conspiratorial wink.

Cabot whipped his handkerchief, the one that was just for show, out of his breast pocket and mopped his forehead with it. This problem was one he hadn't anticipated, that Faith might actually be mistaken for Tippy. In fact, it came as a surprise to him that Tippy already had fans who'd recognize her, and he was her publicist! Pondering his inadequacies, he marched forward behind Faith's slender, graceful figure to his doom. No, not his doom, his dinner. All too soon, it would be bedtime. Cabot stifled a moan.

7

BEDTIME.

If the rest of the day had been a nightmare, spending the night with Cabot in this room was the part of the dream in which you fall two hundred feet and wake up just before you hit the ground. That kiss in the restaurant had almost sent her over the edge, and it was really important that she wake up before she hit the ground. Or go to sleep before she made any moves on Cabot. Whatever. Just inside the doorway, Faith closed her eyes for a moment and tried to imagine what Hope would tell her to do.

Hope would say, "Behave with self-confidence. Treat the situation as an objective one. The kiss was all in his imagination. You don't remember any kiss."

Fine, if you were Hope. Faith's feelings about Cabot were so *subjective* she couldn't imagine carrying the night off with style. Still, she'd have to give it a try.

She gave Cabot a bright smile. It wavered a little when she saw the expression on his face, a look of uncertainty, almost of pain, but she forged ahead. "I'm more than ready to call it a day. And I'm sleeping in the hammock. No arguments. I'm smaller. I'll be more comfortable."

"No, you're..."

She slammed the bathroom door on his words.

When she emerged, he was nowhere to be seen. He must be in his own bathroom, trying to avoid the thunderstorm switch, perhaps even making himself a bed in his Jacuzzi.

What to wear to bed had been a big problem. She'd finally decided the sheer black pajamas were the better of the two choices. She would not, of course, take off the hotel-issue thick terry-cloth bathrobe for even a second. Dressed in the pajamas and robe, she tiptoed over to the hammock with a glass of water and the romance novel she'd brought along, arranged the pillows at one end and then looked around for a blanket.

She found a tiger-print blanket in the top of the "hers" closet. Assured of total coverage, she lay down gingerly on the hammock, let out a little cry when it began to swing and tip, then righted herself in the center and hung on to the sides.

People napped in hammocks all the time. Her father loved to stretch out in the hammock in their tree-shaded backyard in Chicago. The difference was that his hammock wasn't mostly filled up by a slippery pad. She'd be fine, though. She reached back with her left hand and switched on the end table lamp—the one with the elephant base—and out with her right hand to capture the book off the glass and tree-trunk coffee table without unbalancing herself. Now everything was perfect. When Cabot emerged from the "his" bathroom, where the sound of running water indicated that he was taking a shower, and heaven knows what else he was doing, because he'd certainly been gone awhile, she would look both comfortable and busy, forestalling any more argument. She rested the book on her chest, tugged the blanket up under it and began to read.

"Thaddeus's hand rested lightly on Lucinda's shoulder, and yet the electricity of his touch traveled a fiery path into the very center of her body. She moaned."

Faith closed the book. This was not the sort of book she should be reading at this particular time. She wondered if there might be an old *Engineering Weekly* lying around somewhere.

The likelihood of finding an *Engineering Weekly* or a *Journal of Neurosurgery,* say, was too low for Faith to let go of the book in her hands. As tense as she was, she really needed to read herself to sleep, and she also needed to give Cabot the impression of a person who was perfectly content in a hammock. Her finger twitched inside the pages—my goodness, she hadn't even lost her place—and Faith couldn't imagine how, but the book opened of its own accord.

"'I've longed to touch you like this since the day I came upon you cleaning the fireplace in Lady Estelle's castle,' Thaddeus whispered harshly, 'but I dared not, because I knew that one touch would destroy my resolve. One touch, one taste of you and I could never wed Lady Estelle. And my whole life, my fortune, depends on my marriage to Lady Estelle.'"

"'I know,' Lucinda groaned, 'and I understand. You mustn't go furthur, Thaddeus, or I will be unable to restrain myself. I will give myself to you, body and

soul, at the cost of diverting you from the life that will make you happy, will satisfy your true needs. Let me go, Thaddeus, let me go.'''

Tears came to Faith's eyes. Poor, poor Lucinda. She wasn't a bad person, just a simple servant girl who'd found the man of her dreams, but knew he could never be hers.

"From the moment she'd seen Thaddeus watching her as she scrubbed the mortar between the stones of the baronial fireplace, the look in his eyes had told her the depth of his wanting, the intensity of his need for her. She knew the look in her eyes answered the look in his eyes fourfold. For herself, she wanted nothing but Thaddeus's love. But for Thaddeus, in order to have her he would have to give up everything he'd dreamed of, respectability and wealth. She couldn't deprive him of those things. She had to send him on to his true destiny, his life with Lady Estelle."

Faith needed a tissue by the time she'd put herself totally in Lucinda's worn shoes, but if she reached for a tissue, she'd fall off the hammock. Instead, she sniffed deeply and read on.

"'But today is the feast of Saint Valentine, my darling,' Thaddeus rasped, and—"

Faith flung the book to the floor. Thaddeus was about to give up everything he wanted just because Valentine's Day approached, while Cabot...

...strode very suddenly across the jungle-grass-green carpeting and scooped her up out of the hammock.

"Let me go, Thaddeus," Faith screamed, struggling in his arms.

"Who the hell is Thaddeus?" Cabot demanded to know, coming to a full stop between hammock and bed.

She felt too intimidated not to answer. "He's the hero in the book I'm reading. I don't know why I said Thaddeus instead of Cabot, but I did it for the same reason! You can't, I can't let you give up—"

"Give up the bed for the hammock? The hell you can't. I said I was sleeping in the hammock and I meant it. You work for me, damn it, so follow instructions!"

With that surprising statement, he tossed her into the supersoft center of the water bed, then folded his arms across his chest, which was discreetly covered in a Stewart plaid pajama top.

She admitted to a deep disappointment when she observed he was also wearing the pajama bottoms.

With a few little changes—she was in terry cloth instead of Passion, he was in Stewart plaid instead of paisley and there wasn't a shred of desire in his dark chocolate eyes—it was her daydream come true, of Cabot tossing her onto the king-size bed.

The bed rocked her in its waves, so she had to wait until it settled down to say, "I was *trying* to accept the blame for having to share this room. I was *trying* to be thoughtful."

Myriad reactions crossed his face, so many that Faith couldn't keep up. "I don't know how to deal with thoughtful," he finally said. "I understand the bottom line, which is I sleep on the hammock and you sleep on the bed. Tomorrow you can start lobbying the front desk again. Some couple's going to get mad at each other and get an annulment in the morning. We just have to get through tonight.''

Just tonight? No way could she think of it as ''just tonight.'' ''Of course,'' she said, resurrecting her professional self. ''So, just for tonight, could you hand me my book?'' The water bed still rocked her, but more gently.

''Coming right up.'' He strode across the room. ''How about this glass of water?''

''That, too. Thanks.''

''You got it.'' He deposited the glass on her night table, glared at her and said, ''Good night.''

''G'night,'' she murmured. She discreetly wiggled her way under the comforter and between the sheets—tiger striped—and opened her book.

She could see him just fine over the top of the paperback. He approached the hammock, sized it up, slowly sat down on it, slowly leaned back—and somersaulted over the edge onto the deep pile carpet with a muted thud.

''Cabot!'' she said, already half out of bed. ''Are you all right?''

''I'm *fine*.''

He didn't sound fine. He sounded furious. Still, she slid back into bed, listening to a long silence. Unable to stand it anymore, Faith peered around the edge of the book—nothing was happening in the story, anyway, except Thaddeus endlessly examining his soul and Lucinda her conscience. He seemed to be all right, sitting up on the rug and staring at the hammock. After he'd stared it down, he got up and approached it again. This time he sat down closer to the middle and instead of leaning back, he gripped both edges and attempted to put his head down and swing his legs up at the same time.

"Oof" was the only sound he made as the hammock folded into itself. As he struggled to release himself the hammock began to twist. Faith leaped up out of bed. By the time she'd reached the hammock, he was tightly twisted inside it, like a butterfly in a cocoon.

"Ood uuu a east *try* t'gi me ow of ere?" His words were muffled in the thick pad, but Faith had no difficulty intuiting them as a cry for help.

"Of course!" she said, and reached out to begin the untwisting process.

"'Lowly!"

"I'll go slowly and carefully." She managed to flip him over once, hoping some law of physics would take over and unwind him the rest of the way, but he was too heavy. So she gave him another roll.

Now the hammock made its decision to take over. It spun suddenly three times before Faith managed to dive forward, trying to slow it down. When she dived, it caught the sash of her terry robe and tore the robe off her body just before it deposited Cabot on the carpeting with Faith splayed out on top of him. The pad flew out to cover both of them.

As Cabot's body took form and shape under hers, and it was a very specific form and shape, all Faith could focus on was the way she felt, pressed so tightly against that form and shape, wearing nothing but pajamas so thin they might have been hair spray. "I'm sorry," she said at once, knowing instinctively that the way to begin was to accept all the blame.

"Wasn't…your…fault." He sounded breathless.

What did he mean, "wasn't"? What was happening was all too obviously in the present. She couldn't keep herself from moving against him, and she felt him respond, felt that very specific form and shape pressing hard against her sudden moistness.

It was another one of your rain-forest effects. Desire was taking over, desire as raw and primitive as the jungle itself. "You Tarzan, me suddenly Jane." There was only one possible way to handle their isolation, by finding everything they needed in each other.

She searched for it even now, for the warmth of a human's touch, the sense of connection, and felt him responding, searching, too. She could also feel his reluctance, feel the fight going on inside him as his arms gripped her, then loosened and pushed her away, as his hands slid down her back, then shot rapidly upward to her shoulder blades. It felt so right to her that she couldn't imagine why he was holding back. Afraid to do anything as bold as to kiss him, she rested her head beneath his chin and nuzzled his throat.

One minute Cabot would tell himself there wasn't a single reason he shouldn't make love with Faith. The next minute he'd remember the reasons. He hadn't known her long. Long enough to figure out she wasn't a one-night-stand kind of woman, but not long enough to know if they were really right for each other.

Then there was the small matter of Tippy.

Faith's mouth against his throat, instinctively kissing him there, was driving him out of his mind. When he was able to rise above his state of nearly painful arousal and conjure up an image of Tippy winning an Academy award, he was able to push Faith away, but not for long, because he found it difficult and frustrating to hold on to the image of Tippy while Faith was in his arms, warm, silky, as light as a…a…Nerf ball.

Of course, he knew he wasn't being unfaithful to Tippy. As long as he married her and got her name in the industry news, she didn't care who he made love with. But Faith didn't know that, and furthermore she didn't know he knew that. As far as she knew, he was locked in an all-too-warm, all-too-seductive embrace with his bride's double. What kind of man would do a thing like that?

What kind of man would have his hands where his hands were right now? Quickly he put them flat on the carpet, where they began to twitch with frustration.

It was fate. The hammock had made the decision for them. *The hammock did it,* he could tell himself, his own worst judge, and, relieved of all responsibility, he could enjoy this small, deliciously sweet woman for a long, ecstatic night.

No, even better, he could tell Faith the truth about his marriage to Tippy. Then she'd know that he knew it was all right to…

What is wrong with this picture?

As he tried to sort it out in his mind, his dazed and

confused state only increased. But one thought pushed even harder at him than the desperate wanting he felt for Faith. Tippy's career. The importance of not letting the truth about this sham marriage leak out. Faith wouldn't tell anyone intentionally, but things had a way of getting around in the film industry. He couldn't tell her. He couldn't make love with her. He couldn't do anything he'd like to do—yet!

IT ONLY TOOK FAITH another agonizing moment to remember why Cabot couldn't take her to bed and rouse her to heights of ecstasy. He was engaged to another woman. What was she doing nuzzling the neck of an engaged man? She wasn't the kind of woman who'd deliberately set out to seduce another woman's man! She was like Lucinda—courageous, willing to sacrifice her own passion to retain her honor. Like Tippy in *Kiss*. Specifically thinking of Tippy gave Faith the momentum she needed.

"Cabot, we mustn't..." she moaned just as he groaned, "Faith, we can't..."

They parted as abruptly as two magnets turned negative to negative. She rolled off him, he gave the tiger-striped pad a violent shove and came up on his feet in one smooth movement. Getting up was more of a struggle for her. She could see him wanting to give her a hand, then thinking better of it.

"Sorry, that was pretty silly, wasn't it. Me getting rolled up in that hammock and both of us getting dumped on the floor. Lethal hammock. Just an accident, that's what it was. Not something that would ever happen again."

While he rambled on and she scrambled up without any help, he busied himself putting the pad back on the hammock. She noticed that he'd tied the tiger-print blanket over his pajamas.

"So we'll forget all about it. Right. It was just a little spill on the floor. No harm done. You're not hurt, are you?" He turned to her so suddenly it startled her.

"No, I'm fine. Well, sort of fine." She surprised herself by saying it. Most of the time, unless something really mattered to her, she just went along with whatever the prevailing opinion was. Cabot must really matter to her. The thought made her feel shaky.

"What hurts?" he asked. His voice was gentle, which made her feel worse.

"My conscience," she said, "and my pride. I'm embarrassed by the way I behaved just now. I took advantage of you, of the position you were in. I'm appalled at myself. I don't know what came over me."

A smile played around the corners of his mouth. "I think I do," he said. His eyes were dark and warm.

"Oh, no, you couldn't possibly." Her face was flaming. "I'm not that kind of person. I would never, ever come between you and Tippy. I just forgot myself. I…"

"Then can you explain what came over me?"

She halted, staring at him. "Nothing came over you," she said, "except me."

"I have to confess something," he said slowly.

"No, no, you mustn't confess anything," she babbled.

"I'm going to anyway, and you're going to listen." He tilted her chin with one finger and gazed into her eyes.

This was unbearable. With one fingertip he could send this searing heat through her, make her knees wobbly, recreate all the sensations that had assailed her while they were pressed so close together. She wished desperately she'd just said, "I'm fine," and hopped back into bed. And pulled the covers over her head. And hadn't come out until morning. Hadn't come to Reno in the first place. That was really what she wished. That poet who said it was better to have loved and lost was an empty-headed idiot.

"...felt that spark from the beginning," he was saying when his words finally got through to her. His face was shadowed now. "From the minute I saw you in the travel agency, really. I've even caught myself wishing I'd seen you first, before..."

"No! You mustn't say that. You're just missing Tippy," she cried, "and I have a slight resemblance to her, a purely superficial resemblance," she hastened to say, not wanting to sound presumptuous, "and you got confused. Sharing this room, which was all my fault, was the most terrible thing that could have happened. It will all be fine again when you're back at home with her. Promise me it will."

A deep sigh rose from him. "I've made a commitment to her," he said, his voice very low. "I will honor it."

"That's the spirit," Faith said, limp with relief. She began backing away from him. "Okay, nothing happened, what didn't happen is all over and we'll never

mention it again. So I'm off to bed. Good night.''
She'd reached the bed at last and jumped in, turned
over, closed her eyes.

It seemed like forever before she went to sleep. She
felt hot, agitated, frustrated—and guilty. While she
lay there she heard one more thud, the kind of thud
a large body would make after falling from a hammock onto thick carpeting, and then silence.

A HAND TOOK HERS, spreading her fingers apart,
gently caressing her fingertips, pushing lightly at the
nails with something cool and pleasant. Still buzzing
with frustration her dreams had only increased, Faith
rolled toward the source of this attention and smiled
without opening her eyes.

He'd decided the spark was brighter with her than
it was with Tippy. This time she couldn't say it was
her fault, because he'd come to her, had taken her
hand in his and would soon take all of her into his
arms.

She shrieked when her hand plunged suddenly into
warm water. ''Manicurist,'' said a disembodied voice.
''I'm here to do your nails.''

8

FAITH'S FIRST THOUGHT was to look for Cabot.

"He left you a note," the manicurist said.

Faith tried to get at least one hand out of the warm water to grab the note, but the manicurist shoved it back down. "I'll read it to you," she said. *"Faith, I'll be back at ten with the crew. We'll film the breakfast-in-the-room scene. Please wear the dressing gown.* The hairdresser's waiting in the bathroom. We'd like to shower before she does your hair and I finish your nails."

"Cabot said all that?" Faith wanted to know.

"No. Just the part about the dressing gown at ten."

A personal touch, like *"Dear* Faith," from the man she'd been close to making love with the night before would have been nice. "Is there coffee?" Faith inquired, figuring coffee might ease the pain.

"As close as room service," the manicurist said in her extraordinarily dry voice, and tucked a receiver between Faith's ear and shoulder.

Faith ordered coffee. "We already have your order, miss," room service said.

"Oh, fine, then," Faith said.

"Hit the showers," the manicurist said.

"Yes, coach," Faith muttered, and hauled herself

out of bed. She didn't care what the manicurist must be thinking about a bride who had worn the hotel robe to bed.

AT NINE-FIFTEEN Faith sat very still on a tree-trunk stool, the blue satin dressing gown spread carefully around her on the floor, her feet pinched into little blue satin mules. Her hair was perfect. Her makeup was perfect. Her fingernails and toenails were pink and perfect. Three thoughts were vying for her attention.

The first was that she still hadn't had any coffee.

The second was that she no longer wondered why Charity, however beautiful, didn't want to be a model. The Sumner sisters simply hadn't been brought up to be groomed to states of perfection and told to stay that way for forty-five minutes. The Sumner sisters knew how to get down and dirty.

The third was that Tippy Temple could not, absolutely could not, want to spend the early morning hours of her honeymoon the way Faith had just spent her early morning hours. Tippy would want to spend that time exactly the way Faith wished she could spend it, getting very messy making warm and dreamy love with Cabot. Faith was so sure she was right that she felt an urgent need to do something about the situation.

Cabot would thank her later. She was also sure of that.

She would simply call Tippy and ask her what kind of honeymoon she wanted. All she needed was Tippy's telephone number.

It was important that Cabot not catch her going behind his back to talk directly to Tippy. Faith got up carefully, took a hotel notepad and pen from the night table and removed herself to the "hers" bathroom, then rearranged herself on a terry-cloth-covered tree-trunk stool just below the bathroom wall phone. Being careful not to nick her fingernail polish, she punched in the number of directory assistance in Los Angeles. It didn't surprise her to hear that Tippy was unlisted. But an agent wouldn't dare be unlisted. Jack Langley, Cabot had mentioned once in passing. She got Jack Langley's number and dialed it.

It's show time, folks.

"Jack," Faith said, when, miraculously, the secretary put her through to the man himself. She said it warmly, fondly, acting as if he and she were the closest of friends. "It's Faith. There are a couple of little honeymoon details I'd like to discuss with Tippy personally. But Cabot's not here and I don't have her phone number."

There was a brief silence, in which Faith imagined Jack Langley desperately trying to figure out who Faith was and why she needed to discuss Tippy Temple's honeymoon with her. "Faith," Langley said at last. "Let's see. Jog my memory."

Even though it didn't suit her own purposes, Faith was relieved to know that Tippy had the protective kind of agent. "Faith Sumner," she said, trying to sound amazed that he couldn't place her immediately. "Wycoff Worldwide Travel. I'm the honeymoon specialist," she added, trying the title on for size, "who's doubling for Miss Temple on the dry run."

"Of course." He seemed reassured. "How are things going?"

"Well—" That ought to shake him.

"Problems?" A worried note crept into his voice.

"Oh, no," she said, then added, "not really."

"What?" he said sharply.

"Nothing really important," she said, back to her warm, reassuring self. "There are a few little things I'd like to discuss with Miss Temple herself. I've just finished the whole routine—the manicurist, the hair-stylist—and I wanted to be sure their methods were up to Tippy's standards. That sort of thing." She held her breath.

"I don't see what harm that could do," Langley said after an alarming hesitation.

Whoosh!

"Here's the number," he said at long last. "Give me a minute to call her first so she'll be expecting your call."

Faith's heart thudded so wildly with the thrill of victory that the only words of his she could focus on were the numerals of Tippy's phone number. Her hands shook as she dialed. She waited through one ring, two rings, then heard, "Yo," and "pop!"

Yo? "Miss Temple?" Of course it wouldn't be Tippy herself, it would be a minion who'd be flattered out of her skull to think she'd passed for the legendary Tippy.

"Who's callin'?" Suspicion dripped from the hard-edged voice.

Faith felt flustered and suddenly uneasy. "Oh, I'm

sorry. I'm Faith Sumner, Miss Temple's travel agent, and I wanted to discuss a few matters with her.''

"That's me!" The voice brightened, then Faith heard another loud popping sound. "Hey, you're the chick that's in Reno with Cabot! How's it goin'? Pretty keen, huh?''

Faith's mouth opened and closed a few times. "Yes. You don't mind that I'm here with him, do you, because—"

"Oh, hell, no! And you check things out real good, okay? But listen, hon'—'' the gravelly voice dropped a couple of decibels ''—when the time comes, you gotta get me a smokin' hotel, okay? Between us girls, no way can I get through a weekend of hair and makeup and shooting schedules without a cigarette. Between my fingers every second. Read me? Hang on a sec. My other line's ringin'.''

Faith hung on. She hung on to the phone with one hand and the closest towel bar with the other. The harsh nasal voice seemed to be coming through a wad of chewing gum, and the woman wanted cigarettes, and what was she saying about a weekend of shooting schedules, when it was going to be a weekend of hot and heavy sex and a little footage for the old memory video.

"Faith?''

"What!" Faith snapped to attention. Someone else had taken over the phone.

"Sorry you had to hold.'' This person sounded soft and sweet, yet familiar. "That was my agent on the other line.'' She paused. "What did you think about my reading?''

Faith rested her head against the marble bathroom wall. "Reading?" she said weakly.

"Why, yes. I was going over a part in a screenplay I might be interested in doing. A rough, tough kid from the projects, a complete change from my character in *Kiss*. Except for her heart of gold," Tippy added. "And I thought, 'wouldn't it be fun to try out the character's personality on the first person who calls?' So what did you think? Be blunt."

"You certainly fooled me," Faith said. She lifted her head away from the wall and patted delicately at her forehead, relieved to be breathing normally again. "You were a completely different person."

"So, Faith, what can I do for you?" Tippy was asking her. Sweetly.

Faith warmed to her topic, just as she had warmed to Tippy. "Cabot is a considerate, thoughtful man, I'm sure," she said diplomatically.

Tippy interrupted. Gently. "Isn't he?" she said. "I can't tell you how I appreciate what he's doing for my career. And I appreciate your going through the rehearsal—I mean, checking everything out—for me. I just didn't have the time."

Faith felt off balance again. Maybe it was just because she'd rehearsed her speech, it wasn't going quite the way she'd imagined, and she'd lost her place. What *had* she been saying? Oh, the part about how wonderful Cabot was. At least he was wonderful looking. Wonderful feeling. She really had very little information about his true character, his inner being, his...

Faith did a little exercise Hope had suggested to

her. She gathered up all the fluffy bits that were floating around in her head and squashed them into a small gray ball, the way she and her sisters used to do with slices of white bread when they were kids. Then she mentally swallowed it and imagined her stomach acids going to work on it.

"I was saying that he's also a very, ah, strong and determined person, and in this case, he's so determined to honeymoon here in Reno that I wasn't sure an old-fashioned girl like you would speak up and tell him what you really want."

"Old-fashioned girl." Tippy sounded as dreamy as Faith usually felt. A rush of air came through the receiver that Faith interpreted as a deep, heartfelt sigh.

"Yes. I saw your movie," Faith said shyly, "and your television interviews—to tell you the truth, I'm one of your biggest fans. I admire the kind of person you are, and I'm so glad you and Cabot are getting married, because even though I haven't known him long, I'm sure you're the kind of person he deserves, and he's so good-looking and strong and forceful, he's just the kind of person you deserve." It startled her when tears welled up in her eyes, and she paused to pull herself together. She'd been treating her attraction to Cabot like a game, or a private joke. Until last night, when she'd gotten an all-too-brief, all-too-frustrating glimpse of how real it was.

She wished she could get all those fluffy bits of her brain back. She needed distractions.

"Are you all right?" Tippy asked.

"Allergies," Faith said, and faked a sneeze. "Anyway, all I want to know is if Reno is really okay with you or if you're just too kind and polite to tell Cabot you'd prefer someplace more romantic.''

"Oh. Well, Reno's okay.''

"This particular honeymoon suite,'' Faith said, pressing the point, "is a jungle fantasy. No chairs, just hammocks and sawed-off tree trunks. Sound effects. The occasional thunderstorm. Water bed. Is it still okay?''

"It sounds so cute,'' Tippy said.

Faith's eyes narrowed. "What about the routine I went through this morning,'' Faith persisted. "Do you really want your day to start this way, with a manicure and a pedicure and a woman working on your hair?'' She didn't add, *Don't you want to stay in bed all day with Cabot? I would.*

"It's part of my job,'' Tippy said, and sighed. Softly. "I have to look perfect every second for my fans.''

Faith couldn't hold it back any longer. "But what about Cabot?''

"Cabot?'' A little tinkling laugh. "The whole thing was Cabot's idea—the marriage, the honeymoon, the publici—'' Tippy's soft, sweet voice skidded to a dramatic halt before she burst out with "Oh sh—'' which was followed by a brief, thunderous silence, followed by "—oot!''

A vein in Faith's forehead throbbed so violently she thought it might burst. She'd die right there on the gleaming marble floor of the "hers'' bath in the Tahoe Jungle Suite. "She died of love,'' the newspaper article would say. "You're getting married for the publicity?'' she managed to gasp with her dying breath. ''You mean you're not really in love?''

''I didn't say that!'' Puff, puff. Maybe it was Tippy's dying breath, too. ''I wasn't supposed to tell!'' Puff, puff. ''Oh, my goo-awd, please don't tell Cabot I told!'' Puff, puff, rustle, snap, crackle, pop!

What was she doing? For that matter, who was she? Because the voice of the first Tippy was back, and this didn't sound a bit like a reading. It sounded like a desperate woman, a desperate woman from one of those boroughs around Manhattan, a woman from one of those boroughs who was desperate enough to be smoking and chewing gum at the same time.

In a moment of pure shell shock Faith had been able to focus on a single possibility—Tippy Temple had a severe case of multiple personality disorder. Now the ramifications of what she'd just learned flooded her, dizzied her. But only one mattered.

Cabot and Tippy weren't really in love.

And Cabot, who had clearly wanted her as much last night as she wanted him, hadn't told her that his relationship with Tippy was nothing more than a publicity stunt.

That…that…cad!

He'd put her through that drill—the desire, the regret, the embarrassment, the soul-searching, the guilt, plus a dream-ridden night reliving every second of it, all for nothing. All he had to do was tell her nothing stood between them and that ridiculous water bed. Thaddeus, at least, was honest with Lucinda!

Unaccustomed anger climbed her face, prickled her

scalp. She owed him one. More than one. She owed him a lifetime of restless nights.

"Tippy, I'll make you a deal," she said smoothly. "I won't tell Cabot you spilled the beans if you'll promise not to tell him I called you. And I also want you to call Jack Langley and tell him to keep a lid on it."

"I promise," Tippy whimpered. "Cabot would kill me if he knew I'd told."

"Not literally."

Tippy hesitated. "I don't think so. No. He probably wouldn't actually kill me. But he'd kill me professionally!" She suddenly burst into sobs.

"We have a deal then?" Faith refused to be sucked in by tears.

"I'm at your mercy," Tippy said pitifully.

And Faith would be merciful—to Tippy. For Cabot, that…that…words failed her. But for him she had plans. Big plans.

She'd been telling herself all along that she didn't really know him. That she could only call what she felt for him "lust" until she understood his true character. The way he'd deceived her, the way he'd made her feel guilty about that spark between them, was an indication of his true character, and the news was bad.

He was everything she didn't need in a man. He was too strong, too powerful, manipulative. He'd ride over her roughshod, never give her a chance to figure out what she wanted to do with her life, because he'd already have figured out what she ought to do with her life.

Exactly what she didn't need in a man.

If he was exactly what she didn't need, why did she still want him so much?

The telephone receiver still dangled from the cord in her hand. She replaced it in the cradle, stood up and took a really hard look at herself in the mirror.

She needed more makeup on her forehead.

Forget about makeup, focus on fury!

She wasn't without resources. Her anger would fuel her, her determination would steer her and her imagination would take care of the rest. Once she gave it free rein, let out all the stops, she'd give Cabot Drennan a weekend he'd never forget for as long as he lived.

"We're here," Cabot called from the doorway. "Are you decent?"

"Almost," Faith trilled. Still looking into the mirror, she unbuttoned the top button of the dressing gown and leaned over, unbuttoned the second button and leaned over. That was far enough for this morning.

"Good morning," she said, holding back the bathroom door to make an old-movie sort of dramatic entrance. The gesture also opened the neckline of the dressing gown to its fullest. "I hope you actually brought breakfast, because I'm—" she glided to him, the dressing gown brushing the floor, took his arm and looked up into his startled eyes "—starving." She breathed the word, letting her mouth pucker into kissing position.

Flash! "Great shot," Raff said.

"We're not ready yet," Cabot said irritably, shaking Faith's hand off his arm.

"The candids are the very best," Chelsea said. "Faith, you look gorgeous in that dressing gown. Where'd you get it, Cabot? I didn't know they made those anymore."

"Room service," said a voice from the doorway.

The video crew moved aside to make way for the waiter. Pushing a loaded table ahead of him, he struggled his way across the thick carpeting. When he'd arrived at a promising-looking spot, he reached with a flourish toward the lid of one of several chafing dishes.

"Wait!" Raff said. "Let's set the scene. Faith, sit down at the table, okay? Cabot, across from her, that's it. Chelsea, get the lights? Now, you two, give each other a breakfast-the-morning-after look."

Faith wondered briefly if there was anything creative about acting, or if one just did this look or that, acting by numbers, so to speak. But then, realizing this was not the time to seek an answer, especially not from these people, who would only deny it, she got right into the mood of the scene. She parted her lips and leaned forward.

The impact on Cabot was highly satisfactory. His gaze dove down into her cleavage and floated back up. The little nothing of a bra she'd bought yesterday had amazing push-up powers. She'd hooked him. She waited until his gaze had returned to her face, then ran the tip of her tongue across her lower lip.

"Cabot, you look like you just ate a pickle. Loosen up," Joey scolded.

One side of Cabot's mouth smiled. As he used his napkin to pat his forehead, Joey dived forward with the powder puff and plunged it first at Cabot and then at Faith.

"That's better, Joey," Chelsea said. "They were glaring."

"Ooh, we mustn't glare," Faith cooed at Cabot. "It won't look like the real thing."

"Chelsea was talking about our foreheads." Cabot seemed to be talking through his teeth.

"Oh, of course. Silly me. Shall we eat?" Faith said in what she hoped was a sultry voice.

"Now you can take the top off," Raff said.

Faith gave him a shocked glance, but Raff was addressing the waiter, who whipped the top off a chafing dish. Steam emerged invitingly.

"That's good," Raff said. He was using his camcorder now. It was making a rather pleasant whirring sound. "Now put the serving spoon in, that's it, that's it. Cut! Let's try it again, and this time, Cab, could you look a little less like a guy with acid indigestion?"

Faith wished they hadn't cut before the waiter served them. Images formed in her mind of softly scrambled eggs, sausages, a toasted English muffin. But the lid was back on the chafing dish.

"What difference does it make?" Cabot was arguing.

"All the difference in the world," Chelsea said in her slow Southern way. "A smile photographs entirely differently from a frown. If you want the final product to be perfect…"

"Okay, okay," Cabot grumbled, and curved his mouth into a skeleton's grin.

"Yuck," said Joey.

"You wouldn't feel like smiling either if you'd spent the night on the floor," Cabot growled.

"Why didn't you sleep in the hammock?" Joey asked. He stepped over to it, flipped neatly into it, stretched his arms out over his head and said, "I think it's great."

"How did he do that?" Cabot said. "How the hell did he do that?"

"Oh, Cabot," Faith whispered, "you know you didn't have to sleep in that hammock. I was dying to share that big, soft, warm bed with you. Maybe tonight?" She quirked up one eyebrow, encouraged by what was happening to his face. "I'll be good, I promise."

"That's a take," Raff called out. "Much better, Cab. Thanks for cooperating. Want to do the over-the-threshold scene while we're on a roll?"

For a second the expression clung to Cabot's face, a look of longing, his mouth slack, his lips parted, his eyes deep, dark and heavy lidded. Just as suddenly he seemed to come out of a dream. "No," he said. "We'll have plenty of chances to do that one. I'm going...I'm going to the business center to make some calls." He got up so fast he knocked over his chair, then tripped on it as he bolted toward the door.

"Don't you want some breakfast first?" Faith called after him. She opened the chafing dish. It was filled with steaming water.

"That's showbiz," she said. "It's empty." Had she imagined the scents of bacon and sausage?

"Oh, yeah," Raff said. "Just a prop. The muffins

are real. Have a muffin if you're hungry. It's almost lunchtime.''

She watched Cabot flee the suite with the rest of his troop flowing behind him, and she already had her teeth into a muffin when she remembered something important. "Cabot," she yelled out into the hallway, "don't forget to call Tippy!"

She closed the door and finalized the bite into the muffin. It was blueberry and really quite delicious, although not as delicious as that look of pure desire on Cabot's face.

All in all, her plan was going quite well so far. She was scheduled to wear the white silk suit to lunch. She'd unbutton it as far as she dared without getting arrested.

9

CABOT PARTED COMPANY with his film crew and slid
through the first doorway that opened up to him before he hit the cacophony of the casino. He found
himself in a bar.

Driven to drink. He'd been driven to drink. He collapsed onto one of the sofas and groaned. What could
be happening to him?

"You okay, sir?"

Cabot opened one eye to see a waiter hovering over
him. "Oh, fine," he said. "Headache, too much
champagne last night, you know the story."

"There are a million stories in this place," the
waiter said. "You on your honeymoon?"

"Well, I…"

"I knew it," the waiter said. "You have that
dragged-out look about you. I have just the thing for
what ails you." He hurried away.

Oh, Lord, now he was going to have to slug down
some awful concoction on an empty stomach. The
headache would become truth. Then he could use it
as his excuse. For everything. All day. And all night.

Don't think about tonight.

He really had to think of a distraction for tonight.
Let's see, he could activate the thunderstorms in both

bathrooms with the doors open, and while Faith was screaming too hard to notice what he was doing, he could puncture the water bed with the point of his fountain pen. Their room would flood, and the water would seep down into the rooms below, and maintenance would arrive, and all the people staying in rooms below them would be screaming, too, and the house detective would wade through the disaster to snoop around. He'd find the hole Cabot had punched in the water bed and the telltale ink stain marking the spot, and he'd call the police, who would arrest Cabot for vandalism and take him off to jail.

Jail. It sounded wonderful. Solitary confinement, if at all possible. His own thin, lumpy cot, his own scratchy gray blanket, and no Faith. He might wait days to call his lawyer. They might forget him entirely and he could grow quietly old in the Reno jail instead of...

"Here you are, sir. These will fix you right up."

Cabot looked down to see two dozen raw oysters staring up at him from an ice-banked platter the waiter had placed on the table in front of the sofa.

"I brought you a Virgin Mary to go along with them," the waiter added. "Save the hard stuff for later in the day, but the hot stuff will do you good."

Cabot read a great deal of symbolism into his words. "Thank you," he said, directing a weak—he hoped—smile at the young man. He'd give him a big tip. Better than a smile.

He stared back at the oysters. They certainly looked good, cool and refreshing.

Exactly the way the apple looked to Eve! He would not be tempted by these oysters!

He was acting stupid. The old saw that oysters increased the libido was just that, an old saw. No truth to it.

He gazed at the oysters again. Occasionally, there was truth in the old home remedies. Was now the time to take a chance? He forked up an oyster, dipped it into a spicy-looking red sauce, tore the plastic wrapper off a pair of saltines, looked up to see the waiter watching him anxiously from across the room and gave the guy a reassuring nod.

Embarrassed that he'd been caught watching, the waiter faded away.

Cabot tucked the whole shebang—oyster, sauce and cracker—into his handkerchief and palmed the handkerchief.

He glanced around the bar. He was virtually alone. Several tables away was a man who appeared to be finishing his evening instead of beginning his day. Cabot could stand on his head and that guy wouldn't notice. So he got to work. The crackers crumbled pretty well inside the plastic wrappers. He'd gotten a couple of packages of those stashed away and almost half the oysters into his handkerchief when he heard the murmur of voices, people coming into the bar. He swiveled his head and found the waiter hovering again.

"How is everything?"

"Fantastic," Cabot said. "I'm a new man already." He took a big swig of the spicy tomato juice to emphasize how well he was doing, then tried again to turn his head toward the door.

"Let me see you get one of these babies down," the waiter said. He forked up an oyster, dipped it in sauce, ripped a cracker out and approached Cabot's mouth.

Now this was too much. His libido—or his hangover, whatever it was Cabot chose his problem to be—wasn't the business of this waiter. "I'll take care of myself," he growled. "I'm not a..."

"Perfect, Cab, take the oyster, put it in your mouth and chew, look desperate for it—Cab, why won't you cooperate?"

His video crew had suddenly surrounded him, *him* surrounded by empty oyster shells, with the camcorder rolling. Cabot leaped up. "What the hell are you doing?" he shouted.

"We're tracking down candids," Chelsea said in her soft voice. "This was just too perfect, Cabot, the bridegroom desperately eating oysters after the wedding night."

"Desperate?" Cabot said. "Yes, I'm desperate. I'm desperate for a little privacy. I'm desperate for a crew who follows orders." He could hear his voice rising, but he couldn't help himself. "I'm desperate for a little predictability! And that means—" he lowered his voice to a harsh whisper "—that means I predict, and you make it come true!"

Raff lowered his camera and Cabot could tell he was offended. "You don't want any creativity here?"

"None. Zip. Not a shred of creativity. Got it?"

"Yessir."

There were times when he knew he was too tall, too muscled, too intimidating to engage in a fair fight. This was one of those times. Most of the time he tried to back off and give the other side a chance, but damn it, he was stretched to his limits here.

"So show up for lunch."

"Yessir."

"And not before."

"Yessir."

"And middle-class American newlyweds do *not*—" Cabot paused, searching for a word.

"Make love to each other in public places?" Chelsea offered.

"God bless your parents for bringing you up right, Chelsea," Cabot said, thinking all he needed right now was a flag to wave. "So ditch the prurient stuff and show a couple having a good time."

"Now *and* then," Raff said. "In July? When we make the real video of the real honeymoon? Just thought I'd ask, so I'd know what to expect."

Cabot thought it over. "Now *and* then," he said. "What Faith would do now is what Tippy would do then."

Was he wrong, or did Joey snort into his powder puff?

"I have an idea for tonight," he said next. "Can't imagine why it didn't come to me sooner."

"CASINO NIGHT?" Faith said. She opened her eyes wide as she said it, because she wanted then to gape as widely as the cleavage of her second-night's-dinner outfit, a confection of pastel silk flowers hooked together with invisible thread and molded over a layer of cream silk that outlined her body. She felt that the white suit had gotten him pretty heated up at lunch, and it was a nun's habit compared with this little number.

"Yes, casino night."

Cabot was darkly handsome and deeply distant in his ever-so-correct suit, which Faith longed to rip off his body in order to have her way with him. "It's not on the schedule," she informed him.

"I just put it on the schedule. How could we come to Reno and not have a casino night? You were in charge of the arrangements. Why didn't you include the casino in our plans?"

"Because I'm not a gambler." What she wanted to say next was that she was a lover, and what she wanted to do was bring him here after dinner and seduce him into telling her she was welcome to have her way with him, because his marriage to Tippy was nothing more than a—

No, she intended to be more subtle than that. This suite, she decided, was an inspiration to her. She was a panther, stalking her prey, traveling the secret paths of the jungle on soft, silent feet, keeping the elk always in sight. His proud horns would be hers before the night ended.

Did elk live in the jungle? Probably not, and you didn't call those branching things *horns,* you called them *antlers,* and she didn't really want his antlers. What she wanted was him begging her to make love with him, admitting his desire for her, while she, after bringing him to this point, would say, "But no. Your heart belongs to another." And then he, consumed with passion, would be forced to admit that he—

"I'm sorry, what did you just admit?" she asked Cabot. "I mean, what did you just say?" This time she remembered to bat her eyelashes down once, then up again.

"I said," Cabot said, gazing down at her with a faint, indulgent smile, "I'm not a gambler, either. You don't have to be a hardened gambler to spend a pleasant evening in a casino."

"I know, but it scares me," Faith said. "I've heard what happens to people. They think they're just gambling for fun, then something takes hold of them and they can't quit. They spend every cent they have, go into debt and ruin their lives."

"Gambling won't ruin your life if you follow a few rules."

He was wearing a professorial expression, so she assumed an appropriately attentive one. "What rules?"

"Decide beforehand what you're willing to lose." He pulled out a slim roll of bills and said, "I'm staking myself to a thousand dollars. When it's gone, so am I."

"How very sensible," Faith murmured, thinking what an impact a thousand dollars could have on her life. Tires *and* brake linings.

"Be careful not to drink too much. You'll lose your inhibitions."

Aha. She'd ply Cabot with alcohol! Her attention wandered, thinking of Cabot without inhibitions. She gazed at him, thinking he was born to wear black suits and white shirts. Tonight it was a white turtleneck, resort casual. The sweater matched his teeth and set off his tennis tan. With his dark hair and chocolate eyes, he was a hot-fudge sundae to be spooned up and eaten slowly. She could feel that magical mixture of heat and coolness on her tongue already, making her mouth water for—

"…slot machines are your thing, look around for one with a big jackpot and watch it for a while before you…"

His eyes seemed to bubble hotly as hers lost their focus. She should be paying attention to the important information he was giving her about gambling, but it occurred to her that she'd been neglecting the equally important job of seducing him for the past several minutes. She moved closer to him, breasts first, then looked up at him and gave him a slow smile.

"Just like a scene in a James Bond movie," she said at the first pause in his lecture. She ran her tongue over her lower lip, a gesture, she'd noticed, that seemed to start up a tic under his left eye. "I'll be your lucky lady, tell you what numbers to bet on…"

"Something like that," he said, the tic fluttering wildly. "Raff will supply the direction." He cleared his throat. "Time to go to the restaurant. I believe it's the one up in the mountains tonight. Better put on your coat." He grabbed the fluffy white coat from the closet and shoved one of her arms into it.

"Not yet, silly," she said, giving her body a wriggle that started in her knees and went clear up to her neck. "Wait until we're actually out in the cold." She reversed the wriggle.

"I think you should put it on now," Cabot said. She saw him close his eyes before he gave her a half spin and shoved her other arm into a sleeve of the coat.

"THAT WAS FANTASTIC," Faith breathed into his ear, snuggling up to him in the back seat of the white limo she'd engaged for the evening. "What a view! The mountains were so mysterious looking in the dark, with the lights of Reno down below. Oh, it was so romantic."

"My steak was overcooked," Cabot growled, moving an inch away.

By infinitesimal bits Faith followed, and soon had him hugging the door on his side of the car. She let the coat fall open, slipped off her shoes and tucked her feet up in a way that allowed her knees to brush against his thigh. He stiffened. She hoped more of him was stiffening than met the eye.

"That restaurant is a winner," she went on, pulling her knees up a little tighter, which increased the pressure on his thigh. "I think Tippy will like it, don't you? Have you talked to her?" she asked innocently.

"Of course. We're engaged to be married. We talk constantly," he said.

She knew he was lying.

"I just wondered, because I never see you call, and you're right there in the same room with me." She let her arm slide up and down his.

She hoped his door was locked. He was in danger

of falling out. Or leaping out. "Of course I don't call her when you're listening," he said. His voice was tight. "I call at odd times, when you're showering or something."

"Well, good. Because women need lots of attention." She put her face right up in his. "You know that, don't you, Cabot?" she breathed, letting the tip of her nose brush his cheek.

"Is it hot in here or is it just me?" Cabot said.

Faith fluffed her coat a little. "I'm comfortable." Slowly she stretched her legs out across the seat and leaned harder against him. "Ooh. Very comfortable."

Cabot scooted forward suddenly and she slammed back against his window. "How far are we from the hotel?" he asked the driver.

"Not far now," the driver said, and chuckled.

Faith knew what that chuckle meant. The driver knew an impatient bridegroom when he saw one.

Cabot tried to scoot back, but she was in the way. "Oh, sorry," she murmured, and swirled around his solid shape, touching him everywhere she could as she got back up into a sitting position.

A moment at the restaurant began to torture him again, Faith lifting a bite of heart-shaped raspberry tart to her lips and running her tongue lightly across the raspberries before she slowly put it between her lips. The memory made him want to groan, so he cleared his throat instead.

For the hundredth time that day, he did something he hadn't intended to do, didn't want to do, just did it. He closed his arms around her. As soon as he'd done it, he wondered why he'd done it and how he could get out of it.

"Interesting coat," he murmured, trying to still the other impulses he was having. "What's it made of?"

"I think," Faith said dreamily, relaxing with dangerous ease into his arms, "it's made of a synthetic that's intended to look like curly ermine. Charity gave it to me for Christmas. She said it looked a lot like my hair."

Her hair, that fluffy blond cloud, was tickling his ears. It felt much too good. Carefully he lifted his arms away from her. There was nowhere to put them but over his head, so he did that, stretching to hint at the need for a little more space in the damned car, please. All she did was tuck a little deeper into his stretched-out body.

As the blood ran down his veins and his hands began to get cold, he acknowledged that her sudden personality change was very surprising. Last night really had been an accident, but from breakfast on, she'd clearly been trying to stir him up. It proved a point. You had to spend time with a person, even live with her, to know what she was really like. Two days ago he'd have bet his last dollar she'd behave like a nun on this trip, careful to act fully professional and especially careful not to come between him and his intended, her heroine Tippy Temple.

He hoped he did better at the table tonight than he had on that bet.

Maybe there was a reason. Maybe she'd bumped her head last night when the hammock dumped her right on top of...

An increased and more insistent pressure in his groin suggested that the less time he thought about Faith sprawled out on top of him, the better.

Maybe… He felt a smile forming. Maybe she *was* the woman he thought she was. Maybe she was testing him, testing him to see if he was good enough for Tippy.

He found this thought cheering, so he clung to it while he wiggled his hands, trying to get some circulation back into them. Two could play that game. If she could test him for fidelity, he could test her for professionalism.

He'd start testing now. He lowered his arms and folded them around her again. "I shouldn't be doing this," he murmured against her forehead, "but it feels so comfortable. Friendly. Know what I mean?"

She snuggled into him, but he'd already felt the startled jolt of her slim little body against his. He was on the right track!

10

"THINK JAMES BOND," Raff said.

Cabot gave Faith a sharp look, wondering if they'd been colluding.

"Yeah," Raff said. "The two of you stroll up to a window all casual-like, then Cab, you flash a roll of bills. We'll ham it up a little, right? Aw, hell, Cab, haven't you got a bigger roll than that?"

Cabot viewed his high-priced cinematographer with disgust. "They're hundreds. Want me to go switch them for ones?"

"Yeah."

"The hell I will."

"Okay, okay," Raff said. "Then forget the flashing and just get the chips."

Cabot glanced down at Faith. The dress with the little flowers had some kind of lining, but the lining was just about the color of Faith's skin, which made it look like the flowers were pasted directly onto her body. What that made him want to do was put his fingers through the little spaces between the flowers and stroke the creamy skin beneath. He felt himself kind of collapsing all over and whirled abruptly back to Raff.

"Faith can do this scene in her coat," he said.

Raff brought the camcorder down from his shoulder and held it in both hands like a kid with a football. "Why?"

"I just think it would—"

"—look ridiculous," Joey snapped.

"She's so pretty in that dress," Chelsea said. "She looks like a nosegay."

One woman's nosegay was another man's...any man's...

Oh, hell, I need a writer even when I'm talking to myself.

He held out both palms. "All right, I know when I've been outvoted."

What was worrying him was that, as a man whose business involved seeing a lot of movies, he'd seen all the James Bonds. He had a distinct memory of Bond, whoever was playing him in that movie, sitting at the chemin de fer table with a beautiful girl on his lap. Cabot's first defensive move was to avoid chemin de fer and go straight for the roulette table. As for the second, if Faith was going to sit on his lap, he'd like to have as much insulation between them as he could pack onto the woman. But it wasn't going to happen, the insulation, that is. He sat down at the roulette table with his chips, and, as he had feared, Faith slid onto his lap.

She was as light as a meringue cookie. The dress, now that he was getting intimately acquainted with it, was more like a sausage casing than a dress. It molded around her, outlining every curve, and although she was no more than a twig, her twig had some very nice curves, a rounded little bottom and breasts that were small, perfect mounds. He knew the nipples had to be tiny pink peaks, his favorite kind.

As she settled in more comfortably, he knew he was in deep, deep trouble.

"Whoo," Joey said, tittering. Before Cabot could stop him, Joey ran one of those pitchfork-like combs across the front of his hair and shot him with a poof of spray.

"Joey, damn it…"

"That's good," Raff said. "Chelsea, could you get a light here on Faith's chest?"

"Why my chest?" Faith said.

"Why my lap?" Cabot muttered.

"What?"

"Nothing. Pick a number, I'll place a bet."

They had attracted quite a bit of attention due to the fact that three people had stuck lights around them, were pointing a camera at them and, furthermore, were fiddling with their hair. All this in addition to the fact that a beautiful, possibly half-naked woman was lounging across a nervous-looking man. He guessed he looked nervous. He sure felt nervous.

"Four," Faith said. "Place your bet on four."

"Why four?"

"It just came to me."

"Shouldn't it be a number you have some special feeling about? A number you're superstitious about? Your lucky number." It had taken him three tries to remember the words "lucky number," but how could a man think with a nosegay wiggling around on his lap as she tried to figure out the game. *Another man's deadly nightshade.* That's what he'd been trying to think of earlier—deadly nightshade. Faith was beautiful, sweetly scented—and deadly.

"Well, let's see." She screwed up her pretty face in a puzzled way that reminded him of the woman he'd met in the travel agency, before she metamorphosed into deadly nightshade. "I guess that would be—four."

Cabot let out his breath. "Looks like we're pretty stuck on four here," he said to the dealer. "A hundred dollars on four." He tossed in a hundred-dollar chip.

Everyone surrounding the table seemed to fall into silence as the dealer spun the wheel. "Round and round and round she goes, and where she stops... Nine." As coldhearted as a fish, he reached out and raked in Cabot's chip as the crowd around the table chorused, "Aw-w-w."

He actually took heart when he observed that the dealer had noticed Faith and was letting his eyes flicker in her direction. He had no doubt the Mata Hari on his lap was sending back a flicker or two of her own. Still, if the game *was* fixed, he'd just as soon the dealer fix it in his favor.

"Place your bets."

"Seven," Faith said. She wriggled back on his lap and slung a slender, perfect arm around his neck.

Okay, that was it. She was going too far. He already had an erection, it was already throbbing painfully, and now she was literally massaging it. There wasn't a chance in hell she was innocent enough not to know what she was doing. He'd promised himself to pay her back, and now was the time to start. He opened his legs a little wider and let her sink more solidly onto him. It was driving him crazy, but it was worth it, because he could tell it was driving her crazy too, and he received some satisfaction from that little fact. To make sure, he slid his hand right around that curvy little bottom and when he'd dug his fingers just barely beneath it, he let them stay there, wiggling them a little bit, too, as if he were doing it absent-mindedly.

He felt her surprise, felt her struggle to move away, to rest on his thighs again, but he held her tight, right where she was, and let his fingers sink into that soft flesh.

"Eleven." He could barely hear the dealer through the buzzing in his ears, but he did register that he'd lost again.

"How long are we going to do this?" he hissed up at Raff.

"I haven't quite got the perspective right," Raff said. "Chelsea, if you'd move that light over just a smidge to the right. That's it, that's better, maybe that will do it. Can you remember all this until you get a chance to block it out on paper?"

"Hold it," Joey said, and attacked Cabot with the powder puff. "You're sweating, man," he said. "And you—" he directed a sharp glance at Faith "—look washed-out." He began to brush blusher on Faith's cheeks.

"Place your bets."

"S-s-sex," Faith said. She seemed to notice everybody was staring at her and she said, "What? I said six." Funny, she didn't look washed-out anymore.

"Six it is," Cabot said. It came out a lot like a moan, he was afraid, but he tossed a chip on the six and dizzily watched the wheel spin. He was paying quite a price for teaching Faith that she'd better not mess with him.

"Eleven," said the dealer, and reached out with his rake.

"Well, hell," Cabot said. "Raff, have you got the setup yet?"

"Almost. It's still not quite…tell you what, Cab. Move around to the other side of the table."

He leaped up with such alacrity that he almost dumped Faith onto the roulette table. He caught her in midair, which was good, and in mid-body, which wasn't. His hands brushed her breasts, those perfect breasts, the breasts that appeared to be covered by nothing but flowers with spaces between them. "Sorry," he muttered.

"My fault," she murmured back.

But damned if she didn't slide right back on his lap when he'd evicted a guy from his seat and taken it over himself. Reading his mind, Cabot knew the guy was so excited to be at the table with somebody he was sure was a movie star, if he could just think of her name, that he didn't seem to mind.

"I think it's time to double your bet," Faith whispered to him.

"Why? I haven't won anything."

"What does that have to do with it?"

"Oh, nothing, I guess," Cabot said, feeling drained. "Two hundred on…"

"This is much better," Raff said. "I'm going to

get it here in a minute. Just repeat everything you did before.''

''...on...five,'' she said triumphantly.

The wheel spun. ''Five it is!'' said the dealer, losing his cool for once.

''See? You won twice as much,'' Faith marveled. ''Double it again. On five.'' Did he imagine that her voice shook a little?

Ten minutes later he was flat broke.

''But I got everything I needed,'' Raff said, sounding perfectly happy with the outcome.

Faith had not in any way gotten everything she needed. Cabot was driving her crazy with his hands, with the hardness that burned into her. Now, though, he was mad at her for not coming up with winning numbers.

She had a strong feeling she needed to vanish to give him a little time to cope with his loss. She had an even stronger feeling that she needed time to calm herself down. ''I'll just wander around by myself for a little while,'' she said, backing away. ''Maybe play a slot machine. I like the sound.''

''Wear your coat,'' Cabot growled.

Surprised, she took it from Chelsea and slipped it over her shoulders. ''If you insist,'' she said.

''And don't talk to any strangers. I'll find you ten or fifteen minutes from now.''

Who did he think he was, her *father?* She slithered away toward one of the cashiers' windows, hoping none of them saw her get a mere twenty-five dollars worth of nickels from the cashier. That was what she'd decided she could afford to lose—twenty-five dollars—and nickels would last longer than quarters. Carrying her bucket of nickels, she strolled around the casino looking at the gamblers. Now here, she would tell Hope, were people who knew how to focus. They put in the money and pulled the lever, over and over and over. She watched their faces, anxious faces, optimistic ones, people who really cared whether they won or lost, people who were only there for fun.

She was one of those. She was there for fun. She was there to try to calm down her pounding heart, her racing pulse. She pulled a tissue out of the coat pocket and mopped her forehead. She had to get through a whole night of this, of Cabot too close, too available, too unavailable, too…

What was it Cabot had told her about slot machines? "Watch one for a while…" So she made herself look at a slot machine. Its biggest advantage was that it didn't remind her in the least of Cabot. At the top was a lighted sign telling how big the jackpot was. She watched the sign for a while, then watched a woman playing the machine for a while. That "put in the money, pull the lever" thing had a certain hypnotic rhythm, and the woman sitting at the machine sometimes took more money out of the machine than she'd put in. That must feel good.

Her little popcorn bucket of nickels began to itch in her hand, so she turned to look at an unoccupied machine. It had a smaller jackpot. No wonder nobody was playing it. Why play for less money than more? Okay, the thing to do was find the nickel machine that had the biggest jackpot and then knowingly, with purpose and forethought, add her twenty-five dollars to it.

Because that's all she'd be doing, having fun losing twenty-five dollars she'd planned to lose.

She cruised up and down several rows and finally found a machine she felt she could bond with. Unfortunately, someone else was sitting at it. While he played, the jackpot moved up even higher. In a few minutes he got up, looking frustrated.

She wouldn't feel frustrated no matter what happened. She put in a nickel, pulled the lever and got three nickels back. Talk about fun! Now she had twenty-five dollars *and* ten cents!

She happily fed coins to the machine. Sometimes she made a little profit and sometimes she didn't. Although it was more fun when she did, it was fine when she didn't, because she was just having fun. Another nickel, another nickel. She didn't have the slightest chance of winning the jackpot, but she was having *so much* fun that she really hoped Cabot wouldn't find her anytime soon, so much fun that she was thinking she really could spare another twenty-five dollars. She glanced into the bucket. A few nickels rattled around in there looking lonely, so lonely…

She grabbed an attendant who was passing by. "Another twenty-five in nickels," she demanded, and handed over the cash, then used the last of her nickels slowly until the attendant returned.

She was aware of the mist of perspiration that dampened her forehead, that moistened her palms, but that was Cabot's fault, for heating her up and then insisting that she wear this coat. Another nickel, another nickel…

In fact, she hoped Cabot never found her. She still had a liquid net worth of one hundred thirty-six dollars and change minus fifty dollars, which was—whatever that added up to—and by morning she'd be worth millions! It was very important that she stay right here, playing this machine, because it was a lot more fun than putting on an act with a lying, deceiving…

"Faith! I thought you'd been kidnapped."

She registered the fact that he actually did have that sound of a person who'd been frantically worried and was now blessedly relieved. But who cared! "Don't bother me," she snarled. "I'm almost there, almost there. The next nickel's gonna do it, I just know it."

"Faith!" He gripped her by the shoulders and tried to lift her up out of the chair. "Don't get crazy on me. Remember what we talked about? You plan ahead of time and then you quit."

Thank goodness, he got coat instead of shoulders, but she sensed him throwing the coat aside and definitely felt him gripping her waist. "I said, come on, Faith. You've had a taste of gambling, but enough is enough."

Her hips rose out of the chair, but the rest of her didn't. "I said leave me alone! I'm busy here."

Now he was hauling her legs out. It was very inconvenient, because she had to balance herself with her left hand and do everything else with her right hand, but hey, you do what you have to do. "One more nickel," she burbled. "The next one's gonna do it, gonna do it…'' and with her last bit of strength she fed her last nickels to the machine.

Lights suddenly flashed, gongs sounded, coins poured from the machine, and from her position in midair she saw the word, ''Jackpot!''

Cabot let go of her legs, leaving her hanging over the back of the chair scooping up coins, clutching them to her breast, sobbing wildly.

''Fan-frigging-tastic!'' someone yelled, and in the dim haze of her mind she realized it was Raff. ''She hit the jackpot!''

And then there was another voice, a stranger's voice, saying, ''Hey, isn't that Tippy Temple?''

Attendants rushed to the scene, helping Faith gather up the money. ''Can I get in here with a light?'' Chelsea's voice.

''Forget the lights! We got us a moment!''

''A powder opportunity, puh-leez. She's sweating like a *common laborer*.''

Joey hitting her in the nose with his powder puff was the last thing she remembered.

11

"I WON."

A long, drifting period of silence seemed to pass before she heard a voice that was Cabot's say, "Faith. Are you all right?"

"No," she said. She was floating, but not in space. On water, she thought, and wondered where the oars were.

"What's not all right? What hurts?" She heard panic in the voice that was disturbing her peace.

"I don't know how much I won yet." She frowned. "Steer a little to the left, would you?"

"Steer…Faith, we're back in the suite. You're in bed. I've got the house doctor coming up."

Her eyelids shot up. She stared at him, seeing the tanned, chiseled features and fathomless eyes against the backdrop of the familiar, hideous Tahoe Jungle Suite. She struggled to sit up. "Doctor? I don't need a doctor! Do they have a house psychiatrist?"

"You're babbling. Calm down. The doctor will be along…"

"Because I've become a compulsive gambler! One taste of the slot machine and I was hooked." She turned her face to the side to let the tears roll down. "I need therapy."

"No, you don't. It was a momentary, ah, momentary…"

"A momentary loss of everything I was brought up to believe. My entire set of standards and values." The tears flowed more freely. "I gambled and *won*."

"I was going to say personality change." After a long pause, he said, "Did you hit your head on anything when the hammock attacked us last night."

She sat up, wiping away the tears and feeling dangerously irritable. "No, for heaven's sake. You just want to find a way to sue the hotel. The hotel will refuse ever to work with Wycoff Worldwide Travel again, and Mr. Wycoff will say it's all my fault and he'll fire me. And besides, the hotel will probably win, because the lawyer will point out—" she broke off to point at his chest "—that it was all your fault for being so determined to sleep in that hammock, when you should have been sleeping with me in this b—" She came to an abrupt halt.

A deep flush climbed his face. "Where is that damned doctor?" she thought he muttered.

"If they don't have a Gamblers Anonymous group in Reno, they should," she said.

"We'll find one in Los Angeles." There was a desperate sound to his voice.

"The sooner the better. I can already feel my fingertips starting to itch again for the feel of that lever. How much did you say I won? If I tripled that by morning…"

A brisk knock on the door interrupted her serious and important investment plans for the immediate future. Cabot literally ran to open it. She heard mur-

murs, and then a small, dapper man approached her, carrying a large bag.

"Is that my money?"

A deep sigh came out of Cabot.

"No, Miss Temple, that's my bag of magic tricks. We're going to look you over, give you a little something to help you sleep."

"Oh, but I'm not Tippy. I'm just…"

"She means she doesn't want to be recognized," Cabot interjected smoothly. He grabbed the doctor by the lapels. "It's very important not to let this leak out, Doctor. She's had a shock. She's not herself. Whatever she says, whatever she does, has to be kept quiet. Understand?"

Faith reflected that it would be pretty easy to understand Cabot when he was lifting you up off the floor by your lapels, and indeed, the doctor did seem to understand perfectly.

"It goes without saying," the man squeaked.

"I thought so," Cabot said, lowering him to the floor and giving his lapels a straightening out. "I just wanted to make sure."

"Let's take a look here," the doctor said.

"I'll leave," Cabot said.

"No, no, as the next of kin you should be here."

"I don't want to be here."

With his feet back on the floor and his thermometer aloft the doctor seemed to be gaining courage. He gave Cabot a hard stare. "You don't want to know whether your wife is all right?"

"Wi—of course I want to know if she's all right."

"Then sit down and pay attention.

Cabot sat.

"Should I peel off this dress?" Faith asked. A giggle escaped from her. She couldn't imagine where it had come from.

"I'd rather you didn't lift your head until I've made sure there's no sign of concussion."

"I suppose that's a good idea," Faith agreed, and stayed put. "But it's not concussion."

"No?" The doctor lifted an arrogant eyebrow.

"No. It's compulsion. I'd know it anywhere."

"I'm the doctor. I'll tell you what it is."

Faith grumbled a little, but she let him peer into her eyes and wave his finger in front of her and make her eyes cross.

"It doesn't seem to be concussion," he said, turning off his little light.

"I could have told you that," Faith said.

"You did," Cabot said. She darted a glance at him. He was looking a little more relaxed, which was good, because when she made her move, she wanted him to be as loose as possible.

The doctor pursed his lips, but carried on with his stethoscope, his blood pressure machine, his fingertips on her pulse and his tongue depressor. He even stuck another little light into her ears.

"She seems to be just fine," he said. "A good night's rest—" and here he paused, swiveled his head and gave Cabot a meaningful glance "—and she'll be back to normal. Did she have dinner?"

"Oh, my, yes," Faith said. "I had…"

"She did," Cabot said. "If she wants something more I'll have it sent up."

"I couldn't possibly," Faith said. "Although a milkshake would taste good."

"A milkshake."

"No, changed my mind, a malt. How about a chocolate malt?"

Cabot walked the doctor to the door, then got on the phone and ordered a chocolate malt and a bottle of brandy from room service.

"You're hitting the sauce, Cabot," Faith said. "We're both going to need twelve-step programs if you're not careful."

He walked back to the bed, folded both arms across his chest and gazed down at her. "Who are you, really?" he said in a low, quiet voice. "Because I have to tell you very frankly that you're not the same person I chose to be my travel agent."

"I am a person who's under a good bit of stress," Faith said, after thinking it over.

He unfolded his arms and sat down on the edge of the bed, making waves and rocking a little with them. "That's the first sensible thing you've said in hours. Want to talk about it?"

It occurred to Faith that she could talk about it and at the same time, take the first step toward her goal. "Well, okay, for one thing, I'm under job stress...."

He nodded, a fount of wisdom in a navy blazer and white turtleneck. "You've lost so many jobs you keep expecting to lose this one, like waiting for the other shoe to drop. Don't worry about it. I'm going to tell Wycoff you did an excellent job on these arrangements."

"You are?" She was touched. "Even after all the mistakes I've made?"

"Yes."

"That's sweet of you."

It encouraged her when a smile twitched at his lips. "Downright noble, I'd say." He stopped smiling. "You're good at this job. You need a little self-confidence, that's all."

"And brake linings."

His brow furrowed. "What?"

"I also need brake linings. *And* tires. But you were saying..."

"I was saying Wycoff won't want to fire you after I tell him I'm sending all my business to him."

"Oh!" Faith breathed. "He'll be thrilled!"

Job stress, though, and brake linings and tires and even her newly discovered gambling compulsion were putting far less stress on her at the present time than Cabot was. She needed to get him out of this avuncular mood and into a loverly mood. She had to arouse him to the point of confessing that he was not in love with Tippy, nor was he engaged to her. She needed to steer the conversation in a different direction, wondered again where the oars were, and knew they rested entirely in her imagination. She'd have to put it, her imagination, to its most challenging test.

HER FACE HAD TAKEN ON that dreamy look that Cabot had once found so charming and now saw as a distant early warning that she was planning something, something that would undoubtedly increase the physical and emotional discomfort she'd subjected him to all evening, all day, all weekend in one way or the other. Mostly the other.

"Time for you to get some sleep."

Faith yawned. "Okeydokey." She edged her way out of bed and moved like a sleepwalker toward her bathroom, stopping on the way to collect something or other from the chest of drawers where she'd stashed her things.

While Cabot waited for her return, he examined the small vial the doctor had left. One sleeping pill. Well, yes, that should be safe enough.

He stood up, stretched out his tense muscles and took off his blazer. He went to his own bathroom, ran water into a glass and brought it back to the night-stand. He realized he was assuming he'd get that sleeping pill into Faith.

The knock on the door was a welcome distraction. It was room service in the form of a waiter pushing another tiny table, this one bearing a chocolate malt in a tall, frosty glass on a saucer topped with a paper doily and a bottle of brandy with two glasses, no saucer, no doily.

"On the house," the waiter announced. "A congratulatory gift to Miss Temple—oops, sorry—" and he laid a finger on his lips "—for winning the lottery!" He peered around the suite, obviously hoping to catch a glimpse of Madame X.

Cabot glowered, thought about shaking down the waiter and decided against it. The situation was so complicated that the less he said, the better. Instead, he gave the man a large tip and shooed him out the door.

"Is she all right?" the waiter whispered anxiously. "I heard she fainted."

"Just stress," Cabot said firmly. He closed the door in the man's face, then wheeled the table to the bedside and poured himself a brandy. Thoughtfully he gazed at the malt, wondering how much brandy he could add to it without making it overflow, then realized that even he wasn't manipulative enough to mix alcohol with her sleeping pill. To remind himself of his duty to responsible social behavior, he hid the second glass in his underwear drawer, then pulled a tree-trunk stool up beside the bed and sat down, sipping the brandy.

She thought she was under stress! She was so beautiful, so desirable lying there so incongruously in that god-awful bed. He had a smile threatening to break out behind his gravity, too, because he'd realized she was a stronger person than he'd imagined, and a sassier one. If he ever managed to work their relationship around to a personal one, she'd stand up for herself, put him in his place.

That came as a relief to him. He didn't mean to be a bully. He was just, well, large and opinionated. Controlling, that's what his colleagues sometimes said about him, which was nonsense. All he wanted was for everything to be *right*. Right as *he* saw it.

He was as tough on himself as he was on anybody else. For example, what he wanted to do right now was confess all, tell Faith about the publicity stunt, tell her he was making the "wedding video" to supply footage to every television station that would run it. Tell her about that fly in the ointment of his life,

Josh Barnett, and that this whole thing with Tippy had come about out of professional necessity.

But that wasn't the *right* thing to do. He'd made a promise to Tippy and he would keep it. If it killed him. And the longer he sat here mooning over Faith, the surer he became it was going to.

Erection Drains Blood from Publicist's Body. That's how the headline in *Variety* would read. He had to do something about his miserable condition, and what he was going to do was act mature and settle for deferred gratification. Someday he could moon over her, he just couldn't moon over her now. In the meantime...

He didn't want to thrill Wycoff, he just wanted to blackmail the guy into giving Faith the job security she needed. He'd say, "I'll be sending my business to you from now on, as long as Faith handles my account."

What he wanted was to keep Faith where he could find her when the time was right.

Time was his enemy at the moment, and he had to use every weapon on hand to fight it.

The sounds of tooth brushing had ceased, and her bathroom was suddenly too quiet.

He tensed up again, sensing an ambush from the rear. Out of the corner of his eye he saw the bathroom door open, saw Faith start across the room, then actually saw her, head to toe.

If he fainted, would the doctor come back? She was wearing a nightgown that was nothing more than a leopard-printed shadow of silk over not very much of her skin, hiding nothing and making her look more mysterious, more desirable than if she were naked. His groin tightened, his heart rate sped up and his mouth went dry.

"Into bed," he tried to say, but it came out in a hoarse garble of sound.

She poised herself over the bed and slowly turned down the comforter, then gracefully slid in and gave him a slow, sensuous smile. She didn't pull the covers up, so he'd have to do it for her in a minute, and when he did, he'd tie the a sheet at the back of her neck.

He shoved the malt into her hand. "Drink," he rasped, cleared his throat and added, "this."

She took the paper off the straw with long, languorous gestures, wiggled it down into the malt and let her lips close lightly on it. Cabot had to turn away. "Um, yummy," she murmured.

He summoned up a little adrenaline. "You're probably cold," he said, trying for brisk. "Let me pull up these…"

"Oh, no," she murmured. "I'm quite warm enough, thank you. Maybe just a sheet would feel nice."

He'd barely had time to take a deep breath of relief when she pulled the sheet up just barely over her breasts, where it immediately slid a little, showing him a tempting glimpse that, again, was more seductive than if she hadn't bothered with the sheet at all.

He sat back down on the tree-trunk stool and took a gulp of brandy. "Now that you've had some of the malt," he suggested, "take the pill and give it a chance to work."

"I'm not sure I'll need a sleeping pill," she said thoughtfully. "After I drink this I think I'll just pop right off."

"Doctor's orders." He shook the pill into his palm and picked up the glass of water. It was time for him to be very firm—okay, controlling, damn it!

"Oh, okay." She gave him an innocent smile, then stuck her little pink, pointed tongue out at him.

Trying not to react at all to this outrageous, cold-blooded intent-to-arouse-with-malice-aforethought behavior, he dropped the pill into the center of her tongue and handed her the glass of water. She sipped, choked a little and said, "Oops. Would you hand me a tissue from—thanks," and mopped daintily at her chin. Then she gave him that innocent smile again and went back to the slow enjoyment of the chocolate malt.

Cabot went back to ruminating and sipping. The brandy wasn't relaxing him at all. The entire lower half of his body was sending him dangerous messages. Faith could be trusted. She'd never tell a soul. They could have a secret affair, hot, delicious and private, starting as soon as she finished that malt. No one would ever know.

And she would watch quietly from afar while he married Tippy and got the footage of the honeymoon video on television and...

Sure she would.

"Are you going to watch me until I fall asleep?"

"That's what I had in mind."

"Have some malt. It's really wonderful."

"No, thanks."

"Okay, if you're sure."

"I'm sure." It was the only thing he was sure of. Because if he accepted, she'd lean forward, and her breasts would be even more visible than they were now. He was already fighting for control. He couldn't handle any more.

She leaned forward anyway, and his heart nearly stopped beating. She scooted a little toward the middle of the bed and patted the spot she'd just vacated. "Come sit a minute," she said. "I want to talk to you."

Cabot hesitated, then rose like a doomed man and sat down on the very edge of the bed. He kept his feet flat on the floor with his right foot a little forward, ready to take off running, and fixed his gaze on the door to the suite, which would be his goal if he did feel the need to run.

"There is simply no need for you to spend another night on that hammock."

Cabot got up, but she grabbed the waistband of his pants and pulled him back down. "I'm about to fall into a dead sleep," she said, lecturing him, "and this is a huge bed. More than that, I'm quite aware that your heart belongs to another."

He gave her a suspicious sidelong glance, but there was nothing in her face but the most earnest goodwill.

"*That* person," she went on inexorably, "is someone I deeply admire. Even if I didn't admire her, I'm not in the business of breaking up other people's relationships. Not even in the early stages," she assured him, "and certainly not when marriage plans have been made."

Uh-huh. So put some more clothes on.

"So now that we understand each other, you might as well sleep on the other side of this bed."

Cabot observed that she hadn't released her grip on his waistband. "I don't think that would be wise," he said.

"Why not?"

She didn't sound a bit sleepy to him. She sounded like a crocodile with its eyes closed and its jaws poised to spring open. "For appearance sake," he said. "I mean, what would Tippy think?" What Tippy would think was that he was close to reneging on his promise to marry her, and she'd be right.

"It's not the sort of thing you'd need to mention to Tippy. And of course, I wouldn't."

"But it would be on my conscience." He felt like slime mouthing these lies. But then he already felt like slime for dreaming up this sham marriage, so what was a little more slime.

"Just lying here on this nice soft bed? Sleeping? Don't be silly."

Maybe she was right. If… "Maybe I'll do that—after you're sound asleep," he said, more to end the discussion than anything else.

"Okay, then." Oddly enough, she sounded satisfied. "I'm going to sleep right now." And to his amazement, she turned off her bedside lamp, pulled the covers up to her chin, rolled over on her right side and closed her eyes.

He eyed her for a moment. He got up, and she let him. He walked all the way to his bathroom door and then spun around to look at her again. Her eyes were still closed, and her mouth had taken on a peaceful, relaxed look.

Maybe she was serious.

He went into the bathroom, closed the door, then opened it swiftly and peered at her. Resting like a baby.

He brushed his teeth, splashed cold water on his overheated face and changed into pajamas. He never wore pajamas, but some sixth sense had told him to bring the stack of pajamas that had been Christmas gifts from his mom, whom he could hardly tell not to bother because he never wore them. They were still folded and pinned together, straight from the store, and it wasn't until he started taking the pins out that he realized how sorry he was that this pair was not only silk, but leopard printed.

He peered out the door again. Faith really did seem to be asleep now. Wearing just his trousers, he looked at his other set of clean pajamas and discovered they were white silk with short pants. Disgruntled, he went back to put on the leopard pair.

He turned off the lights one at a time as he tiptoed across the floor and around the bed. He wouldn't even get under the covers. He'd just pull the same blanket over himself he'd ended up using last night. It was all going to be fine.

He slid onto the bed. It felt great. He was exhausted, physically and emotionally. If he could sleep tonight and wake up early, well before Faith's sleeping pill wore off, he'd be like a new man, ready to face the many challenges life was presenting him right now.

He sank down, his head in a nest of pillows, and closed his eyes. Beside him was a sudden flurry of movement, and in a split second Faith was beside him, half on top of him, all silky skin and silky nightgown and a tickle of curly hair.

"Gotcha," she said, just as he'd known she would.

"Damn it," he said, and kissed her.

12

IT WAS WHAT FAITH WANTED, and still she wasn't prepared for the shock of his kiss, the pressure of his body against hers.

Cabot's hands splayed across her back, pulling her closer, stroking her as if he wanted to hold all of her at once. His lips against hers, his tongue teasing at the corners of her mouth, had captured her complete attention, so it was far too late to protest when she realized he'd pulled her across his body. She felt his hardness, his unspoken promise of delights undreamed of, and moved against him, seeking more.

But those delights couldn't be hers until she…until he…

His tongue was no longer teasing but openly exploring, and she moaned, unable to remember what it was that made what was happening impossible, an event that needed to be slowed down in order to take steps, several important steps. If only she could remember what they were.

How could she think when his hands were sliding down her sides, scooting the silk of her gown upward? The fabric moved against her skin like the caress of his long, warm fingers, higher and higher. His mouth slid away, blazing a trail of kisses across her cheek to her ear. He outlined it with his tongue and then nibbled lightly on the lobe.

A deep, hard shudder made its way through her body and straight down to her center, which she pressed closer to him, demanding release from the fire that licked at her, and all at once his hands were on her buttocks, helping her out, tugging her closer, caressing the sensitive skin there with his fingertips. Fingertips…fingertips…tips…

"We can't do this." Her hands captured his and tugged them away, but the effect was only to drive her tighter against him. "You can't be mine. You're…"

"Just for a night," he groaned. "Or two…" And he captured her mouth again. The pressure was hot and sweet. The ache that rose through her body was far more compelling than any thought going through her mind, but she forced herself to remember her mission. There were things he had to say first, assurances he had to make to her.

"I can't handle a night or two," she said against his cheek. "It's not fair to me or to Tip—"

"Shh." His hands roamed her body, tugging at the silk. "Just think of now." His voice grated, hoarse with desire. "Don't look at the future. Don't…"

Suddenly she couldn't think of the future. She couldn't think at all, only feel the silken slide of his body against hers, the delicious melding of his mouth with hers, the probing velvet of his tongue, the all-too-knowing stroke of his fingertips against her skin.

His movements were urgent but not hurried. His hands slid up to her breasts and she let out a little cry against his cheek when he cupped them, his thumbs caressing nipples that felt hard and aching, then smoothly slipped her gown over her head.

She lay naked against him, hardly able to breathe, knowing only that she wanted the feel of his skin against hers. Her fingers reached for the buttons of his pajama top, and he groaned as she slipped them out of the buttonholes one by one.

He rolled her over to his side when she began to tug at the waistband of his pajamas. Her hand encountered him, hot, aroused, silky smooth, and she knew at once that she had to have him, now. "I found these in my bathroom," she whispered to him, hearing the catch in her voice as she handed him a foil packet.

"In mine, too," he said, and in a few seconds, sprawled her across him again, driving her to ecstasy when her center met his. Their bodies joined effortlessly and she collapsed against him with a moan, rocking with him in an age-old rhythm that heated her blood to boiling. He thrust deep and hard, bringing tears to her eyes from the pure pleasure of it. The sensations were suddenly too great, driving her over a cliff into freefall. She cried out and then, feeling a groan rise through Cabot's body, she gripped him tightly and carried him along with her.

It was several minutes before her body calmed down enough that she was able to accept reality again, but when it happened, her first thought was what might be going through Cabot's mind.

He still held her tightly, her sweat-slicked body nestled in the curve of his, but he was oddly still. She waited, feeling happy and contented, knowing he was looking for a way to tell her what they had just experienced was all right. It had not been infidelity on his part or improper behavior on hers. It was okay, and soon they would experience it again.

Of course, she already knew that, but he didn't know she knew.

CABOT HOPED he was never captured by enemy agents, because it was clear he couldn't stand up to torture. In spite of a deep regret that he was so weak, he lay there feeling more euphoric than he could ever remember feeling after making love to a woman. He wondered what the difference was, and knew it had to be Faith herself. She wasn't like any other woman.

The problem was what to do next. He knew what he *wanted* to do next. His libido was already stirring with new excitement, and he felt it would take many, many more varied but similar events before it would be too tired to stir.

Could he, did he dare allow himself the pleasure of doing that? No. In the first place...in the first place, the telephone was ringing. He froze.

"Want me to get it?" Faith asked sleepily.

"No!" Feeling as if he'd been in a coma and was just coming out of it, Cabot slid over Faith, grabbed the receiver and turned on the lamp.

"Tippy!" he said, hearing his voice crack as if he were a thirteen-year-old kid. He glanced at Faith, whose eyes went from heavy lidded to narrowed in a split second. Naked beneath a sheet, she gazed at him.

"Sweetheart!" Wondering what was meandering through Faith's mind, he'd added that for her benefit.

"She there with you?" Tippy demanded to know. "Well, it's no never-mind to me as long as you don't back out on me. You're not gonna back out on me, right?"

"Of course not." Cabot got himself in an upright position on the edge of the bed and reached into the tangle of bedclothes for his pajama bottoms. He hadn't really known the answer to her question until the phone rang, jarring him out of a pleasant dream and back into a world of onerous responsibilities. "How are you, Tippy?" Did he sound fond enough? He hoped so.

"Rich, apparently," Tippy said with a snap, crackle and pop. "I was watching the news, y'know, and there I was, magically shorter and a dress size larger, winning a big jackpot in Reno. And then I *fainted,* if you can believe that. So what's up, Cabot?"

He wasn't, not anymore. "Joey did too good a job of turning Faith into your double," Cabot said. On the bed beside him, Faith put her hand over her mouth, tugged the covers up over her again and gazed at him with newly widened eyes. "In fact, we were just sitting here talking about *what we should do.*" He tried to stare Faith down, and failed.

"Yeah. What are we going to do?" Tippy said. "Was I in Reno this weekend or not? We haven't made the everlovin' announcement yet! So am I already a bride, or did we just enjoy a stolen weekend together?"

Cabot suddenly felt very tired, and it wasn't the pleasant exhaustion he'd felt a few minutes before. "I'm working on it," he lied. "Here we've been denying that she's you, but apparently no one believed us. I'll get a statement together by morning."

"I can't leave the house until you get our little *statement* together," Tippy informed him. "But then I can't leave the house anyway until the Mercedes guy brings my car back, and I don't know how he's going to do that without getting attacked by reporters, because there are three big trucks parked out on the street. One says FoxNews in great big neon letters on the side. I can read that one in the dark. I don't know what the other two say, but my guess is they aren't from the electric company."

Cabot groaned.

"So I'd say we got us a problem. Either I'm in two places at once or you're being unfaithful to me. Figure out which one it is, Cabot, because if the story is that you're being publicly unfaithful to me, your intended, I might want to be publicly unfaithful to you. With the Mercedes repairman, maybe. Call me first thing tomorrow, which it already is." With a loud snap, she slammed down the receiver. Cabot hung up more thoughtfully. *What next? What the hell do I say now?*

"That was Tippy," Faith said unnecessarily. "How do you feel about...about what just happened?"

Knowing he was merely heaping one lie upon another, Cabot buried his head in his hands. "I feel wretched," he said. "I gave in to temptation, and you *are* a temptation,'' he emphasized, turning to her with a pleading expression on his face. He didn't want to leave her with the impression that he wasn't crazy about her, because when this thing with Tippy was over, he was going to burn rubber getting back to Faith, explaining why he'd done what he'd done, making everything right.

It was disturbing to realize how much it mattered to him that everything be made right. It wasn't possible in this short time, was it, to develop a set of deeper feelings about a person? Then it hit him, right in the pit of his stomach, what kind of person Faith really was.

He'd thought she was testing him, making sure he was the kind of man who'd be faithful to Tippy. If she'd been testing him, she wouldn't have let this night happen. She would have said something like, ''Aha, so you're not worthy of her after all!'' and, at the very least, would have gotten out of bed and hopped into the hammock to plan the little talk she'd have with Tippy about her fiancé. But she hadn't done that. She'd protested a little, making herself look good, and then had enjoyed making love as much as he had.

She'd even produced the complimentary condoms from her bathroom. That was consent, any way you looked at it.

This revelation was making him feel sick. His long-range plan for love and happiness had just gone down the drain. It was much worse than a blip in his electronic calendar. It terrified him to realize how much worse.

So he wouldn't go there. He got up, moved on leaden feet to his briefcase and pulled out his laptop. Apparently people didn't use desks in the jungle, so he put it on the tree-trunk coffee table and pulled up a tree-trunk stool to sit on.

He was booting it up when Faith said, "What are you doing?"

He glanced at the bed to see her huddled entirely beneath the covers except for one eye and the bit of face and hair above it. She looked so cute, so sweet, he almost lost it again, but he reminded himself that that was her schtick—cute, sweet, deadly nightshade. "I'm drafting a statement to the press," he said.

"What are you going to say?"

He heard waves coming from the bed and desperately hoped she wasn't getting out of it. "I don't know. It'll come to me."

"Just don't mention my name."

He felt his mouth tightening. "I'll do my best to keep your name out of it."

"Because if my parents and my sisters hear about this there will be coast-to-coast hysteria," Faith went on. "I have this way of causing hysteria in my family, and now isn't the time for it. Hope's starting a new business with the man she's going to marry and Charity, well, I don't know what's going on in Charity's head right now except visions of parasites, but then I've never been smart enough to figure out what was going on in Charity's head, certainly not why she prefers parasites to—"

Cabot rose, stalked to the wall switch and turned on the audio effects. The room filled with the sounds of tropical birds and ominous rustlings-in-underbrush. He gave Faith a hard, meaningful glance before returning to his makeshift desk, and was alarmed to see her legs emerging from under the covers. He whirled, went into her bathroom and brought back her robe, the one that matched his, holding it out in front of him like a shield.

"Put this on and keep it on," he growled.

"Oh. Thanks," she said, and thrust both arms into it.

"Now go back to bed and let me work."

"I'm going to help you. This is all my fault. Want some coffee?"

Help! It was a shout that rose inside him, but he managed to swallow it before it got out. "Yes." It would give her something to do.

"I knew the twenty-four-hour room service would come in handy."

Actress Tippy Temple issued a denial this morning...

"Pie? Cabot, would some pie taste...no, let's go with the plate of sandwiches and the plate of cookies. This is going to be an all-night thing."

Cabot winced.

"I'm not Miss Temple," Faith said patiently, "but I hope that won't affect the speed of your service."

He gritted his teeth. *In a statement to the press this morning, actress Tippy Temple denies being in Reno last night to win a major jackpot. "I'll be happy to take the money," she said, snapping her chewing gum, but..."*

Backspace, backspace, backspace... *"I'm not a*

gambler," Miss Temple assured reporters. *"Even if I had been in Reno, which I wasn't, I wouldn't have…"*

Delete. *"I don't know who was mistaken for me,"* Miss Temple said, *"but I imagine she was in one of those look-alike contests, something like that, or maybe it was a publicity stunt. No, of course I'm not pi…"*

Backspace. *"…angry. Public figures have to be prepared for moments like these. In fact, I find the whole thing very…very…"*

"…amusing," Faith said over his shoulder.

"funny," Cabot typed.

"You know we're going to have to talk about what happened sometime," Faith said, pulling up another tree-trunk stool and perching on it.

He stopped typing and gave her his full attention. "I don't think so," he said firmly. "All we have to do is decide it didn't happen and never mention it again."

"But it did. And there was a reason it did."

"No, it didn't." He'd gone back to his statement, but he'd lost his momentum. "I thought the sleeping pill would work."

"You have to swallow them for them to work," Faith said.

"You didn't swallow it."

"No. I wrapped it up in a tissue."

That bit of information sealed her fate, as far as Cabot was concerned. Tonight had been a seduction in cold blood. She was nothing more than a woman who wanted to boost her own self-esteem by cutting out a glamorous starlet. How could he have been so stupid as to believe in her innocent gray eyes?

Sick at heart, Cabot said, "I have to write a statement." He directed a condemnatory frown at her. "We're *not* going to talk about what happened, but we're going to *not* talk about it in the morning. First things first."

At last he'd made his point. She sat back on the silly tree-trunk stool looking a little pale, a little sad, and just waiflike enough to make him sorry he'd hurt her feelings.

He had no reason to feel sorry! She was an opportunist of the worst kind!

FAITH HAD MADE a terrible, terrible mistake. She'd thought Cabot had feelings for her that were greater than a need for sex. She'd misjudged him.

He hadn't confessed that his marriage to Tippy was a publicity stunt because he wanted to hide behind his supposed engagement. He didn't want anything more than sex. And she'd thrown herself at him like a…like a…

A *wanton!* The most cautious person in the world, she'd behaved like a wanton woman. Lucinda hadn't thrown herself at Thaddeus. She'd counseled him to keep the faith with Lady Estelle! And that was exactly what Faith would have done—if Cabot actually were engaged to Tippy. Which he wasn't.

Lucinda didn't have to throw herself at Thaddeus, because Thaddeus filled up the chapters throwing himself at her. If she'd waited for Cabot to throw himself, she'd still be waiting. But it wasn't because

Cabot was a stronger man than Thaddeus, it was because he wasn't in love.

Just look at him sitting there. Even with his hair tousled, even in that robe and pajamas—for heaven's sake, his pajamas were leopard printed!—he was the most compellingly attractive man she'd ever met, the most thoroughly masculine man she'd ever known. Testosterone dripped from his every pore, if he had any pores. His skin was so smooth and tanned you couldn't tell. His eyelashes would be beautiful on anybody, man or woman. And he was so big, so muscular, so…infinitely desirable. Beside him, she was insignificant and mousy. Why would a man like that fall in love with an insignificant, mousy woman?

She hadn't even asked him for love, not yet. Just passion. And he *had* felt passion for her. It was still practically branded into her, still making her crazy!

On the other hand, any man who found himself in a bed with a woman dressed in nothing more than a smile, and furthermore, was being attacked by that woman, however insignificant and mousy she might be, might feel a little passion whether he wanted to or not.

It was something to ask Hope. Or Charity. She glanced at her watch. But probably not now. It was either too late or too early, depending on how you looked at it.

Room service made itself known at the door. Faith stood up, ready to hide, but Cabot pushed her back down onto the stool. "I want him to see us here working," he said.

Apparently he meant it, because he said to the

waiter, "As you can see, my colleague and I are working late."

She bet the waiter wished he had a dollar for every time he'd heard that one. When she caught the man glancing at the tumbled bed, she smiled sweetly at him and said, "Ooh, cookies. My, won't those taste good right about now," just as if she hadn't had her "colleague" flat out on that bed and panting for her not thirty minutes ago.

Then Tippy called. Cabot called her "sweetheart," just to show Faith how little he cared about *her* and how much he wished Tippy were there to make love with. When it wasn't true. Faith was feeling worse by the minute.

The waiter left, and she stood up. "If you really don't need my help," she said, "I'm going to leave the coffee to you and take that sleeping pill after all."

"Good idea," Cabot said briskly, typing.

"You might want to be sure I'm awake before the manicurist and hairdresser come."

"I'll have another round of coffee sent up."

"With cinnamon toast, please." Cinnamon toast was Maggie Sumner's special comfort food for her daughters when they were down in the dumps. Faith had a strong need for comfort food. "Thank you. Good night."

"Good night." The keys of the laptop clattered.

Faith made a face at the back of his head, then got into bed, took the sleeping pill and picked up her book. Thaddeus was still throwing himself and Lucinda was still righteously resisting.

Lucinda, Faith decided, was a tiresome prude who

didn't deserve a man like Thaddeus. Then she turned off her light and ducked under the covers. She had a terrible feeling she was going to cry.

NOW SHE REALLY WAS ASLEEP. Cabot stood beside the bed for a moment, gazing down at her hair spread out on the pillow, at the soft, light-brown eyelashes that were so long and thick it didn't much matter whether she put any stuff on them or not. She was beautiful, just as she was.

He'd thought he was the one who had to make everything right as soon as the marriage and divorce were over. Now he realized Faith had some things to make right, too. But he knew she'd be able to explain why she'd seduced him. No matter what she was, what she'd done, he had to accept the fact that he was in love with her. If she could convince him she was a halfway decent human being—oh, hell, he didn't even care about that. He had to have her. Be she saint or vixen, he was crazy about her.

Or maybe just crazy. He picked up his blanket, paced the distance to the hammock and addressed it. "I'm going to sleep here, like it or not, so you might as well adjust to it."

He couldn't say he slept well, but he did sleep some. A hammock was really pretty comfortable once you got it under control.

SUNDAY WENT BY like a bad dream. They blocked out the Sunday Brunch scene, the Back-to-La-La-Land scene, and even backtracked to the Over-the-threshold scene.

Cabot, picking her up, cradling her in his arms, giving her a final memory of his warmth, his energy, had come close to polishing Faith off. But her biggest challenge was the Kiss-beside-the-pool scene. In his trim black swimsuit, Cabot was so nearly like the man in her many daydreams she could hardly bear it.

He should be the actor, not Tippy. He could act as if he loved her, while in truth, he was an opportunist who'd seen a chance to score.

Not the man of her dreams. In her assessment of Cabot, she'd been wrong once again.

But this was to be expected. If there was a way to make something go wrong, Faith could always find it. And she'd found it this weekend with Cabot.

Using the excuse that they'd finished shooting and she wouldn't need all that grooming on Monday morning, she discreetly moved in with Chelsea on Sunday night.

On Monday morning she packed up her jackpot money and her personal belongings and endured the ride to the airport. She raised "small talk" to its highest level during the flight to L.A. "Just drop me off at the travel agency," Faith said. "I need to discuss something with Mr. Wycoff."

"Of course. I'll be in touch," Cabot said vaguely. "For travel arrangements."

"Of course. Travel arrangements."

Those were the last words they exchanged until the limo pulled up in front of the agency and she said, "Well, goodbye and good luck," and he said, "Thank you," and gave her a wave.

She'd kept herself under control as long as she

could. In Mr. Wycoff's office she wailed, "I need to see my mother!" and burst into tears.

He gave her a week's vacation and a free ticket some airline had given him. That was the thing about people. They constantly surprised you.

And broke your heart. Not constantly, of course. Faith didn't know how anyone could live through it more than once.

13

"I HAD CINNAMON TOAST in Reno," Faith said, snuffling, "but it wasn't like yours."

Maggie sat beside the bed Faith had collapsed into on arriving home. She had risen only briefly, when Hank came upstairs the night before and told her in his inimitable way to come down to dinner. She, Hope and Charity had always done exactly what Hank asked them to do. There was something compelling about his voice, Faith thought. There was also the fact that he rarely asked them to do anything.

They'd been so happy with Maggie and Hank. They'd called them Mom and Dad almost from the beginning, and no one could have had better parents. Faith knew now that the Sumners had engaged in a fierce, lengthy and expensive court battle for the right to adopt them when their mother's family proposed to split them up. But at the time, the Sumners had let nothing ruffle the gentle surface of their new daughters' lives. They'd helped them through the grief of losing their parents, had hugged them when they cried and had smothered them with love and attention.

That's how Faith wanted to rear her children, except she wasn't ever going to have any children, because there was only one man she wanted to have children with, and he didn't want to have them with her.

"Oh, baby, you're crying again," Maggie said, producing a tissue and moving over to the edge of the bed to rub Faith's back.

"I thought I should try to get it all out of the way at once," Faith said brokenly. "More efficient."

"I see," her mother murmured. "I'd never thought of crying as something one did efficiently."

"It's Hope's influence," Faith muttered. "In more ways than one," she wailed suddenly. "When Hope found her wonderful, wonderful man it seemed like an omen. Charity and I thought she'd *never* get married, and here she is getting married first! So I thought if Hope could find a man, anybody could! Oh, I didn't mean that the way it sounded," and she buried her face in her pillow.

Maggie sighed. "I did hope the cinnamon toast would help a little."

"That's just how bad it is, Mom, too bad to fix with cinnamon toast."

"Do you think there's a way to fix it?"

"Not for me." Faith clamped a tissue over her eyes. "I gave Cabot every chance to tell me the truth about himself and Tippy. If he'd been interested in me, he would have."

"Dad and I were talking about it last night. I suppose we shouldn't have been. It's your life. We've never wanted to interfere."

"Interfere," Faith said, "please."

"Well, then, we were just wondering. If Cabot had

told you the truth, would he still have gone ahead with the plan to marry Tippy Temple?''

Faith felt something grow still and thoughtful inside her. ''Well, I guess he…no, I don't see how he could… Omigosh, Mom, I hadn't really figured out what Cabot would do.''

''He doesn't sound like the kind of man who'd tell you he loved you and then go ahead with a plan to marry and divorce another woman before the two of you could be together.''

Faith looked at her suspiciously. ''How do you know he's not that kind of man?''

Maggie smiled. ''When you three girls showed up on my doorstep that day so long ago, I took one look at you and knew you were the idealistic one. I can't imagine that little girl growing up to love that kind of man.''

Faith's eyes widened.

''Moving on a step,'' Maggie said, and Faith had a feeling there was nothing, absolutely nothing that could keep her mother from moving on a step, ''this publicity-stunt wedding must have been extremely important to Miss Temple. And to Cabot's career. It was something he'd promised to her—a wedding that would attract media attention and get her the publicity she needed. I don't think you could love a man who'd back out on a commitment.''

''But don't you think it was a smarmy sort of thing for him to do? Marry somebody to get publicity for them?'' Even as she said it, Faith couldn't imagine Cabot doing anything smarmy.

Maggie hesitated. ''It's not the way we do things

around here,'' she admitted, ''but he may have had a reason. Maybe he couldn't trust anybody but himself to be discreet about it. I'm just speculating. I have a feeling that one day he'll explain it to you himself.''

Faith sighed deeply. ''The things you're saying about Cabot sound more like the man I love than the things I've been thinking about him. I guess it was pretty selfish of me to try to force him to renege on that commitment.''

''You're the least selfish person I've ever known,'' Maggie said firmly. ''You're just too much in love to think straight.''

''I'm too flighty to think straight,'' Faith said.

''You? Flighty? Don't be silly, dear,'' said Maggie, gathering up Faith's teacup and empty toast plate. ''You girls have always put such pressure on each other to be perfect. When it's so unnecessary. If you were any closer to perfect, you'd be intimidating.''

She turned back at the doorway to give Faith a wry smile. ''I'll be in the kitchen if you need me. I'm going to try to reach Hope the second she walks into the office. Catch her off guard. See if I can pry some information out of her about wedding plans. Is she making any, is what I'd like to know.'' She tossed her head as she turned into the hall.

Faith lay there a few more minutes, shaken by the conversation. Had she been unfair to Cabot? Had she expected him to let Tippy down professionally in order to love her, Faith, personally? He wouldn't ask her to perform her job badly just because she was in love with him.

Of course, she'd never needed to be asked. She could do a job badly without any external incentive.

She moaned, then slowly rose out of bed, her sense of purpose growing as she moved. She'd have two more pieces of cinnamon toast and fly back to L.A.

"SORRY, WHAT DID YOU SAY?"

"Where *are* you, Cabot?" Joey said peevishly. "I said let's give Tippy a darker shade of cream for the wedding-night-supper scene. This one just goes blah. Don't you agree, Chelsea? Blah?"

"Definitely blah," Chelsea said.

"I wouldn't say blah, exactly," Raff said thoughtfully, "more…" He waffled one hand in the air.

"Oh, for God's sake!" Cabot yelled. "Who cares?"

They turned to stare at him. They were sitting in the conference room of his office suite, which also served as the projection room, looking at the honeymoon video rehearsal footage. At least *they* were looking at the film. Cabot was looking at Faith, and his sense of loss was killing him. "*You* do, we *thought*," Joey said pointedly.

Cabot got up, feeling tired and old. "I do, I do," he muttered. "You're right. It's blah. Or at least…" He waffled *his* hand in the air.

They were still staring, so he said, "Hey, it's been a long day. I have some other stuff to do. I'll look at everything again tomorrow and we'll block out the final while everything's fresh in our minds." He started out the door without waiting to hear what they thought about quitting for the day.

Fresh in my mind. The taste of Faith, the feel of her skin against his was just as fresh in his mind and troubling to his body as if he'd just left her after a long afternoon of love. When he unpacked, he'd caught the scent of her perfume on those stupid leopard pajamas and had almost wanted to cry.

"Cab." Some undertone in Raff's voice made Cabot come to a halt just outside the conference room. He turned slowly, and went back in.

The three of them were standing, staring at him. "We've been talking, Cab, and we feel, that is to say, we're together on this thing, well, anyway, we want to know why you don't just admit you're in love with Tippy's double?"

For a moment he felt frozen in time and space, and then something inside him loosened up, thawed, and he felt a surge of energy flow through him. "I have to admit it to Tippy first."

"Oh, well, good, just so you have a plan." And amazingly, they let him go.

He was dreading it, but he had to do it, now, while he still had that energy running through him, that sense of a greater purpose. After a quick phone call to be sure Tippy was in, he reached her house in record time in record traffic. He was going to tell her and get it over with, even if she put out a contract on him. It was about six o'clock on a perfect Southern California evening, cooling down pretty fast but feeling good to his overheated body. A sunset was shaping up over the Pacific that even he ought to take a minute to look at. But it was a minute he didn't have. Some other day.

"Yo, Cabot! Let's sit in the whatchamacallit, the conservatory. Too cold outside. What can I getcha to drink? How about a margarita?" Without waiting for an answer, she poured green stuff from a pitcher into a glass and handed it to him.

One look at Tippy in her bright aqua pants that stopped at the knee and a striped sweater that had shrunk in the wash, and Cabot couldn't imagine how he'd ever thought she and Faith looked alike.

Where Faith was soft, Tippy was brittle. Faith was gentle, Tippy was harsh. Faith was dainty, Tippy was sinewy. Faith looked great in her clothes, clothes looked great on Tippy. However insecure Faith was about her competence, she was comfortable with her soul; Tippy was still looking for her soul. Cabot thought again that Faith was what he'd hoped he could make Tippy become. And he could, if only in the camera's eye.

"You look great," was what he said to her. "How've you been?"

"Fine." She sat down in a wicker chair and eyed him assessingly. "You don't look so hot."

"It's been a long day."

"Well, since you're here, I've got something to tell you. I kinda wanted you in a good mood."

Cabot quirked an eyebrow. As he remembered it, he'd asked himself over to tell *her* something, and no "kinda wanted" about it. He'd been praying to find her in a good mood, which seemed to be the case.

"I'm fine," he said, smiling at her. "Just tired."

"Oh. Well, I'm gonna come right out with it, Cabot." But she didn't. She just snapped her chewing gum.

She's going to tell me she's...changing publicists. She's going to tell me she's...pregnant! Oh, please, no, not that. Anything but that! The media will think

I'm the…no, no, no… He dived into his pocket for a handkerchief to mop his sweating forehead. His ears began to buzz, deafening him.

"I don't want to marry you, Cabot," Tippy said.

"What?" He growled out the word. He thought she'd said:

"I don't want to marry you."

The buzzing dimmed, faded, ceased. Cabot patted his forehead, picked up the margarita and used it to moisten his lips. Apparently he was off the hook, but he still had a responsibility to her career. "It's your choice, of course, Tippy," he said. "Do you have another plan? Something you might want to share with me first?"

"Yes." His sarcasm was lost on her. She could out-sarcasm him any day. "I couldn't help myself, Cabot. I fell in love with my Mercedes mechanic." Her little chin trembled, her big blue eyes filled with tears. "That day when all the news trucks were parked out there? The way he just…just *gunned* my car and *flew* into the garage—he nearly ran over NBC, did you know that, Cabot? Well, it was just too heroic for words. He's the man I want to marry."

Waves of relief, of joy, even, were roaring upward from Cabot's toes to his head, but it was still too soon to feel that a miracle had happened. "Tell me about him," he said. "Is he passably attractive? Not married to anyone else? Not wanted for murder or mayhem in seventeen states and three European countries?"

Tippy laughed. "He's blond," she said, "two years younger than I am and pushing seven-feet tall. If you look at him just right, he reminds you of a Greek god.''

Images spun through Cabot's brain. Tall blond Greek god, delicious-looking blond actress. His professional side began to salivate. ''Does he speak?'' he said. ''Read? Write?''

''Just poetry,'' Tippy said. ''That's what he writes, I mean. He reads everything. But that's not important. He's a racing star in Europe, but he wanted to come to the U.S.—'' she halted, glowing all over ''—to meet me! Can you believe it? So he took a job with a Mercedes dealership in L.A., because he knows cars from the inside out....''

''Tippy,'' Cabot said solemnly, ''when you get bored with acting, you should consider becoming a publicist.''

''You're not mad at me?'' Tippy said plaintively.

''No.''

''You're not disappointed?''

Hell, no ''No. I'm just happy that you're going to be happy.''

''Cabot.'' She smiled, and for a second she reminded him of Faith again, a Faith trying to get out of a Tippy who, in her heart, meant well but hadn't been lucky enough to have whatever it was that made Faith the woman she was. ''You're happy as a pig in clover. You're crazy about that travel agent. I started thinking about marrying Borg right after I talked to her.'' She clapped a hand to her mouth in a way that reminded him painfully of Faith. ''No, actually it was after you mentioned her for the first time,'' she said, but guilt was written all over her face.

The buzzing started up again, but it wasn't quite as

unfriendly as it had been before. "You talked to her? When?"

"She called me from Reno," Tippy said, looking like a child who has misbehaved. "Just to make sure I really wanted to honeymoon in the jungle. She's a real sweetheart, Cabot."

"And you said?" Cabot felt a sudden lightening of his spirit, a sense that the last obstacle to his complete happiness was about to be blown away.

"I said, well, I said sure, it sounded great—" Tippy looked him directly in the eyes. "Okay, Cabot, to be absolutely honest with you, I blew it. I let it slip out that the whole marriage was a publicity stunt."

His mouth fell open. "She knows we weren't in love?"

"'Fraid so. But if you tell her I confessed I'll call home and get a contract taken out on you, so help me, Cabot, I will, because she promised me she wouldn't tell you I'd told and I promised her I wouldn't tell you she'd called...."

The old Tippy, the Tippy who needed cutting and splicing, was back. Cabot got up, hauled her up out of her wicker chair and lifted her off the floor in a bear hug. "Tippy, I love you," he said.

"Oh, go on," Tippy said.

He halted, held her out in front of him. "You're not smoking."

"Borg said I had to stop," she said.

"You *are* in love."

"Told you so," Tippy said. "Can you tell how fat I've gotten? I've gained two pounds. But Borg says that once we're married..."

Cabot didn't really want to hear the rest of it. He

was in love, too, so much in love he'd come over here tonight to end the whole scheme with Tippy even if it meant losing her as a client, even if it meant giving up his career.

And somehow everything had turned out all right.

Well, not everything. Not yet. He had to make things right with Faith.

He picked up the phone and called her. No one answered, not even an answering machine. He called the travel agency even though he knew it closed promptly at five. Amazingly, the call went to Mr. Wycoff's house.

"She went home to Chicago a couple of hours after she got back," Wycoff told him. "A family crisis, apparently."

Cabot didn't ask for the phone number. He didn't have the right to call her at her parents' house at a time of crisis and tell her what had been going through his head for the past twenty-four hours. He didn't have the nerve, either.

"Would you call my cell phone the minute she comes back?" he asked Wycoff.

Not being able to reach her at once depressed him deeply. But tomorrow was Valentine's Day. It seemed like a good omen.

"MY GOODNESS, you're back early," Mr. Wycoff said.

"You're looking at the new Faith Sumner," Faith said. "I'm back, I'm fine and I'm raring to schedule."

Wycoff drifted away to his own office for a while. Soon after Faith had figured out what she'd been doing before she left for her disastrous trip to Reno, he came back.

"Don't overbook yourself," he said, resting his potbelly on her monitor. "Keep yourself open for the showbiz clients."

"Mr. Wycoff, don't count on me for any show-business clients. I'm sorry to have to tell you, but—"

"Here he is now!" trilled Wycoff. "Mr. Drennan, how can we help you this morning?"

And there he was, bigger than life, bigger than her life, anyway, filling the travel agency, her cubicle, her heart, her soul with his presence.

What this giant among mere mortals said was, "Happy Valentine's Day," and handed Mr. Wycoff an enormous heart-shaped box of chocolates.

"Ooh," Mr. Wycoff said, and moved at once toward Miss Eldridge's desk. As Faith watched, he and the four other Wycoff agents gathered around the box and were soon making yummy sounds, leaving Faith uncomfortably alone with Cabot.

"That was a nice thing to do," Faith murmured.

"Not really," Cabot said. "It's an old trick. When explorers needed to cross a river full of piranha, they'd give the piranha something to eat upstream, and when the piranha were involved in a feeding frenzy, they'd cross downstream."

"What a sentimental story," Faith murmured. "Perfect for Valentine's Day." He would never know how fast her heart was racing, how shaky she felt, how the old familiar ache was insidiously taking over the most secret parts of her body.

"That's me," Cabot said, watching her closely.

"Mr. Sentimental. How's everything at home? Wycoff mentioned a family crisis."

"I was the crisis," Faith said, "and the crisis has passed."

"Good," Cabot said, "because I want you to plan a honeymoon."

His words hit her in the pit of her stomach. "Oh, Cabot, please, I can't play this game any more."

"It's not a game, it's a honeymoon. And this time, we'll do it your way. Plan the honeymoon of your dreams. Make it as romantic as you like."

"Last weekend was a failure?" It figured. "You don't like the video? You have to start over?" She really could not do anything right. Except break her own heart. She'd done a pretty good job of that.

"Last weekend was perfect. It's just the honeymoon Tippy wants. Now I need a honeymoon plan for someone else."

"Okay," she said slowly. "I take it this person's a true romantic."

"The most romantic woman I ever met."

Something stirred in Faith's heart. What he had just said and the way he was looking at her gave her a shred of hope. "This one isn't just a publicity stunt? She's really in love with the groom?" She clapped a hand over her mouth. In one unthinking moment she'd broken her promise to Tippy never to tell that she'd learned the truth about her marriage to Cabot.

She gazed at Cabot, expecting a thundercloud to form on his forehead, and instead he smiled. Sunshine seemed to fall all around her. Somehow, and she'd find out how one day, he knew that she knew that he knew...

"I think she is. It's not the kind of question you can just blurt out. You have to work up to it."

"May I ask—" still Faith hesitated "—who the bride is?"

"You."

Her heart pounded. Her body trembled. She longed to throw herself into his arms, but she wasn't going to let him off that easily. "And the groom?" she asked.

"Me, if you'll have me."

"What about Tippy? I have a natural bias against bigamy."

"Tippy has fallen in love with a blond, nearly seven-foot champion race-car driver who writes poetry and worships her. A publicist's dream. He'll look a heck of a lot better in the pictures than I would have, and it frees me up to pursue other options, if you get my drift."

Faith whirled to her computer in order to hide the joy that must be showing on her face. "Okay," she said briskly, "for a honeymoon spot, I suggest—" she fell silent while she tapped at the computer keys "—the Never-Tell Motel," she announced triumphantly. "Fifteen minutes from here, no questions asked!"

The next thing she knew, she was in his arms. Behind them, Mr. Wycoff and his longtime agents still had their backs turned, making yummy sounds.

She and Cabot might as well have been alone.

And on their honeymoon, they would be.

Epilogue

THE CHUGGING SOUND of a helicopter broke the delicious silence of the isolated lodge in the Rockies where Faith and Cabot were honeymooning. She was the first out of bed, and she ran outside in her bathrobe and slippers just in time to catch the packet the chopper dropped.

She slogged back inside, kicked off the snow-burdened slippers and said to Cabot, "You had *Variety* delivered? On our *honeymoon?*"

"I'm trying to change," Cabot said unrepentantly. "The metamorphosis isn't complete yet." He opened the paper, scanned it, then zeroed in on a story and read it aloud to Faith.

"*Actress Tippy Temple and her gorgeous new husband Borg Bergenstern are honeymooning in the Inn of Dreams in Reno. 'When I met Borg,' Temple told our reporters, 'I knew I'd found the only man I could ever love. Those rumors about my publicist and me—who knows how things like that get started. Cabot Drennan is a gifted professional who has done so much for me, and I'm so thrilled that he's in love, too, with an absolute sweetheart of a travel agent, Faith Sumner, presently with Wycoff Worldwide, but soon to start her own agency....'*"

"I am?" Faith said, stunned.

"Heavenly Honeymoons, you could call it," Cabot said, folding his arms around her.

"Heavenly? Hellish with me at the helm! Cabot, this is not a wise idea. You know I'll only—"

"—make everybody who comes to you happy," Cabot murmured into her hair.

"No kidding," said Faith, whose heart was no longer in conversation. "You think I can do that?"

"I'm here," he answered her, "in the middle of nowhere with a chancy electrical system, no phone and absolutely no contact with the outside world. I'm happy. Doesn't that tell you something?"

It told her everything she would ever need to know.

Are You for Real?

BARBARA DALY

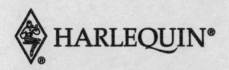

TORONTO • NEW YORK • LONDON
AMSTERDAM • PARIS • SYDNEY • HAMBURG
STOCKHOLM • ATHENS • TOKYO • MILAN • MADRID
PRAGUE • WARSAW • BUDAPEST • AUCKLAND

To Kenneth and Michael, who keep me young
at heart, and to their big brother, Jason.
A very special thank-you to Bob Marshak,
Dean Emeritus of the School of Veterinary Medicine
at the University of Pennsylvania, to his beautiful and
accomplished wife, Margo, for putting up with him
while he read every word of this book three times
and to both of them for being wonderful friends and
neighbors. It goes without saying that everything I
got right about worms in this book is thanks to Bob.
Anything I got wrong is entirely my own doing.

1

"I'M ONLY available until noon. I told you that, the agency told you that, so what's the problem?"

Charity Sumner waved her arms in the air for emphasis and felt one of the pins they'd lined down the back of the red spandex dress pop free. The dress was already so tight she could hardly breathe, but in their wisdom, they'd made it tighter.

Look what they'd done to her. Made her look like the Wicked Witch of the West. They'd pulled her hair back so tightly that her eyebrows stood up in wings, and her slash-of-scarlet mouth looked as if she'd just sucked blood from the throat of an unsuspecting prince.

She'd probably never meet her prince. Right now she'd settle for a frog.

The studio was large and drafty. Through the grimy windows she could see a slice of the Chicago skyline, the mists of winter swirling around the tall towers just as this horde of people swirled around her. The horde included the fashion photographer, a stylist, a hovering minion from the overanxious designer whose dress she was wearing, the makeup man, the lighting man—vultures, all of them, picking at her, poking at her, smoothing her, powdering her as if nothing mattered but the outside of her.

That had always been the case, everywhere except within the comforting confines of her own family, who understood her. Sort of.

Her sisters, in fact, were her immediate problem. She had to get out of here, go home, do what she had to do and get out of *there* before Faith and Hope arrived to spend the night. Because when they found out what she intended to do, they were going to have a fit, separately and collectively.

Her other immediate problem was that no one in the studio was paying the slightest attention to her. Across the room, Celine, a model with whom Charity was often paired, was telling the people who were tugging at her to pronounce her name, "Chuh-leen, not Suh-leen, and certainly not See-leen," but no one was listening to her, either.

The reason they often worked together was that Celine had very blond hair and Charity had very dark hair. They were "such a nice contrast to each other."

They were people. Individuals. Not "a nice contrast." It was enough to make you want to scream. "I said," Charity repeated more loudly, "I have to be out of here by noon."

"Don't move," whispered the designer's minion as she refastened the straight pin and added a few more. "We've almost got it."

"*Don't* wrinkle your nose like that," the makeup man said fussily. "When you wrinkle your nose my makeup cracks."

It's my makeup. All this fuss, and when it ended, when they'd manhandled half a dozen other models in the same way, what they'd have was one more catalog for next Christmas. Today was January second. What if second-skin red dresses weren't in fashion next Christmas?

The big factory clock on the loft wall counted down the minutes. It was already noon. After noon, to be precise, by two minutes. She might feel rebellious, but if she didn't cooperate, the shoot would only take longer.

She made her face a mask. "Mark," she said through her teeth to the hairstylist, "you have a lot of wigs in your van, don't you? Happen to have one in gray?"

He put a hand on one hip, jutted it out and stared at her. "*What* would I be doing with a *gray* wig, one might ask?"

"I just thought you might…I mean, older women do model and I supposed…"

"They're *already* gray, poor things," he snapped, "we don't *make* them gray. You'll be gray soon enough, dollface, with that black hair of yours. Just wait a year or two."

"I need it now. I'm going to a costume party," she improvised.

"In *January?*"

"My friend was sick on Halloween, so she switched the party to January," Charity said, developing her story as she went along.

"Well. If you want gray streaks in a hurry," Mark said, getting into the project in spite of himself, "there's some stuff you can buy."

"Position," yelled the cameraman. Hands surrounded her, tilting her chin, moving her arms around, shoving one red spandexed hip out to the side, tugging at her ill-fitting shoes until her knees were almost touching and her legs were splayed out.

This stage of her life would be over soon. *Had* to be.

THE THREE BIG DOGS formed a semicircle behind her dressing table and stared at her, worried and unblinking, as she wrought the changes in herself. The little dogs were lined up on the foot of the bed with their front paws hanging over, getting a better view that way, and the cats seemed to be everywhere, flicking their tails in her powder and attacking her makeup brushes.

"It's okay," she reassured all of them. "It's still me inside here. I have to get this job. Understand? And it's the only way I can do it."

Her hands shook as she tried to hurry. Faith and Hope would be here soon. This was their "sisters night," the traditional end to their Christmas visit to their parents, and they'd decided to spend it at the country house Charity had bought on the outskirts of Antioch, a suburb north of Chicago. Tomorrow Faith would fly home to Los Angeles and Hope would fly home to New York and her new love, Sam. Unfortunately, Charity's interview was today.

Equally unfortunately, she was putting out fresh water for the dogs when they suddenly deafened her with their frantic warnings, the kitchen door flew open and there her sisters stood. Faith's curly blond hair was setting up a static electricity relationship with the voluminous fake fur coat Charity had given her for Christmas, and Hope, as always, was perfectly pulled together in black, her auburn hair falling right back into place the minute the door closed on the winter wind.

Faith's luminous eyes widened. ''Oh, honey, what's happened to you?''

Hope's green eyes narrowed. ''How could you possibly have managed to gain twenty pounds since New Year's Eve?'' Even when she was glowing with love, some things about Hope would never change.

''You've gone gray. My baby sister,'' Faith said. Her eyes filled with tears. ''Oh!'' she shrieked suddenly. ''What did you do to your face?''

''Whatever has happened to you,'' Hope said, ''I'm not letting you go anywhere in that outfit.'' She hesitated. ''Unless you've joined the Salvation Army. If you've become a Soldier, I want you to know I fully support your—''

''Well, hello to you, too,'' Charity said, looking down at them from her superior height. ''And now, if you'll excuse me, I must run. I have a job interview. I'll be home by six and we'll have a lovely evening together.''

She should have known the words *job interview* would flip a switch in Hope. ''You're going to an interview in that suit? Oh.'' Hope's voice went flat. ''I see what you're up to.''

''What's she up to?'' Faith said, fluttering around Charity like a disoriented butterfly.

''Nobody's going to believe those white streaks in your hair,'' Hope said.

''Women with black hair often gray early,'' Charity said in her own defense.

''But not overnight,'' Hope said. ''The problem is, you didn't have white streaks two days ago.''

''You know that, but Jason Segal doesn't.''

''Who's Jason Segal?'' They did that one in chorus.

Charity sighed, giving up on the silly idea she'd once had that she was grown-up now and could do what she wanted to without having to explain herself to her sisters. While she was the tallest, she was and would ever be the youngest. ''He's a brilliant young veterinary researcher at the University of Wisconsin in Madison. He got a grant to develop a—'' They wouldn't want to know what he was developing. ''He advertised for an assistant, so I sent him my résumé and he invited me to interview."

"I still don't think you can go for an interview looking like that," Hope persisted. "It violates every principle of good business practice."

"I have to interview looking like this," Charity burst out. "I've tried everything else." She flung her hands forward in supplication. "I've interviewed for two dozen positions for which I was perfectly qualified and nobody hired me because I look too... frivolous. I don't want to be a model. I want to be a scientist."

"You're not frivolous. You're just beautiful," Faith said. "Even now." But her voice faltered a little as she said it.

"Whatever. I can't get anybody to take me seriously. Now—" Charity glanced proudly at her reflection in the mirror over the sink "—I look like a woman with purpose, a true scholar, and Jason Segal is going to hire me on the spot. I'll be back where I belong. Studying worms."

Her sisters went a little green around the gills, as they always did when the topic of her parasitology training came up. She hadn't even been able to get them to proofread her dissertation. And she'd chosen a parasite she thought would at least appeal to Faith, *Syngamus trachea,* a worm that mates for life. It was as romantic as you could get in the nematode world.

"If you insist on following this career in worms," Hope said after a deep swallow, "instead of maximizing your personal assets and building your modeling career as any other woman as beautiful as you would do, I still think you've gone off the deep end with the scar.''

Hope could pack a lot of punch into one sentence. That's what made her so successful in business. Charity ran her clear-polished, newly shortened nails down the long gash on her cheek. ''It doesn't look realistic?''

''It's ghastly,'' Faith breathed.

''Good. I'll keep it then.''

''Did you burn off your eyelashes in the same accident?'' Faith wore an empathetic look that said, ''Talk about it. You'll feel better.''

Charity exchanged a glance with Hope that said, ''she still doesn't get it.'' ''I cut them off with my cuticle scissors. They'll grow back. Eventually. I just bleached my brows'' She glanced at the kitchen clock. ''If I don't leave right now, I'll be late, which would violate every principle of sound business practice.''

Hope glared at her. ''Do you really intend to leave us alone with all these animals?'' She waved an arm at their silent audience—a Rottweiler, a pit bull, a white dog of no particular breed, terriers and cats of every size and color.

''Yes. There's a lint lifter on my dresser if you need one. If Oscar throws up, don't give him anything for dinner except some of that rice on the stove. And don't leave a wineglass unattended. Supercat—''

Charity gestured toward a huge gray Maine coon cat that eyed them narrowly from the top of the refrigerator "—has a drinking problem. Bye," she said. "I've cooked you a fantastic dinner."

At the door she whirled. "Did you notice my eyes? Contact lenses. Two different shades. The optician was so sweet and understanding." She smiled at their stunned expressions.

BETWEEN INTERVIEWS in his office at the veterinary school in Madison, Jason Segal picked up a popular magazine for dog lovers and saw yet another article in which he'd been quoted. *"Brilliant young veterinary researcher Jason Segal gave us the following statement in regard to the effect of Interferon on…"*

He squinted one eye, stared at the paper and tried to imagine the story read, *"Sexy young veterinary researcher Jason Segal,"* but his imagination wasn't up to it. No matter which eye he squinted, it still said "brilliant."

He wadded up the paper and threw it at the wastepaper basket. A three-pointer. Didn't anybody notice there was more to him than brains?

Maybe there wasn't.

Not that women didn't like him. From grade school onward they'd sought him out as a friend. In high school they'd fawned over him. From the beginning of his college years, they'd slept with him. But it always followed that they needed help with homework, or a term paper, or lab work or a narrowed-down dissertation topic.

They didn't even lust after his whole brain. Just the left half. Couldn't they see that the right side of his brain was desperately trying to hang on to control of a roiling, seething mass of...

He gave up his soul-search for the moment and let his gaze roam over the résumé that lay open on his desk. Charity Sumner had terrific credentials. He needed someone with her lab training to succeed at the project that lay so close to his heart.

She was even younger than he was, just twenty-six. She lacked job experience, and the two-year gap between the time she'd received her Ph.D. and now was puzzling in light of those fine credentials. But you never knew. Maybe she'd had a baby. The résumé only said, "personal pursuits."

On the other hand, he really couldn't afford to hire an older, more experienced type. His early work had generated enough interest to get him a grant, but not a huge one. Much of it was going toward supplies and sophisticated equipment. So he'd take the best help he could find at the best price he could pay. He was more than ready to finish this project and get on with his life.

Get a life was more like it.

A soft knock sounded on his office door, and when he called out, "Come in," the woman who had to be Charity Sumner paused in the doorway, looking confused, as if her eyes were having to adjust to the light, then stepped in. He had to grip the edge of his desk to still his immediate reaction. This woman didn't look as if she'd had a baby. She looked more like a person who'd survived a plane crash. Barely.

"Don't get up, Dr. Segal," she said briskly. "I'm Dr. Sumner. It's a pleasure to meet you."

"It's Jason," Jason said, and got up anyway to shake her hand.

The woman looked twenty years older than the résumé claimed she was. She was tall, probably five-nine or so, and sort of chunky. Her graying black hair was skinned back into a bun. She had virtually no eyebrows or lashes—they'd probably been burned off in the accident—and her eyes, oh, lord, her eyes were two different shades of brown, each duller than the other. The blouse she wore with her dowdy navy suit was the hideous color of mustard that had sat too long on the shelf, but it did match one of her eyes.

He focused on that eye to keep from staring at the scar that bisected her cheek. At once his heart went out to her. "Have a seat, Charity," he said through dry lips.

"Have you had time to go over my résumé?"

This was not going to be your ordinary interview during which you engaged in small talk, explored hobbies and interests outside the candidate's work, figured out whether you could get along together in the intense environment of a lab. Something tragic had happened to this woman, had aged her before her time, had closed the door to her emotions.

"It's very impressive," Jason said. "I did notice your lack of job experience. With a scholarly history like yours, I would have thought you'd choose to teach, or—"

"Things happen," she said shortly. "Since what I've been doing in the past two years has no bearing on the field of parasitology, I knew you wouldn't be interested in it. And frankly, I'm not interested in discussing it." She fidgeted in her chair.

"I read your dissertation," he said quickly. "Excellent work. Really significant."

For the first time some life sparkled in her mismatched brown eyes. "Thank you," she said. "I can't tell you what a pleasure it is to talk to someone who doesn't gag just hearing the title."

He glanced down at the thick, bound manuscript. "Mapping the Genome of *Syngamus trachea*," it said on the cover. Why would that make anybody gag? "The topic is relevant to a line of research I'd like to get into someday."

"I know," she said, her unscarred cheek reddening a little. "I read your preliminary study...before I sent you my résumé, and I can see where it might eventually lead. But what you're doing now will be a major step in canine and comparative medicine. A vaccine to prevent infection by any known canine gastrointestinal parasite. It's a very exciting prospect." Indeed, she looked very excited. More excited than he'd ever seen a woman look about gastrointestinal parasites. And the quality of her voice had changed. Earlier it had been sharp. Now it was softer, musical.

Jason made a quick decision. Being able to make quick decisions was the upside of having a big brain, he guessed. He cleared his throat. "So you're free to take a job now."

"Yes." The musical tone vanished, leaving a monotone.

"I really mean now. A week from Monday."

"Yes." She thought for a moment. "If I may take some time off in the next month or so to honor several prior commitments. It would be a matter of a half day here and there. I can give you a schedule."

Probably doctors' appointments. Maybe visits to a psychiatrist. "I could work around it," Jason said. "Well, Charity, I've already interviewed two candidates, but you sound like the right person for the job. Want some time to think it over?"

"No." A little expressiveness seeped into her face, although he was sure she was trying to hide it. "I've already thought it over pretty carefully. I know I would enjoy working with you on this project."

"Then consider it a done deal," Jason said, smiling at her. At least she hadn't said, She'd enjoy working with "someone as brilliant as you."

"Let's talk money and benefits," he said, getting serious again, looking down at the papers on his desk. "I'm afraid this job isn't as lucrative as some others you'd be equally qualified for."

"I think it probably is."

It was such an odd statement that he glanced up and caught her with a look of sheer delight on her homely face. Something about that look made his heart beat a little faster. She really did want this job. And he'd bet his National Institute of Health grant she'd be damned good at it.

"In that case," he said, "I'll send you right on to Personnel." He stood up. "Better hurry. They close at five on the dot."

She held out her hand and he shook it. It was a slim hand, and though her fingers were long and tapered, it felt small in his, and soft. She looked up at him and smiled. Either the accident had spared her teeth or she'd been fitted out with a deluxe set of brilliantly white caps. He was aware of sudden feelings of confusion. He couldn't imagine where they were coming from.

She turned and started toward the door. Halfway there she paused, holding very still for a second, then seemed to lock her knees together for the rest of the short walk—more of a waddle, really—out of his office.

Poor thing. The accident had done some damage to her joints. Or maybe to her bladder.

2

CHARITY WADDLED down the hall and into the women's restroom, where she locked herself inside a stall and collapsed onto the toilet seat, her face carefully balanced on her fingertips so she wouldn't mess up her scar.

She had a job. In parasitology. Her disguise had worked. She could renew her acquaintance with worms. Nothing else mattered.

But it did, it did. Softly she groaned. For a minute there, when she first saw him, she'd thought it was the contact lenses playing tricks on her. But no such luck. She'd gotten a job in parasitology, all right, working for a fantastic-looking parasitologist. He wasn't just intelligent, he was a hunk, a blond, green-eyed hunk, muscular and all male. While she looked like a—

She didn't have time to think about it now. It was clear she couldn't keep her padding up by tucking it under the waistband of the panty hose. When she sat down, the towels pulled out. Feeling marginally calmer, she got up, tucked the towels inside the panty hose, which made them so tight she could hardly breathe, and made her way to the personnel office.

It was either the call Jason had made to them or her scar that accounted for their willingness to see her at 4:59.

It was close to seven when she moved on heavy, silent feet into her house to find Hope on the floor tossing toys to the cats and covered with their hair while Supercat circled the glass of wine Hope had poured for herself.

"Thank goodness I left Ch'I with Sam," she was saying to Faith. "I wouldn't want to expose her to these ruffians."

Charity caught this statement in passing and decided not to take offense, even though Hope's new kitten was a holy terror and she, personally, felt that Hope was being much too indulgent in her discipline. Faith— What was Faith doing?

Was she reading to the dogs? Charity's old copy of *Lassie, Come Home*? Whatever it was, the dogs had arranged themselves in formation around her chair and were listening so intently they hadn't even heard Charity pull into the driveway. The bucolic scene ended when Charity tried to dart past them and into the bathroom to scrub her face.

"What happened?" they yelled through the closed door.

"I got the job."

Screams.

"Would you bring me that purple sweater that's hanging on the closet door?" she shouted over the screams. "The socks, too, and a pair of black tights."

Silence, then mutters and scurrying sounds. In a minute the clothes came through the door. Charity skimmed into them and took a quick look at herself in the mirror, trying to see herself through her big sisters' eyes, trying to imagine why they would ever have christened her the family beauty. Her sisters were gorgeous!

She didn't even want to be the family beauty. She had a brain, and that's what she wanted to be admired for. She glanced at herself again and saw, not a model, but a parasitologist.

"Yes!" she said, clenching her fist and making a right angle with her forearm.

But there was that one big problem. This was where interfering sisters came in handy. She slipped out the door and gave each of them the hug she should have given them the minute they arrived.

"It worked," Faith said, her eyes big and wide. "The disguise worked. You were right."

"Maybe it was the disguise," Hope said, "or maybe everything just came together in the right place at the right time."

Charity knew Hope couldn't help being so matter-of-fact. She had an MBA. "Something worked," she said slowly, "but there's one thing I hadn't counted on."

"What?" Hope narrowed her eyes.

Charity knew Hope was thinking clauses in contracts, salaries, stipulations. None of the above. "He's gorgeous," she said in a small, wondering voice. "Jason Segal is the sexiest man I've ever laid eyes on, and all I could think about during the whole interview was how much I'd like to lay my hands on him, in the most secret and forbidden places. Tell me, Hope, is it sexual harassment when the research assistant goes after the boss?"

More screams. Naturally. And they kept it up—the questions, the exhortations, the advice—until at last she sat them down to her famous Algerian lamb shanks with couscous.

LOOK AT HER NOW," Faith said in her dreamiest voice.

Even Hope sighed a little. "That hair," she said, "that figure, or lack thereof, those eyes."

"Like blue violets," Faith breathed. "And skin like porcelain."

"I can't help wishing…" Hope said.

"I know," Faith said.

"But she…"

"I'm here," Charity said. "It's fine for you to talk directly to me. Although I wish you wouldn't, because I've already heard it."

"That's the shortest skirt I ever saw anyone actually wear," Hope said, to Faith, of course.

"It only looks that short because her legs are so long," Faith said, sounding wistful, "and her arms look so pretty in that sweater. She's the only person who could wear that outfit."

Everybody Charity knew was wearing outfits like the one she had on. Black leather micromini, sleeveless black wool turtleneck, black boots. Plain little everyday separates to wear to this afternoon's modeling assignment.

"How anyone can be that beautiful and cook at the same time," Hope said, forking up a bite of blueberry pancake, "is beyond me."

"It doesn't seem fair," Faith agreed.

"After breakfast, I'll get the dog hair off her with that lint lifter," Hope told Faith. "It's the only thing that stands between her and utter perfection."

"Hello!" Charity yelled. "I said stop referring to me in the third person! Oh, Oscar, I'm sorry," she said, dropping to her knees to cuddle a startled Border terrier. "Charity wasn't yelling at you."

"You're doing it," Hope said.

"What? What am I doing?"

"Referring to yourself in the third person."

"Oh, for heaven's sake!" Charity sat down with a platter of pancakes and filled her own plate. "Maybe I am three people," she said, losing her irritation as she grew thoughtful. "The model, the parasitologist—and the person who takes in strays and cooks and lives in a house that looks like somebody's aunt

Agnes lived there once. And don't think it's not tough." She poured a river of syrup over the pancakes she'd just lavished with butter.

"How does she eat that way and stay so thin?" Faith asked Hope.

"Because she has such a tough life," Hope said.

Charity put down her fork. "When do your planes leave?" she asked, gazing steadily at them.

"Mine's at 2:10," Hope said, "and Faith's is 2:23."

"What timing!" Charity said. "Did you make the reservations, Faith?"

"No," Hope said. "I did."

"She didn't trust me," Faith said, an expression of resentment briefly crossing her face. "I'm a travel agent and my own sister doesn't trust me to make a couple of simple reservations."

"Well, you know…" Hope said, and trailed off, giving Charity another of those looks. "How long does it take to get to the airport?"

"Four hours," Charity said.

"Really?" Faith leaped up. "We're going to be late!"

"She's lying," Hope said. "Sit down. Toss me another pancake, okay?"

"More sausage?" Charity asked, inwardly sighing. For a minute she'd almost gotten them pitted against each other instead of against her. It was the only way she could ever win an argument with them.

No, not the only way.

"About this job…" she began. "When I tell you what I'll be working on, I think you'll understand why I'm so excited about it." She took a bite of pancake on her fork. "Jason Segal is developing this single vaccine against all the different worms that infect dogs." She let her mouth curl around the word *worms* as she put the pancake square into her mouth. "And the vaccine's actually made of worms." She speared a piece of sausage. "What? What's wrong?"

They'd laid their forks down on their half-eaten pancakes and were staring at her, their mouths uniformly slack. "How long does it really take to get to the airport?" Faith said faintly. "We don't want to be late."

"We certainly don't," Hope said in a similarly lackluster voice. "Now that I think of it, by the time we return the car, and this and that…"

"And if there's traffic…" Faith said. "Let's pack."

They rushed away.

Charity polished off three pancakes and two links of sausage. She wasn't looking forward to her modeling job this afternoon or to any of the other dozen or so she'd have to do before she could truly say that part of her life was over. All she could think about was the beginning of her new life—the laboratory, an opportunity to work with worms, or against them, actually, and her next encounter with Jason Segal.

What if she went in to the lab as herself and said, "Surprise!"

He was a scientist. It was too soon to know if he had a sense of humor. What if she went to the lab as herself and said, "I really shouldn't be coming to work so soon after the plastic surgery on my scar, the laser surgery on my eyes and the incredible diet I went on to lose...."

What if she went to the lab as herself and said, "I came to the interview in disguise because I knew it was the only way you'd ever give me this job."

He'd say, "Aha! You're nothing but a fluffhead! And a conscienceless deceiver! Your résumé is probably a lie, too."

No. If she handled it carefully, he'd never find out she'd deceived him to get the job.

"Penny for your thoughts," Faith said, coming back into the kitchen with two large suitcases.

"I'm used to getting two-fifty an hour," Charity said. "That's two *hundred* fifty."

"It would only take a minute!"

"That would be four dollars, seventeen cents."

"I still can't afford it," Faith admitted.

"Good," Charity said, as Hope trotted into the room with her single rolling carry-on.

How COULD SHE have been so stupid!

She was a model, for heaven's sake. Why hadn't she taken a picture of herself in a mirror, or drawn a sketch? Charity slumped over the dressing table in complete despair. The large dogs moved a step closer, Rags the Rottweiler put his head on her lap and the little ones fidgeted on the bed. She couldn't remember which cheek she'd put the scar on for the interview with Jason. Nor could she remember which eye was which, but that wouldn't be as memorable. The scar was crucial. She returned a steady gaze to the mirror.

"Concentrate," she told it. "You had the scar here, like this." She made an imaginary sketch on her left cheek. "Although—" her hand halted in midair "—I seem to remember trying to be careful with my right cheek."

She spun on her dressing table stool, carrying Rags's huge head with her, to continue the conversation with the dogs. "I have to tell you," she confided, "that I was so *wasted* the minute I saw Jason Segal that the scar could have been on the left while I was being careful on the right."

There was a slim possibility that Faith or Hope would remember. Also that Hope would remember most accurately, so she dialed her cell phone first.

"Right," Hope said.

Charity was about to move ahead when a thought struck her. Hope was in love. Could she be trusted?

Slowly she dialed Faith at home, realizing belatedly that it was only five in the morning on the West Coast. "What!" her sister answered. "Did I oversleep. Omigosh, I'll be there in a—" There was a long pause, and then Faith said with unaccustomed coolness, "Charity, is that you?"

Charity didn't have time to apologize. She simply asked her question.

"Left," Faith said after thinking about it, "because you were standing on my left…no, you must have been on my right, and I remember looking at that terrible scar and thinking…"

"Thank you," Charity said. "You've been a big help."

So the scar was either on the left or the right. Reflecting on her quandary, she decided to go with the right. Even if Hope was disabled with love, she was more likely to know left from right than Faith. In fact, Jason had probably forgotten, too. If he was a true scholar, he'd be too absentminded to notice. Having made the difficult decision, she did the makeup job with the skill of long practice, then got up to admire herself.

Her hair was perfect, nicely grayed and skinned back into an unrelenting bun. No eye makeup. She'd used a lipliner to draw inside the natural line of her lips, and had found a lipstick of such an unbecoming color—geriatric mauve, she'd call it—that she looked far more washed out wearing it than not.

She was dressed in a suit she'd found in a thrift shop. If she'd been charged with the responsibility of naming the color, she'd call it Grandmother Gray. The skirt hit a spot between knee and calf, which shortened her legs nicely. She wore thick black tights and stumpy black pumps to enhance the impression. The blouse was a real find—maroon. Not ruby or burgundy or garnet, but old-fashioned letter-sweater maroon. It was hideous. She was immensely proud of it, and she'd gotten it for a dollar fifty.

Her greatest victory, though, was the queen-size, high-waisted girdle. Once she'd stuffed it with towels, she was a confident size sixteen. She was ready for the first day of her new life, her real life, well, almost real, as a parasitologist.

"Oscar," she said to the Border terrier, "you're in charge of the canines. Work on your benevolent despot image, okay? I oiled the pet door hinges—" she flipped the door that led to a fenced-in area she kept clear of snow a couple of times to emphasize her point "—and don't let anybody chase the cats. Supercat in particular. He might kill one of you."

"Please don't answer the phone," she continued, since she had Oscar's full attention. "Wait for the answering machine. There's plenty of food and water for all of you...."

Separation was painful, but it had to come sometime, like now. "I'll see you tonight! Bye."

JASON WAS intensely nervous. He could tell he was nervous because he'd put artificial sweetener in his coffee. He hated sugar in his coffee whether it was real or artificial. But he'd been standing there at the coffeepot wondering what Charity Sumner put in her coffee and if he had the right stuff. Skim milk? Cream? Creamer? Sugar? Sweetener? Sweetener in pink packets? Sweetener in blue packets? Then he'd digressed, as he often did, and had started reading the label on a pink packet, and before he knew it, he'd torn it open and dumped it into his coffee.

Why—could someone explain to him why?—was he worried about what she'd want in her coffee?

"Because she seems to be a nice person," he told Candida. Candida was one of his better friends among the beagles whose job was to help him perfect his vaccine. She seemed to relish a bit of conversation while he weighed her, and to appreciate the back massage he gave her afterward for sitting still.

"Because I think she needs somebody to care about the little stuff, like whether she's a pink-packet person or a blue-packet person," he told Lionel, another of the beagles, the one who always seemed to listen so intently.

"Because I've gone bonkers," he said to himself as he went back to his office. "Why else would I be discussing her with beagles? They haven't even met her yet."

"Insane young scientist Jason Segal…"

Given the alternative, he'd better stick with "brilliant."

"Dr. Segal?" She'd arrived. She stuck her head

shyly through the doorway before she eased herself into the small reception area.

"It's Jason, remember? Glad to have you onboard. Charity." He shook her hand heartily, noticing again how soft it was, and how small for a woman of her girth. "Coffee?"

"I'll get it."

She shrugged off a threadbare coat of an odd shade of brown, hung it neatly on the coatrack and edged her way around the perimeter of the room to the coffee counter. The brown probably matched one of her eyes. He reminded himself to notice later, when she left the lab this afternoon.

But now he had hosting responsibilities. He joined her at the coffeepot. "Cream?" he said. "Sugar?"

She turned to face him fully. He looked at her face, felt his vision get a little fuzzy and then go crosseyed, but got himself straightened out. He could have sworn that tragic scar was on her left cheek. But it wasn't. It was on the right.

For the hundredth time he cursed the pitfalls of his profession. You learned to look at people—animals, in his case, but he guessed it had carried over—as test cases, not in any personal, sensitive way. It was a shame, especially for a person who wanted, someday, to have a personal life.

She'd hesitated too, uncomfortable, he was guiltily sure, under his gaze. His guilt increased. "Sugar," she said. After another slight hesitation, she patted her waistline. "I shouldn't, but…"

"Sugar it is!" Now he was being too jolly. He wished he could erase himself and start over.

"And cream, if you have it."

"Cream!" *Shut up, Jason, you sound like Mom hovering over Dad.*

"Thank you," she said. She looked up at him with those mismatched eyes and gave him a slight smile.

He'd give up a Nobel Prize to know what she was thinking.

3

HE SEEMED BORN to wear a lab coat. His teeth were as white as the coat, and it went with everything about him that was blond and clean looking.

She ought to be ashamed of herself, drooling over Jason Segal's appearance when she should be drooling over his brain. Although from the professional journals she subscribed to, it appeared that Jason didn't have a problem getting anyone to notice his intelligence.

"I'll show you around," he told her, "and then let's sit down in my office and I'll start briefing you."

Sitting down now would have been her choice, because her knees were shaking a little, and when you were as tall as she was, you needed steady knees.

"This is your work area," he said, opening a door to a small laboratory next to his. Trying hard to notice something besides Jason, Charity focused on the view of the snow-covered college campus, the tall lab chair, the state-of-the-art computer.

Staying in character, she said, "Quite adequate."

He walked her through his laboratory, which was fitted out with the latest in equipment, showed her the storeroom and then said, "I'll introduce you to the lab animals."

Charity knew the vaccine would have to be tested on dogs and knew that certain breeds of dogs were bred especially for experimental purposes, but still she'd been dreading this part. In her brisk "Dr. Sumner" voice she said, "I trust you keep them in a humane—" He opened the door, and her jaw dropped open.

She was looking at a Disney World of beagles. What could have passed for real grass lined the dog runs, and the lighting created a daytime atmosphere. A walk space ran along the outer edge of the two beagle communities. In the runs, the dogs played and visited with each other or slept contentedly in their own cages.

"The test group," Jason said, gesturing to the kennels on his left, "and the control group." He nodded to the right. "I hope you're not bothered by the informality of the conditions." She could feel his intent gaze on her as he waited for her reaction.

"Ah..." She wouldn't mind living there herself. "No, as long as you're able to control your variables." She felt obligated to let her stuffy, overweight alter ego speak up.

"That goes without saying."

"They do seem to be happy." It popped out of her before she could stop it.

He gave her a look of pure relief. "Thank you for

not telling me it's silly to give them all this exercise room.''

"Of course not.'' She was back in character. "The better shape they're in physically and emotionally, the more accurate the results of your tests.''

He gave her a strange look. What was that she saw in his wonderful green eyes? Was it disappointment?

As she listened to Jason discuss his vaccine with an enthusiasm that would have charmed even a person who tended to faint at the mention of worms, Charity's mind wandered.

How could she have disappointed him? He'd wanted a dedicated scientist and she'd behaved like one. He didn't know it, but he wanted a research assistant with brains, not beauty. She'd certainly achieved that.

His eyes were so green. They weren't hazel. They didn't have brown flecks. They were simply green. And looking straight at her.

"Yes," she said, shifting the weight she wasn't used to shifting in the chair on the other side of his desk. "I can see how you chose to approach the problem from that angle. In fact, I found it interesting that…''

…that he was so muscular. He certainly hadn't gotten those muscles lifting petri dishes or sitting at his computer. Did he work out? Play tennis?

If she weren't in this dumb disguise, behaving as

if she didn't have a personality, she could just ask him. As it was...

"...I'd like to pursue that aspect of the study. That would free you up to..."

...*ask me out.*

"No!" she said aloud before she could sort out the two channels she had playing at the same time in her brain. "No," she said more mildly, "I wouldn't need much guidance. I did a lot of work in that area before I settled on my dissertation topic."

You fool! You should have said you'd need tons of guidance! The kind of guidance that would involve his constant presence, him looking over her shoulder, his hand guiding hers. Nice hands, too. He had really nice hands. Long fingers, neat, short nails.

"I'm sorry," she apologized. "What was that last thing you said?" It was time to clear one of the channels out of her brain. Unfortunately, the one she wanted to shut off was the science channel.

The question, when he repeated it, surprised her. "Of course I'll want to work with the beagles," she said.

"Good." He hesitated. "You may have noticed that I treat them as much like pets as I can under the circumstances. I'd appreciate it if you'd do the same."

"Of course." She managed to say it briskly, as Dr. Sumner would. What Jason Segal didn't know was how much he and she had in common, at least in their attitude toward animals. What the beagles didn't know was that Aunt Charity had come to cuddle them. They'd know soon enough, but it wasn't the time to correct Jason's impression of her as a cold and clinical scientist.

Her predicament was maddening, and she'd done it to herself.

"For the next few days you should go over my data, familiarize yourself with the protocols."

"Certainly." Could she possibly sit on his lap while she went over his data?

As she gazed at him thoughtfully, she realized he was staring directly at her scar. She felt the heat climb her face and knew she was blushing. She was sure of it when his face reddened, too, and he quickly looked away.

She was feeling ever more certain that the scar had been on the left the day they met. Well, it was on the right now, and that was where it would stay.

JASON WONDERED if she'd loosen up a little bit if she got that scar taken care of, got back some of her self-confidence about her appearance. Not that she'd be a raving beauty even then, but she had some features that were quite attractive.

Her eyes were a funny color, but they had a great shape.

Almond, he thought they called it. The accident, or whatever it was that had happened to her, had burned off her lashes, but they'd grow back, and her colorless brows winged up as if she were always about to ask a question.

Ha! She didn't ask questions. She already knew everything. He wondered suddenly if that's what people said about him. He hoped not. His mother gave him annual lectures on humility. Thirty lectures that would be, and he thought he'd gotten the point by now.

Her mouth was a little thin. Made him think she didn't have a sense of humor. Well, she didn't. None that he'd noticed yet.

Her legs looked so good—he hadn't been able to help noticing as she was hanging up her coat—that he wondered why she wore those inch-thick stockings. It was almost as if she didn't want anybody to notice that she had great legs. Funny.

But she was going to be a terrific asset to his project. He could tell already. He needed to spend some time in the lab, and on the way he'd poke his head into her work area and see how she was doing.

So he did. He found her so absorbed in the data on the computer screen that she didn't know he was there, so he gave himself a minute to watch her.

She'd made a window on the side of the screen for her own notes and comments. So she was into it, already feeling a part of it. That was good. Her surprisingly small hands were light and deft on the keyboard, and from this vantage point he could study her profile.

She had a neat nose and small, perfectly shaped ears. He found them so enchanting that he hardly noticed the scar on her cheek.

Study of the nose and ears was not what this laboratory was all about. Jason cleared his throat. She whirled, saw him, and smiled. The smile was so genuine, so brilliant, it nearly knocked him over.

"This is fantastic," she said. Her voice had the musical quality he'd heard in it once before, during the interview. "Your vaccine will elicit an immunological response that will…"

To him it sounded like poetry. Jason hovered in the doorway, mesmerized by her voice, her smile, her excitement. And then she halted, staring at him as though something had shocked her. She seemed to gather herself together, and then she said in the flat, dead voice of Dr. Sumner, "I'm confident I can get into this without any difficulty."

He felt fully deflated. "I'm pleased to hear that," he said in the personality-free voice of Dr. Segal. An oddly disturbing thought occurred to him, that he was pretty sure it was the only voice he had.

SHE HAD TO get her act together. She was the only one in the family with any acting ability, not entirely a good thing, because it only supported her sisters' belief that she should model and then break into showbiz instead of futzing around with worms. But now she needed to use whatever talent she possessed.

She'd gotten so excited about Jason's research that she'd forgotten she was playing a role.

What was most frustrating was that when she'd gotten back into character, Jason had drifted away to the lab with that same look of disappointment in his eyes.

He didn't like "Dr. Sumner," but that's who he'd hired. He might have liked her real self, but he wouldn't have hired her. This was a terrible quandary, because she wanted both things, the job—and at least a fighting chance at the boss.

HE WAS HAVING trouble focusing today. He wasn't used to having anyone around except the prevet students who came in to help him with the beagles, so he supposed his distraction was understandable.

At noon Jason wandered back from the lab after a session at the microscope. It occurred to him that taking his new research assistant to lunch would be a polite thing to do, even though he hadn't planned to go out. So he poked his head around her door again.

"How about lunch?" he said.

She jumped, obviously startled out of deep thought. "Oh. Is it that time already?" She glanced at her watch, which gave him an opportunity to notice that her wrist was slim for such a heavy woman. So were her ankles. She wasn't naturally heavy. Stress eating, that's what had done it. The aftermath of the accident.

"Sorry, but I brought my lunch."

Jason came back to the present. "Actually, so did I," he admitted. Knowing it was against federal regulations for biohazard, but feeling unusually bold, he said, "Want to clear off a space and eat together?"

Thin smile. "Yes. Thank you."

There weren't many women, Jason reflected as he led her back to the lab, who could lunch comfortably with the smell of his chemical reagents. Maybe, when he actually started looking for a woman to share his life, the life he really wanted to live, he should look for someone in his field.

He pushed several flasks and notebooks aside and set up stools on each side of one of the metal counters. When he looked up, she was unpacking an interesting-looking picnic. A thermos of something that smelled like hot tea. A tray of chicken wings, just the good part of the wing, the part that looked like a bantam drumstick. Deviled eggs. Potato salad. Cookies. They looked like oatmeal-raisin, his favorite.

Jason set his turkey sandwich and carrot sticks on the counter beside his root beer and sat down opposite her. As she brought item after item out of a cooler that looked too small for its contents, she pulled out a sheet of paper.

"I knew I put this somewhere," she said. "This is a schedule of days I'll have to be away from work.

I'm sorry I have to do this, but they're commitments I made before our interview.''

"I understand," Jason assured her. He glanced at the sheet. Tomorrow afternoon, Friday morning, a full day next week, then an afternoon scattered here and there over the six weeks following.

"I'll get the work done," she said, sounding almost anxious.

"Oh, I'm sure you will. Please don't feel that you have to apologize," he said while she worked away at unwrapping and removing plastic tops. His mouth was watering, and not for a turkey sandwich and carrot sticks.

Her gaze came up from her unwrapping and top-removal chores and met his. "I brought enough for an army. Want to share?" she said abruptly.

"Yes." This was no time for manners. He put down her calendar, then ripped his sandwich in half with his bare hands and put one of the halves on a napkin in front of her.

"I didn't mean..." she began, then simply put everything she'd brought with her in the middle of the table. Maybe it was just his imagination, but he thought her smile widened a little.

"You like to cook?" he asked unnecessarily in the middle of a piece of chicken.

"Cooking and worms are my favorite pastimes." She made this admission after a brief hesitation, as though she were scripting every word. "Besides, I have to eat.'' Another hesitation. ''I live out in the country and there isn't a restaurant close by. What do you do about food? Eat out?''

Since she seemed genuinely interested, Jason said, ''Some. But I have a landlady...'' He sighed. ''The idea was to rent the apartment above hers. Instead I rented a mother. More like a grandmother,'' he corrected himself, thinking about his youthful parents.

It wasn't his imagination. Her smile was growing. ''And she cooks for you,'' she prompted him.

''Well, she...'' He felt helpless just thinking about Mrs. Appleby. He was going to feel even more foolish describing his situation to the self-contained woman sitting opposite him, but there was something in her smile that made him forge ahead. ''There's no stopping her.'' He groaned. ''I get home and she's cleaned my apartment. There's food in the refrigerator. Little notes on the food—'I cooked much more of this than I can eat, and it doesn't freeze well.' Same notes every day. I think she has them printed up at the copy shop. My laundry is either gone or already back. She *irons* my underwear.''

He'd gotten so wound up he'd forgotten to watch his words. ''I'm sorry,'' he said at once, ''that was too personal a thing to say.''

''If your underwear isn't too personal for your landlady, it certainly isn't too personal for me.'' Now the look in her eyes was one of pure mischief.

Jason knew he was turning red. He felt off balance.

There was more to Charity Sumner than met the eye, and one of her characteristics was inconsistency. One person one minute, another person another minute. He liked all sorts of people, he just didn't like it when one person was acting like all sorts of people. Of course, maybe she'd been one person before the accident, and the accident had affected her personality, turned her into a quite different person, and sometimes she forgot which person she was.

He'd made himself dizzy just thinking about it. It wasn't as if he had to find a scientific explanation for her. He'd hired an odd research assistant, that was all. Who did, as it turned out, have a sense of humor. "Anyway," he said, "when you have Mrs. Appleby on your team, you want for nothing."

Once again his face flamed with heat. There was plenty more he wanted. He just had to find the right person to get it from. To give it to. Whatever. How had he gotten into this stupid conversation anyway? It had all started with a piece of chicken.

"You're a Wisconsin grad, right?" he said, getting back to safe territory.

"Yes. Northwestern as an undergraduate, then I came here for my Ph.D." She smiled. "My sisters fled to opposite coasts right after high school, but I hung around close to Chicago where we grew up."

"How many sisters?"

"Two," Charity said. "I'm the youngest. We're

adopted. A friend of our mother took us in when our parents died.''

Jason's tangled thoughts faded away in a rush of sympathy. Orphaned. Adopted. She'd had all the bad breaks.

''What a coincidence,'' he said. ''I have two brothers, one older, one younger.''

''What are they like? Are you all scientists, or…''

''They're both jocks. Michael coaches the high school football team in the town we grew up in, and Kenneth's a professional golfer.''

''You look athletic, too,'' Charity said.

''I do?'' He was so stunned he almost squeaked the words.

''Yes. You look like a man who just came off a soccer field.''

His heart pounded. No one had ever told him that before. It made him want to flex his biceps for her. ''Well, they don't see me that way at home,'' he told her, feeling almost pathetically grateful and trying to seem offhand. ''Mike and Ken are 'the jocks' and I'm 'the brain.' They've been calling me that since I was four.''

''Now that is interesting,'' she said, unnerving him again with her sudden enthusiasm. ''My sisters did the same thing to me. They always called me the family…'' She came to a sudden and complete stop. She'd just closed those perfect white teeth—or caps—on a deviled egg half, and for a moment the egg just hung there, giving her the look of a duck-billed platypus. "—brain," she said at last, then completed the bite she'd begun.

"Do you ever wish they'd see that there's more to you than brain?" It burst out of him. He couldn't help it.

His embarrassment increased when she said, "No. You eat the cookies. I want to get back to work."

Jason sat for a while at the counter. He munched one cookie, then went back to the lab. She was a puzzling woman. She didn't seem to have a shred of sympathy or warmth, but somehow she'd found out almost everything about him and he still knew nothing about her except that she was adopted and had two sisters, and was also the family "brain." Plus she liked to cook. Lunch had been great.

He'd just have to keep plugging away until he solved the puzzle. That was, after all, what scientists did.

"Do you mind if I take a few data books home with me?" Charity asked shyly. "I'd like to do a little more work tonight."

"Not at all. But you shouldn't feel obligated to—"

"To work after hours to make up for missing tomorrow afternoon?" She smiled, remembering to thin out her mouth. "It doesn't feel like work. I'd be doing it for my own pleasure."

His voice was a little gruff. "I know what you mean. So, okay, I'll see you in the morning. Maybe we can discuss whatever thoughts you might have come up with while you reviewed the data."

He reached for her coat and held it out for her. As she slid her arms into it, his fingertips brushed her neck. A bolt of electricity shot straight down her spine, and awkwardly, trying to hide the flush that rose to her face, she wrapped the coat around herself.

When she looked up, he was staring at her eyes. The coat was a whopping seven-dollar thrift-shop purchase. She called this color Indescribable Brown. It picked up the color of one of her eyes. Had he noticed?

From her eyes, his gaze drifted across the scar— for the thousandth time that day, she thought grimly—and then slid away. "Well, good night."

He sounded as awkward as she felt. She left the lab and stepped out into the early darkness of a northern winter day. Halfway to the parking lot, she remembered her briefcase. It was still sitting on the floor just under the coatrack. Some of Jason's disks were in it, but worse, so was her makeup, which she'd brought in case she needed to refresh her scar during the day.

She whirled and scurried back into the building and up the stairs at a run. She used the key he'd given her to let herself in. She didn't see Jason, but she heard his voice coming from the kennel.

"Good dog, Lionel! Okay, your turn, Jeremy, fetch!"

Intrigued, she tiptoed back and found Jason throwing balls to one ecstatic beagle after the other, clapping his hands and petting their heads when they made a successful return.

As if he felt a presence, he whirled to see her watching him. His face flushed a little, and then he said with great dignity, "We sterilize their balls every day."

Hysteria born of tension, tiredness and guilt rose up inside her and threatened to explode into insane laughter. Getting a tight grip on herself, she said, "Good," and quickly left.

On her way home, Charity formulated an entirely new program. Looking beyond his green eyes, appealing sandy hair, broad shoulders and a certain chemical reaction that seemed to be taking place between them, the bottom line was that she was fairly sure Jason Segal was a man she could be happy with. A man who would take time to play with his lab animals before he went home was the kind of man who could understand the things that mattered to her. She realized that all the data wasn't in yet, but the early results looked good.

That was Step One. Step Two was to show Jason that she was the kind of woman he could be happy with. The very idea, and all that it entailed, sent such a shiver up her spine that she almost lost control of the car.

To achieve her goal, she was going to have to murder the brisk, thin-lipped, sexless "Dr. Sumner," a woman who, as far as Charity was concerned, deserved to die. She would have to change, slowly enough that Jason would hardly notice, both within and without. And what she had to change into was her true self.

Shouldn't be that hard to do, should it?

4

IN BED the night before, with Oscar on the pillow beside her and Rags slumbering heavily and rather loudly at her feet, Supercat tucked into the curve of his huge body, Charity had discovered the first fly in her otherwise perfect ointment. There seemed to be a problem in one of Jason's protein purification procedures.

She had realized she was probably too tired to think straight and shouldn't even be looking at the data. It was almost certainly nothing. She'd put it out of her mind until this morning, but now she'd ask him about it, he'd reassure her and everything would be fine.

"Do you have time to answer a few questions?"

Charity had caught him on his way into the lab. "Of course," Jason said. "Come on back." He was surprised at how much he'd looked forward to seeing her this morning and how pleasant answering a few questions sounded.

Science could be lonely work. He probably just appreciated having company, a peer, someone he could really talk to about the project.

Today she was wearing a pair of trousers about the

color of the rust that eventually appeared on every car you drove in this northern climate. He was sorry for several reasons. First, the pants looked threadbare, and it reminded him all over again that she must have been through something terrible in those two "missing" years of her life. Second, it made it more difficult for him to admire her slender ankles.

He cleared his throat with a grumpy harrumph. Wouldn't do to be thinking about his research assistant's ankles.

"If you ate a little something with that it would be better for you," Charity said, gazing at his coffee.

"I'm sure you're right."

"How about a cookie?"

"That would be—"

"Just a sec," she said, leaped up with surprising grace and came back with a little plastic bag of cookies.

"Thank you," he said sincerely.

"Better you eat them than me," she told him. "Now, here's what I was wondering about. You've almost got the vaccine ready for testing, right?"

"I'm working out the last couple of glitches," he said, feeling the small knot of anxiety in his stomach those frustrating glitches always triggered. "I'm counting on your input," he added generously. "The grant money won't hold out forever. I've got to get this show on the road."

"Okay, then, right here, where you're purifying the antigens for the vaccine, why did you…"

When she'd phrased her question, he said, "Oh, that," and answered her as well as he could with oatmeal cookie crumbs flying from his mouth with every word. She listened intently, nevertheless.

"I see what you're saying," she said when he'd finished.

She did, in fact, see what he was saying. She just wasn't sure he was right. This was a very touchy situation. She didn't want to challenge him until she was sure.

In the meantime… She glanced at her watch, relieved to see it was eleven-thirty. "Omigosh, look at the time. I have to run. I'll be here as early as I can tomorrow." She gave him an apologetic look.

"Okay." He waved her on. "Have a good afternoon."

She paused, guilt warring with her firm intention to begin her new self-improvement program at once. Her attraction to Jason, so sudden and overwhelming, wasn't the slightest bit affected by the possibility that she might be barking up the wrong tree. So to speak.

"I hope the news will be good," she said, quashing the guilt. "I'm seeing a plastic surgeon." She gestured toward her scar. "There may be a laser treatment that would make this scar a little less obvious."

His eyes softened, which made her feel about a thousand times worse. "If you need to be away from the lab to have it taken care of,'' he said quietly, ''we'll work around it.''

''Oh, I...'' She hadn't planned to be away at all. She wanted to work on this project! But of course, she'd have to be to convince Jason she'd had the scar removed. ''Let's see what the doctor says,'' she said. ''I, uh, I have a little lunch here that I'm not going to eat. Here, you take it.''

''Absolutely not,'' Jason said. ''You can eat while you drive.''

''The doctor said to come in on an empty stomach. I forgot.''

''Well, okay, I guess, thanks.''

As Charity gunned the engine of her Jeep Cherokee, she hoped something came along, like a whole new, never-before-heard-of parasite, to distract Jason before he got around to asking himself why a person would have to go in for a laser treatment on an empty stomach.

Why hadn't she said, ''I'm dieting?''

Because if she was dieting, why had she packed a lunch that included creamy coleslaw and six oatmeal-raisin cookies? Which, admittedly, Jason had already eaten three of.

Deception wasn't one of the standards and values of the Sumner household. She was going to have to learn it on the job.

An hour later she darted into yet another drafty studio in Chicago just outside the Loop. ''Hi,'' she said to the photographer. "Hey, Mark," she said, seeing her least favorite stylist among the group. Of course Celine would be working today. It was fate. The look of distaste on her face made Charity suddenly feel very protective of "Dr. Sumner," who couldn't help not being beautiful! "Sorry I'm a minute late," she said, turning back to the photographer. "You know I've started a new job, and..."

She was speaking into utter silence. "Who. Are you?" the photographer said at last, looking down his nose at her.

"Charity, of course. I'll explain later." She directed a smile around at all of them. "Won't be a minute," she added breezily, and darted back into the dressing area. She stripped out of her girdle and towels first, whooshing with relief at being rid of them, then scrubbed her face. Mark could deal with her hair. She went back out into the studio at a jog.

The crew didn't appear to have recovered yet. Well, too bad. She was ready. Almost.

Mark was the first to speak. "Was that your costume for the party?" he breathed.

"What party? Oh, yes! The Halloween party. Yes, it was. Fooled you, huh?"

"What were you hoping to look like?"

"Who, Mark, *who* was I hoping to look like?"

"I'll stick with 'what,' thank you."

"Okay. Well, a...ah...a bag lady."

"A bag lady who's been mugged and then overfed

for some bizarre reason." Celine had moved gracefully up behind them to add her two cents' worth.

"I don't think bag ladies get mugged often, do you?" Charity said earnestly, gazing at Celine. "Because they don't have a lot of money with them. If they did, they wouldn't be bag ladies, would they?"

"Oh, for heaven's sake," Mark said. When he came out of his trance, the rest of the crew seemed to follow. "Let's get your hair washed. You look ghastly, darling, absolutely *ghastly.*"

WITH CHARITY OUT of the lab, Jason had a long and productive afternoon. His mind strayed occasionally, wondering what Charity was hearing from the plastic surgeon, but by and large he was able to work.

It wasn't that he cared whether she had a scar on her face or not. He had a scar on his forehead where Ken had kicked him once. Not on purpose. Ken and Mike were scuffling and Ken was wearing his football cleats. Jason had merely been in the same room reading something frivolous like *The History of the World.*

He felt that his scar added character to his face. Obviously, Charity's scar made her feel insecure, while his was a badge of honor. "Got hit by a cleat," he could say if he ever wanted to, which he hadn't yet, leaving the person he was talking to with the impression that he'd played football, soccer, whatever.

In high school he'd wanted to do all those things, and he could have, because he was as tall, strong and coordinated as his two brothers, but his family wouldn't hear of it. While his brothers went to football practice, swimming practice, basketball practice, he took college courses at the nearby University of Illinois, where he'd gone on to undergraduate school and then to vet school. It was great to ace those science courses in a class where everyone was at least three years older than he was, but the euphoria didn't last long after he'd gotten home to that old, familiar, left-out-of-everything-fun feeling.

He reached for another oatmeal-raisin cookie. Charity couldn't have an endless supply. He wondered if she'd make more when these ran out, and if so, what kind. Chocolate chip were good. Also peanut butter.

No wonder she'd put on a little weight since the accident. His mother had always said it was hard to be a good cook and stay thin. She said that to explain why she was such a terrible cook. Mrs. Appleby was a pretty terrible cook, too, but she didn't look like a person who was missing many meals.

It had occurred to Jason that he might have to learn to cook someday in order to eat decently, but not yet. He couldn't let anything distract him from his project. When he'd perfected the vaccine, when he'd run the tests and published the results, then he could do what he really wanted to do with his life.

He was surprised to see that it was six o'clock. He played with the beagles for a while, greeted the vet students who'd be in charge for the night and made his way home.

The house he lived in, and Mrs. Appleby controlled, was close to the campus. He pulled into the old-fashioned garage and made his way across the shoveled driveway to the mudroom, where, as was often the case, Mrs. Appleby was lying in wait for him.

"What's the Latin word for dog?" she asked him, a pencil poised over a crossword puzzle.

"*Canis?*" Jason said.

She frowned. "Hmm. Oh, I see. Then this word is *slime* instead of *jelly*. There! I think I'm actually going to finish this puzzle."

"You're good, Mrs. A," Jason said. He couldn't help smiling at her. With her fluffy white hair and her bustling gait, she reminded him a little of a Bichon Frise.

"You look tired, Jason," Mrs. Appleby said, as she always did. "You're working too hard." In fact, the whole conversation was their usual routine. Next she'd say, "When are you going to take a little time for yourself?"

For once, he had new material to add to the script. "My new assistant came on board yesterday," he told her. "Looks like she's going to be great. Life is looking up." Too late, he wished he hadn't mentioned the sex of his new assistant.

"Is she pretty?"

Bingo. It was no use explaining to his grandmother, or now to Mrs. Appleby, that occasionally in a man's life a woman cropped up who was not a marriage prospect. Or that if a woman knew enough about worms it didn't matter if she was pretty. So forget trying to go another step and explain that a woman who knew enough about worms might look pretty to a man who was largely involved with worms. Or that a man who spent most of his time with worms might find almost any woman pretty.

But that wasn't the case here. "I wouldn't say she was pretty," he told Mrs. Appleby. "But I didn't really notice. I'm a credentials man."

"A what?"

"I was making a little joke," he said kindly.

"Oh. Well." It was clear she was disappointed and he felt bad about that, but he had a greater purpose in his life than to find a woman friend to make Mrs. Appleby feel better.

"I left a little surprise in your fridge," she said next.

"Thanks. I'll go right up and see what it is."

Released at last, Jason climbed the back stairs to his second-floor sanctuary. Most of the single men he knew lived in classy, low-maintenance condos, but this suited him. The house reminded him of the one he'd grown up in, and of the one he'd have someday.

He put down his briefcase, pulled off his heavy coat and boots and then, filled with the usual mild dread, he opened the refrigerator to see what Mrs. Appleby had left for him.

A shape, vivid red and purple-veined, lay inside on a glass plate, and as he leaned on the door for support, the shape wobbled. No, throbbed! The Alien's heart!

He slammed the door fast, held it tight for a second, then walked to his back door and called down the stairs. "Mrs. A, what is this?"

She bustled out of her kitchen and stood at the foot of the stairs. "It's called Cardinal Salad," she said with considerable pride. "It's made with beets and horseradish. For Valentine's Day I'll put it in a traditional heart-shaped mold, but since you're a doctor, I made yours in the shape of a real heart. I julienned some red cabbage for the veins."

He gripped the newel post at the top of the stairs. "You did a remarkable job. Did you work from a picture or straight from the heart?"

"A picture in one of your textbooks, silly. I borrowed it while I was collecting your laundry. I hope you don't mind."

"Oh. Not at all. Any time. Well, thanks, Mrs. A. Can't wait to taste it."

"I hope you like it," she said. "I didn't have any lemon Jell-O, so I used raspberry."

He was about to start on his other dinner treat, Mom Appleby's Special Casserole, whose ingredients he'd never had the nerve to inquire about, when he heard her calling up the stairs again, so he put down his fork and took up his position beside the newel post.

"I don't know that we've ever talked about female visitors," Mrs. Appleby said, "but I wanted you to know I'm a liberated woman with a raised consciousness. Also a sound sleeper. And I expect you to adopt the same attitude if I should ever bring a man home with me." With that surprising statement she whisked back into her own kitchen and slammed the door.

Jason shook his head and went back to his dinner. He stuck an experimental fork into the Cardinal Salad, which set it throbbing again. He withdrew the fork in a hurry. Mrs. A should have been a sculptor. The heart was way too realistic, and it took him a minute to decide it was okay to take a bite. It tasted of artificial raspberry flavoring and horseradish. Interesting, but he wasn't sure it was going to start any culinary trends. As it slipped down his throat he felt his sinuses open from the impact of the horseradish, and he wondered what Charity was bringing for lunch tomorrow.

CHARITY WAS ALREADY in her lab and working when Jason arrived the next morning. She looked like the kind of person you shouldn't interrupt even to say hello, and that wasn't all bad, because it gave him a chance to sneak past her door undetected and go straight back to spend a little time with the beagles.

Not completely undetected, because one of his students was hard at work taking samples for testing. "Morning, Ed," Jason said. "How's everybody doing?"

"Roger's in a funk," Ed said. "Dr. Sumner noticed it too."

"She's already checked on these guys?

"She was here when I got here. Anyway, she said to tell you as soon as you came in."

A funny, tender little something happened to his insides at the news that Charity began her day by checking on the beagles. "I'll do some tests," Jason said, looking Roger over carefully, then scratching him behind his floppy ears. "Could be a sign of a problem we need to know about." Or maybe Roger just needed a little more ball-playing time. He'd pay him some special attention today.

"Other than that, everybody's in great shape. I think Lionel's got a crush on Candida."

"Candida's a vamp." He had a thought, which was that Ed was a gifted student who spent every spare minute working on Jason's project and might deserve special attention, too. "An unfortunate thing has happened, Ed," he said slowly. "Some investigative reporter from the campus television station has gotten curious about what I'm doing here and wants to tape an interview with me in the lab. I can't really tell her anything until I've published my results, but, well, I told her to come over and we'd talk. A week from today. Would you be sure to be around then? They might want to see how we treat the beagles. You could give them a tour of the kennel.''

Ed's face lit up. ''Sure thing. Happy to, Dr. Segal.''

''I'll count on you,'' Jason said gruffly. He spun on one heel and went to his desk, where he had some housekeeping details to work out. They involved grant expenditures, mostly. What a waste of time. But somebody had to make sure the money held out.

He had to get the vaccine perfected, and soon. Damn those glitches.

5

JASON HAD BARELY sat down at his computer and opened his accounting spreadsheet when he sensed a presence in his doorway and looked up to see Charity standing there. He was glad to see her, because he wanted to know how the visit to the plastic surgeon had gone.

"May I ask you a few more questions?" she said, "or should I wait until you—"

"Until I finish my monthly budget report?" Jason said. "You couldn't have come at a better time."

The faint wrinkles of worry on her forehead puzzled him, but her questions were intelligent to the point of scary. She seemed satisfied with his answers, though, and when she was out of questions, she volunteered the information that her visit to her plastic surgeon the day before had left her very optimistic.

"There's a laser treatment he can use that will clear up the scar a little at a time," she told Jason. "Painless, and I won't have to miss much work at all. I had the first treatment yesterday. Nothing to it."

"That's great news." When Jason smiled at her,

she felt dreadfully guilty, but there was nothing to do but forge ahead with her plan.

"It made me feel so much more positive about myself that I think I'm ready to start on a diet."

"A diet?"

She tried to hide her surprise at his crestfallen face. "Well, yes. You must agree I could stand to lose a pound or two. Or twenty." She'd succeed, too, because all she had to lose were towels. And it couldn't happen any too soon for her, because she was sick of them.

"I guess this means you won't be baking any more cookies."

"Cookies? Of course I'll be... Oh, because of the diet." Another look at his face was all she needed to tell her he was lobbying for more cookies. He liked her cookies. The thought filled her with a startling feeling of warmth. The man was clearly food deprived, at least deprived of food that tasted good. If she could trap him in her house and feed him steadily for a reasonable period of time, he might fall for her no matter how she looked, even if she looked great.

But would he keep her on at the lab? "If you'd like," she said as emotionlessly as she could, "I'd be glad to bring a tin of cookies to the office and put them out here in the reception area for anyone who'd like to help himself."

The way his face lightened up, she knew she'd hit the mark. It wasn't surprising that he said, "Oh, no,

I couldn't ask you to do that. It would be like asking you to make the coffee, or one of those demeaning things.''

"No, it wouldn't.'' She decided to go all frosty on him. "You didn't ask. I volunteered.''

"Thank you for your generous offer. What's your position on peanut butter?''

"Very strong.''

"Chocolate chip?''

"With pecans or walnuts?''

"Pecans.''

"The house specialty.'' She'd managed to keep a straight face, but wasn't sure how long she could hold out. "If you'll excuse me, I'll get back to my primary purpose here, which is lab work.''

"Fine. See you at lunchtime?''

She couldn't help softening. "Yes.''

She'd reached his doorway when he remembered to tell her about the interview. "I glanced at your schedule and noticed you'd be here next Tuesday.''

"I'll just hide out in my lab,'' Charity said.

"No! No,'' he said more calmly. "I told you so you'd be sure to be on hand. There will be questions. If I can't finesse the answers, maybe you can.''

"I can't go on television looking like this!''

"Don't be silly. This isn't about looks, it's about worms.'' He paused. "That sounded funny, didn't it? What I meant was—''

"I understand what you meant,'' Charity said

kindly. ''And I appreciate it. It's a lesson I need to learn.'' Without thinking, she'd laid a hand on his arm, meaning to show him she hadn't taken offense, but she was getting a very different reaction, both from herself and from him.

She felt him jump, then felt the heat coming from his skin—smooth, tanned skin with a crisp cover of blond hair. It startled her, but then she was already startled by the tingles of pure pleasure that her fingertips were conducting to the center of her body. She wanted to caress his skin instead of merely touching it, to run her hand up under his lab coat to his flexed biceps, to grasp his other arm, too, and pull herself closer to him. To look up at him and feel his mouth coming down to hers, to close her eyes and let his kiss surprise her.

What kiss? She'd probably scared him to death. He'd undoubtedly flexed his biceps in preparation for warding off her attack. ''I'll be around for the interview,'' she said hurriedly.

She went back to her lab feeling shaken, but very glad she'd embarked on the route to improving her appearance. Not a minute too soon, her sisters would say.

She brought up the program she'd been studying, but as she stared at the monitor, her thoughts strayed. She'd have to figure out a way to ''diet'' while still bringing things Jason could share at lunchtime. He liked her cookies. How lovely. Now that he wasn't watching, she could let herself smile.

The smile faded at once. He was supposed to like her brain, not her cookies! What was she thinking?

SHE COULDN'T IGNORE the facts much longer. Although the work Jason had done was excellent, he'd made an error in one step of the procedure for purifying the antigens, the proteins taken from the worms themselves, which were the components of the vaccine.

They'd fallen into such a pleasant work routine that it was doubly difficult for her to think of ruining it all by pointing out his oversight. On the other hand, if he continued the way he was going, he'd never correct those last few glitches.

She was staring at the numbers on the screen, worrying over Jason's error again, when Faith called with her big news—she was going to Reno to stand in for the bride on a honeymoon rehearsal. It sounded like just the sort of crazy situation Faith might get into, had gotten into, in fact, because it was clear that she had also fallen in love at first sight—with the groom. When the call ended, Charity returned to her computer, very grateful that she was too intelligent to get herself into a mess like the one Faith was heading for.

Her hands froze in midair, poised over the keyboard. Intelligent. Right. So intelligent she was bobbing around on her lab stool in a queen-size girdle stuffed with towels under a puce suit with a poison-green blouse. And while she certainly hadn't fallen in love with her boss, which was almost but not quite as bad as falling in love with some other bride's groom, she could easily see herself falling in love with him, eventually. After years and years of getting to know him.

She focused on the screen in front of her, but the data went fuzzy. The next thing she'd have to announce to Jason was that she'd enrolled in a Fashion for the Working Woman course, or hired a personal shopper. The clothes had to go if she was to change back into herself. She'd wait, though, until she'd lost a towel or two. It would not be intelligent to buy a whole series of wardrobes in gradually diminishing sizes.

What would she do about her eyes? Tell Jason she'd bought a set of violet-blue contacts? Then spend the rest of her life pretending she wore contacts? But what was she doing, talking about the rest of her life?

"Anything wrong?"

Startled, Charity almost rolled off the lab stool. "Oh, no, no. Why would you think anything was wrong?"

"Your hands are hovering over the keyboard like *Toxocara canis* plotting to invade a cairn terrier."

She faced him with a cool stare. "If I were a different sort of woman, I'd be offended by having my fingers compared to oversize roundworms."

"Oh, gosh…" He clapped a hand to his head. "I'm sorry. It was the image that came to me and I…"

She decided to take pity on him. "And I'm sure the same image would have come to me." She sighed. "We belong to a very small and exclusive club, Jason, those of us who are fascinated by worms."

"Very small," he agreed. As if he felt more comfortable, he moved closer and took up a position over her shoulder. "I should watch my words."

"Not with me. I'm a member of the club." She turned to face him, and found him very close to her. Of course, he was only looking at the monitor, paying attention to whatever it was that had led her to the frozen state he'd surprised her in, but it didn't matter. She was staring into the angle of a strong jaw, a square chin, an unconsciously sensuous mouth, and when she dropped her gaze just a little she could see a pulse in his throat, a few curls of crisp blond hair in the V of his lab coat, the promise of more crisp blond hair that would cover his broad, muscular chest. And worse, she could feel the warmth coming from him, smell the deliciously fresh scent she loved most, the scent of the chemical reagents she'd lived with throughout her graduate training, and then been forced to trade for whiffs of expensive aftershave during these two miserable years she'd spent dating the sorts of men who sought models to wear on their arms.

Jason had a certain magic for her, and the magic was affecting her right now, sending impulses from her brain to the secret parts of her body, impulses that told her to lean a little closer to him, to let her lips brush his throat, her tongue tangle with those blond curls. She would have to take the first step, she knew. Would he take the second? She swayed a little on her high stool, rethinking the idea of "years and years" of getting to know him. She could feel herself waking up inside, imagining...

Had the worst possible thing happened? Had she suddenly become as romantic and flaky as her sister Faith?

Not on your genome! After all she'd gone through to get this job?

Disguise or no disguise, she had a mission. She turned abruptly back to the monitor. "What's wrong with these gels?" she said.

"We'll talk about it after lunch." His voice sounded strangled, and he left her lab as suddenly as he'd appeared there.

WHAT WAS happening to him? He'd been looking at an equation, then suddenly founded himself looking at a nose, a pretty nose, and then at her chopped-off lashes and bleached-looking brows. It had occurred to him briefly to wonder why, if she'd spent two years healing, they hadn't already grown back in. Maybe there had been damage to the follicles. He was sure there was a reason. The accident that scarred her face and destroyed her confidence in femininity, leading to stress-eating and overweight, must have been an explosion.

A laboratory explosion.

How you could have an explosion while studying *Syngamus trachea, Toxocara canis* or *Trichuris vulpis* under a microscope was a mystery to him at the moment, but someday she'd tell him how. His heart swelled with sympathy for this woman, but he was uncomfortably aware that his heart wasn't the only part of him that was swelling and sympathy wasn't all that was driving him.

He felt a connection with Charity, had from their first meeting. He couldn't imagine where it was coming from, unless it was from their mutual interest in worms, but the way he felt when she turned her head to look up at him didn't have anything to do with worms. Brilliant young veterinary researcher Jason Segal was at least smart enough to figure that out.

She was an employee. More than that, she had to be especially vulnerable to masculine attention, feeling as she did about herself. He couldn't do anything to take advantage of her.

What he wanted from her was her knowledge and intelligence, the contributions she could make toward the perfection of his vaccine, and that's how he would treat her, as a nameless, faceless, valued assistant, from this moment on. No, starting yesterday. Better make that retroactive to the day she stepped so shyly into his lab for her interview, then waddled out.

He hadn't noticed her waddling since then. So her waddling that day had undoubtedly been the result of a little nervousness on top of a little bladder problem. Quite understandable. It was even possible that the oddly padded look of her hips might be a...one of those whatchamacallits, those things elderly people used.

What a tragedy for someone her age. Again he felt his heart going out to her, and he grimly went to his lab and his worms, the only things he truly understood.

"REMEMBER THE interview this afternoon."

If Charity hadn't been so upset by the news she had to give Jason, she might have smiled. Jason made his announcement a split second after she walked in the door in one of her best "Dr. Sumner" outfits. This one consisted of a pair of Burnt Toast trousers, somewhat unevenly burned due to their age, which she wore with a turtleneck in a pinkish tan she'd decided to call Sahara Mauve. The sweater had pilled nicely while it hung on the rack at the thrift shop, and a wire hanger had permanently shaped the shoulders into humps. She'd hoped the image of how this ensemble would play on television would get her sense of humor going, but as she looked at Jason's face, so ap-

pealing, so sexy, but also so sincere, she was afraid
it wasn't working.

"May I have a minute with you in my lab?" she
asked him. Her fingers shook as she put on her lab
coat over the sweater.

"Sure. A problem?"

"I'm afraid so." She pulled up a stool for Jason
and brought her monitor to life. She was glad to have
something to do with her hands. Otherwise she'd be
wringing them. "I thought I'd better tell you before
the interview."

"What?" He sat, looking at her monitor with interest.

He was so unsuspecting that she almost lost heart.
She might be wrong. But she'd never know if they
didn't talk it over. "I've found what I think may be
some staining problems with these gels. Some of the
bands from identical samples don't match up."

Delivered with the appropriate concern and humility, this beginning to a much lengthier explanation
was one she'd rehearsed after consulting Hope the
night before. They'd started with her first idea—
"Your technique...is...doo-doo, Dr. Segal!"—and
worked their way toward the sentence Charity had
just delivered. First Charity had to put Hope through
an introductory course in antigen purification, in
which Hope hadn't done particularly well and Charity
had had to employ all the patience at her disposal.
Then it was Hope's turn to put Charity through an

intro course in productive communication, at which Charity had chafed, undoubtedly forcing Hope to employ all the patience at her disposal.

She thought she'd heard Hope's new love Sam laughing in the background as the conversation took its natural course, which was to go with Charity's scientific terms and Hope's wording. So according to Hope, she had just communicated productively with Jason and after a calm, clarifying dialogue, Jason would say something like, "Oh, I see! You're right! Thank you for pointing this out to me!"

Still concerned and humble, Charity glanced at Jason, and saw that he'd drawn his sandy brows together in a deep frown.

"There's no way I could have made a mistake like this."

Her courage faltered. He already didn't like the idea of being wrong, no matter how carefully she'd told him, and when she got more specific, he was going to be even more upset. But she forged ahead.

"Here's where the problem is," she said. "I suspect you used the wrong…" Her explanation went on for quite a while. As she forced herself to the finish line, she could feel Jason's mood growing colder by the minute. He possessed such masculine energy, it was a force she could feel merely working beside him, and when it went away, it was as if the sky grew dark.

Mirroring the weather outside the warm comfort of

the lab, her sky was growing very dark. She finally made it through her spiel. She turned to him and waited.

"I disagree completely."

He could use a session with Hope on the topic of productive communication. She knew she was getting mad, and forced herself to rein in her emotions. "Where am I going wrong?" That was the ticket. She was probably wrong, he was probably right, and all he had to do was show her.

"Here," he said, gesturing toward the protein bands on the gels. "You assume that..."

His explanation was no less lengthy than hers had been. She listened carefully, willing to see the error of her ways, but when he finished, she was even more certain she was right. Regrettably, his know-it-all attitude was also making her even madder.

She rarely got mad. Okay, irritable, but rarely mad, and she only got mad or even irritable at people, never at her dogs and cats, just at people who refused to respect her intelligence.

People like Jason! He didn't respect her brain even though she was no longer beautiful! After the work she'd gone to to make herself homely, it was the lowest blow he could have delivered.

"I'm sorry, but we'll have to agree to disagree," she said, being as cold as he was.

"I don't agree to anything. You've challenged my technical competence."

"You've refused to look at my observations objectively. You've challenged my—"

"The WEDU people are here." Ed broke in at the moment of highest tension, shattering it, but not dispelling the shards that flew into Charity's soul like darts.

"I'm trusting you to choose your words wisely, if you're asked to comment at all." Jason looked her up and down, and she felt he wasn't seeing anything but jarring contradictions in brown.

"Of course." All she could see was a man who refused to recognize that she had a brain. "I will speak when spoken to. Even lie, if necessary. I don't intend to sabotage your project."

"What do you mean, lie?" Now he was furious.

"I mean I wouldn't dream of telling the media your *technique* needs more than a little fine-tuning!" she snarled. "After all—" She knew she'd gone well beyond permissible professional disagreement, but she couldn't stop herself "—I have something to lose, too."

"Your temper." He glared at her.

"My job."

Sparks shot between them as they slid off their respective stools and went out to meet the interviewer and her cameramen.

6

"SO THE SHORT WAY to say everything I've just said," Jason summed up with a smile Charity was certain would charm every female in their limited audience, "is that we are in the preliminary stages of testing a multivalent vaccine against the entire spectrum of canine gastrointestinal parasites."

The interviewer, Kathy Kimball, was a college student majoring in communications. She was such a pretty girl. If she chose to be a model instead of a student of communications, Celine would have a run for her money. She was also sweet and cooperative, a really nice person. As a result of Jason's "short and simple" summary, her big blue eyes crossed and she began to finger the heart-shaped locket at her throat. She was still a little pale from hearing Jason's long and, to your normal, ordinary person, boring disclaimer that he was doing anything that would be at all interesting to anyone who was not a parasitologist.

"What Dr. Segal is saying," Charity said, hoping to put Kathy at ease, "is that he's working on a vaccine against the worms dogs pick up. Here's a chart showing the various worms that infect dogs...."

"Cut!" said the cameraman, also a student, also youthful. He rushed out of the room. Kathy patted her forehead. In a moment, the cameraman came back. "Okay," he said weakly, swallowing hard and sweating, "pick up right after 'dogs pick up.'"

Jason had turned a hard, cold stare on Charity in the interim, but after they'd had a look at the chart, he focused his attention on the interviewer. "I can't be specific until I've published my results," he said smoothly, "but when we're sure we have a pluripotent vaccine, we'll challenge the dogs with the whole range of gastrointestinal parasites."

"What Dr. Segal means by 'pluripotent,'" Charity interrupted, "is—"

"What Dr. Segal *means,*" Jason growled, "is 'pluripotent.'" He paused for a moment. "That means it will be effective on a number of parasites rather than just one. *Pluri.* Many."

"And when he has this pluripotent vaccine," Charity persisted, "he'll—"

"And I will have that vaccine soon." Jason seemed to have lost all interest in Kathy Kimball and had eyes, angry eyes, only for Charity. "If nothing happens to slow down our progress. If we don't have a lot of silly roadblocks thrown in our way. *If too many cooks don't spoil the soup!*"

"It's not soup. It's a vaccine," Charity murmured. "I really wouldn't use the word *soup,* Dr. Segal, in a dialogue about worms. I mean, worm soup isn't a particularly pleasant concept. And of course Dr. Segal means to say that he won't want to produce anything less than a perfect product. If some new bit of information should slow down his progress, that would be all to the good, because—''

''Not necessarily,'' Jason said. His glare intensified. ''This new bit of data would have to have considerable weight behind it. Intellectual weight.'' The look he gave Charity wasn't exactly a sneer, but it was close enough to infuriate her.

''Dr. Segal.''

Charity had momentarily forgotten Kathy, and from the look on Jason's face, so had he.

''Dr. Segal, what did you mean by 'challenging the dogs'?''

''Well, Kathy,'' Jason said smoothly, although a pulse throbbed visibly at his temple, ''I mean that after we inoculate the test group, we'll introduce the parasites into their food.''

''Can we stop right there for a second?'' Kathy said, taking her turn to stagger from the room.

While they waited, Jason merely fumed. Charity had never noticed that fuming made a sound, a cross between a mumble and a snort. At any rate, that was the sound Jason was making.

Kathy came back looking pale but pulled together. ''So the inoculated test group should repel the parasites,'' she said rapidly.

Jason looked surprised. ''Yes.''

"How long do you expect the entire process to take?" Kathy was reading her questions now from a little list she held on her lap.

"In a couple more weeks the vaccine should be ready for clinical trials." He turned on Charity briefly, then turned back to Kathy. Charity decided not to interrupt him. "If it does allow the test group to repel or kill the parasites, the university will probably license it to one of the large drug companies for further testing, manufacture and marketing. On the other hand, if it doesn't work…"

He gave what Charity supposed he thought was a humble little laugh. Humble, ha!

"…Or if there are serious side effects…"

"I see," Kathy said. "What area of research do you intend to tackle next?"

His jaw clenched. "I was thinking about changing fields altogether," he snarled, swiveling to glare directly at Charity, "and getting into *mad cow* disease."

Charity gasped. So, she thought, did Kathy. Maybe even the cameraman.

"Well, thank you, Dr. Segal, Dr. Sumner, for this very enlightening interview. We at WEDU wish you the best of luck in your effort to make life happier for our little canine friends. And thanks, Ed, for the tour of the kennel. Aren't those beagles precious?" Kathy Kimball turned an insipid smile on the camera and the interview was over.

Charity got up very carefully, went to her lab and for the first time since she'd been working here, shut the door.

Leaning against it, she closed her eyes and willed herself not to get angry. Well, no angrier than she already was. She could resign, but she didn't want to. She could certainly stop bringing cookies to the man, but that seemed childish and the vet students enjoyed them as much as he did. But Jason's yummy lunches would end, and that was that.

Quietly she packed her briefcase and went home. At least the dogs appreciated her. She wasn't sure about the cats. The other people who appreciated her—sometimes—were as close as the nearest phone.

"He called you *what?*"

Faith was flabbergasted, but Hope was enraged.

"He didn't exactly call me a mad cow," Charity admitted, "but he might as well have."

"Did you speak to him tactfully, the way we agreed you would?" Hope wanted to know.

"You can be a little blunt sometimes, honey," Faith said.

"I said it just right. Just the way you told me to. I wrote it out. I memorized it. I said it with abject humility. And then he blew up."

"Sue him."

"No, Hope, I'm not going to sue him."

"Then quit."

"I'm not going to quit, either. I like the work."

"I hear heavy breathing," Faith said. "Is somebody listening in on the line?"

"That's Rags," Charity said. In her care, the Rottweiler had metamorphosed from deadly potential killer to lapdog. He had no idea how big he was.

"I feel," Hope said, "that you have to do something to show him he behaved dreadfully. It's a matter of pride."

"You're right, and I've decided what it will be," Charity said. "I'm going to stop bringing him lunch."

"You're bringing him lunch?"

That came from both of them. In stereo. At moments like these, Charity sensed it was time to hang up.

SHE GOT TO the lab early the next morning and closed her door again. She sat down at her lab bench, looked at the gels and the methods manual one more time, and was even more certain she was right. Her anger diminished slightly while she concentrated on her work, but close to noon, she decided calling home would make her feel better.

She couldn't get her cell phone to work. Of course, she'd locked herself into a tight space filled with all sorts of sound-bending equipment. Cautiously she opened the door to the reception area. Jason's door was closed, too, so she dialed her own number, let the phone ring until the recorded message came on, and then at the beep, started speaking.

"Oscar?" she said. "Hi, sweetie. How's everything at home? Everybody getting along okay? I'm sure you are because you're such a dependable guy. Don't let Jimbo overeat, okay? He had a little bit of an upset tummy last night. I'll see you at the usual time and we'll have fun together tonight—"

"Who's Oscar?"

She hadn't heard Jason's door open. Startled, she said, "Bye," pushed End and turned off the phone. It wasn't as if Oscar might call her back. Her anger momentarily forgotten in her embarrassment, she said, "Oscar. Oh, Oscar. Oscar is…"

If she told him she'd been talking to a dog on the telephone, he'd feel he'd hit the nail right on the head when he looked straight at her and said, "mad cow." Remembering how he'd treated her yesterday enraged her all over again. "My cousin," she said coldly. "The son of one of my…my father's sisters. He's visiting me…with, ah, yes, with his younger brother, so of course he's in charge while I'm at work."

As Jason listened to her babble on, he was careful not to show how relieved he felt. For a minute there, he'd supposed Oscar was her lover, the way she was talking to him, so affectionately, so warmly, the way she'd accidentally spoken to him a few times. If he didn't apologize and do a darned good job of it, she'd never speak to him that way again.

"I'm sorry I interrupted," he said. He cleared his

throat. "I came out here to apologize for my behavior yesterday."

Her dull brown eyes narrowed. They also brightened, but only for the purpose of flashing angry fire at him. "Mad cow," she muttered. "I should report you to someone."

"I did *not* call you a mad cow! For all you know about it, I might go back to school, take the courses I need and actually go into mad-cow-disease research. It's a terrible thing. Looking for a preventative measure would be a worthwhile use of my—"

He flushed red, then started over. "Yes," he said with all the regret he could muster, "you probably should report me. I behaved despicably, and I'm truly sorry. I'm..." How should he put this? "I'm just not used to having my work questioned. Everything else, yes. But not my technical competence."

The fire in her eyes dimmed to a curious flicker, which he took as a good sign.

"Of course, I'll look at all the gels again and see if you might be on to something," he assured her. "Sometime. When we're not so busy. But in the meantime, I hope we can go on working in an atmosphere of friendship. May I take you out to lunch?"

She glared at him. "Yes."

"We'll laugh about this someday."

"I doubt it."

"Okay, we'll be able to discuss it like two adults someday."

"That's a possibility."

"Put on your coat."

"Where are you taking me?"

"To the best restaurant in Madison."

"Well, all right," she mumbled ungraciously. "But I intend to have dessert." She announced this departure from her diet as if it were a challenge.

"Of course. This place makes a great warm chocolate cake with ice cream, and a…"

Talking to her gently, escorting her almost tenderly out to his SUV, he told himself the worst was over. Unless she turned out to be right about the damned gels. In the unlikely chance that should happen, the worst was just beginning.

THE RESTAURANT was bright, loud and cheerful. "Have you been here before?" Jason asked her. "When you were a student?"

"I couldn't afford it when I was a student."

"I wouldn't have been able to, either. It's great to be grown-up and rich, don't you think?"

The smile he gave her was self-deprecating. He wasn't going to get rich doing what he was doing, and he knew it. He'd be amazed to know how much money she'd made modeling. It amazed her, too, and she'd put most of it into investments against the lean times.

She devoutly hoped those times were starting now. She had a half-dozen more modeling jobs to do, and then that phase of her life, when she'd been rich and discontented, would be over.

Jason opened his menu. "We're going to blow it all out," he said. "I'm going to start with the mussels, and then...the tuna, I think."

"Well. I'm going for the crab cakes and the halibut."

"The halibut with the tomatoes and olives or the one with the mango salsa?"

"The spicy one."

"You like Thai food?"

"Love it."

"There's a great Thai restaurant not too far away. We'll have to go there for an early dinner some night after work."

"I, uh, I wish I could do that," Charity hedged, "but I have a long drive home and, uh, responsibilities when I get there. But thanks."

Was it possible he'd gone straight from calling her a mad cow to asking her for a date? Of course, people who worked together often went out for drinks or dinner, but Jason was wearing the look of a man who's just been turned down and is trying not to show that he feels rejected. Her anger dissipated, replaced by a little thrill as she realized Jason had asked her out looking just as she did now, overweight and awkward. And she would have loved nothing more than to say yes to his invitation. But she had to get home to her dogs and cats. They were alone until nearly seven most evenings as it was.

"But some night," she added quickly, "if we plan ahead, I might be able to work something out." A baby-sitter, she wondered? Maybe she should hire someone full-time now that she was working regular hours.

"Wine?" Jason asked her. He looked a little happier now.

"Thanks, but I don't want to fall asleep with my head in a petri dish this afternoon."

"Good point. Okay, then." He got the attention of a waiter. Charity let him order for her. He seemed to want to. When he'd finished, he rested his chin in his hands and contemplated her from across the table.

"What *do* you want to do when this project is finished?" She said it softly, trying to say she accepted his apology, if not his procedure.

"What I want to do…" He hesitated, then sighed. "What I really want to do is set up a veterinary practice."

"Really? You're not going to continue in research?"

"Oh, I guess I'll always be doing research. But I want to work with animals. Live in the country. Be a small-town vet." He smiled. "Big animals, small animals, deliver the occasional baby—the human kind—in a pinch."

"No kidding." She was too surprised to stay in

character. Her mind immediately went off into a daydream—Jason as country vet, she as his assistant. On winter evenings they'd curl up on her sofa in front of the woodstove and discuss worms.

Her heart pounded and she felt a little faint. It was her idea of the perfect life, and sitting across the table from her right now was a man who wanted the same kind of life. Maybe a larger cottage. Maybe a different sofa. But the same life.

Jason was talking about his plans. For him it wasn't merely a daydream. He'd worked out the details, had a fairly clear idea of the costs, knew where he wanted to settle—not too far away from Madison, because he'd like to teach a class or two, and also because he could easily refer his customers to the veterinary specialists on the campus.

She'd give a million dollars for the nerve to propose to him right now. Of course, he'd be in for quite a shock on their wedding night.

"Dessert?"

"I can't. Oh, I know I said I was going to, but I'll never get rid of this weight if I keep on stuffing myself—" she paused, thinking how appropriate that phrase actually was "—with things like dessert."

"Don't be silly. Everybody has to have a special treat now and then."

"I guess you're right," she sighed.

"Charity…"

"What?" She was busy scanning the dessert menu

the waiter had put in front of her while simultaneously planning her life with Jason.

"There's no need to think of yourself as fat or unattractive. You're quite a lovely woman right now."

She gazed at him, then swallowed hard. Last night Faith had reminded her that sometimes she was too blunt. She supposed that meant she shouldn't come right out and say, "Then will you marry me?"

"Thank you, Jason," she said softly. "That means a lot to me."

If the waiter hadn't appeared, he might have said more. She might have said more if she hadn't, while looking up at the waiter, spotted a disaster on the horizon. A photographer Charity had worked with many times stood at the reception desk waiting to be seated, and beside him, tall, blond, cool and elegant, wearing her trademark disdainful expression, was Celine.

7

CHARITY HELD the dessert menu right up in front of her face. "Let's see. I'll have…" What could Celine and Todd Anderson be doing in a restaurant in Madison? They belonged in Chicago! Not here, blowing her cover! "What was it you mentioned, Jason? Oh, here it is. The warm chocolate cake with ice cream. I'll have that."

"The warm chocolate cake. Yes, madame." The waiter took the dessert menu in his fingertips and Charity yanked it back. He tugged harder. She dug her nails into it and held on for dear life. "I want to read about the other desserts," she said, gritting her teeth. She could feel both Jason and the waiter staring at her through the menu. "Ooh, the floating island sounds wonderful, too."

"Would you rather have that?" Jason said. He sounded puzzled and a little nervous.

"No! No, I'm definitely sticking with the chocolate cake, but ohmyohmy, read the description of the bread pudding! Does that come with a whiskey sauce or a hard sauce? Oh, a bourbon flavored *crème anglaise.* Wow, does that ever sound yummy."

"Bring us the cake, the floating island and a bread pudding," Jason said. "We'll share everything." His fingers—she'd know them anywhere—firmly gripped the menu and handed it back to the waiter, just as Celine walked past their table and looked directly at Charity.

Celine's beautiful, sculpted mouth opened. Her heart-shaped chin dropped. Her baby-blue eyes widened to the size of robin's eggs. She allowed herself to be seated, then engaged in a moment of excited conversation with Todd the photographer. Todd turned, stared at Charity, then shook his head at Celine. She nodded hers emphatically. And to Charity's horror, she got up and came toward their table.

"Charity," she said when she reached the table. "What a surprise to see you here."

"I'm even more surprised to see you," Charity said with a silly-sounding laugh she felt was due to the adrenaline rushing through her bloodstream, but sounded as if she'd inhaled some helium. "I work here. My new job is here. I belong here. The question is, what are you doing in Madison, of all places? Oh. This is my boss, Jason Segal." While she babbled, she implored Celine with her eyes.

Celine turned the full effect of her gaze on Jason. "Well, hello," she said, the two words rife with none-too-well-hidden meaning.

"He's a professor here," Charity rattled on to Celine's back, "a doctor of veterinary medicine engaged in research, a parasitologist. You knew I was a parasitologist, didn't you? I'm sure I must have mentioned I'm a parasitologist. There's a market for parasitologists here in Madison because of the vet school, and that's where I'm working all right, in Jason's labora—''

''I'm very glad to meet you, Celine,'' Jason said, pronouncing the name perfectly. But he wasn't looking at Celine, he was looking at Charity, so Celine turned and looked at her, too.

Charity felt it must be her turn to speak. ''So tell us what you're up to,'' she said with a wide, weak smile.

''I'd much rather know what you're up to,'' Celine said in her low, sultry voice.

''Oh. Not with lunch you wouldn't,'' Charity hastened to say. ''We work with worms.''

Celine went gratifyingly green. ''I didn't mean—''

''I know. You didn't mean to get me started on that,'' Charity said with another squeal of laughter. ''Now your turn.''

Celine gave her an odd, contemplative look. ''I'm consulting on the *Mademoiselle* college issue,'' she said.

''I think you may have mentioned it to me the last time we talked,'' Charity said.

''Have you two known each other long?'' Jason said. He, too, was gazing contemplatively at Charity.

''Forever,'' Charity said.

"Two years," Celine said.

"Two years can seem like forever," Charity said. "It all depends on how you spend them." This time she gave Celine a hard stare, and saw a look of understanding cross Celine's face.

"You're certainly right about that," she said with a smile that was more gracious than Charity had ever seen her wear. "Give me your new work number. We'll talk more later. It's nice to see you looking so...happy. And a real pleasure to meet you, Doctor."

With a last, lingering glance at Jason, she returned to her table. Charity mopped her forehead with her napkin and returned it to her lap covered in makeup. "A good friend," she said.

Jason watched her with unnerving concentration. "What does *she* do for a living?"

The way he said it, he must be thinking she was a high-priced call girl.

"Celine's a model."

"Oh? Where did you meet?"

"Oh, at a party somewhere or other," Charity said with a generous wave of her hand, waving that hand directly into the warm chocolate cake the waiter was positioning on the table between them. She smeared the chocolate on her napkin and heard a tiny exasperated sigh come through the waiter's tightened mouth.

"You seemed upset about seeing her," Jason said, but his green eyes had suddenly softened into fresh-water lakes and Charity had a grim certainty of what was coming next. "Don't feel that way, Charity. Don't be afraid to see the people you knew before...well, before. If they're friends, they'll still be friends. If not, then you don't need them around anyway."

"Thank you, Jason," she said in a small, embarrassed voice. Embarrassed? Humiliated! This lovely man was being so kind to her, while she built lie upon lie, deceiving him outrageously. She suddenly felt she'd gotten herself into something she couldn't get herself out of.

That's how Faith must feel all the time. How could she stand it?

"You know," Jason said thoughtfully, "when I was interviewing here, somebody told me about a woman who'd just graduated with a degree in parasitology, terrific student, he said, who went into modeling. Charity, are you all right?" he said when she choked on a bite of bread pudding. "Have some water." He half rose from his chair. "Should I do the Heimlich maneuver?"

IN THE MIDDLE of the next morning, just about the time Charity was reassuring herself that the Celine incident was over and forgotten, Jason said, "What's *Mademoiselle*?"

She stifled an irritated sigh. Since she sat beside Jason in his lab, both of them with an eye glued to a microscope, at least she didn't have to look at him. "It's a fashion magazine. They do a college issue each September, go around to various universities and photograph actual students modeling. Celine's working with the girls on their posture and makeup and so on. She called last night and told me all about it." It was the truth. Celine couldn't wait to find out what Charity was up to.

The words, *up to,* when applied to herself, had upset Charity out of all proportion. Not really. She deserved to feel upset. She'd taken a big chance by telling Celine the truth, too. *That's right. Lie to Jason, whom you worship and admire, and tell the truth to Celine, a person you don't even like.*

"Never thought of UW as a fashion leader," Jason mused.

"Do you ever think about fashion at all?"

"No."

"Then it's not surprising you hadn't recognized UW's place in the fashion swim."

"Do you ever think about fashion?"

"Frequently," Charity said, and decided to leave it at that. Jason would of course feel even sorrier for her, a woman who thought about fashion and just couldn't achieve it.

They were silent for a while, working. "Don't you want to have lunch with Celine while she's on campus?"

Can we forget about Celine already! For one thing,

she hadn't liked the come-hither looks Celine had given Jason. "Celine doesn't eat."

"What was she doing in the restaurant then if she wasn't having lunch?"

Charity raised her eyes briefly from the slide she'd been examining. "I'll bet you an electrophoretic protein she ate one lettuce leaf, dressing on the side."

"Call her and find out. I could use one of those for the vaccine."

Charity slid off the lab stool. "Guess I'd better write up this report and go on to my...doctor," she said.

"Sure," he said absentmindedly. "See you tomorrow."

"Bright and early," Charity assured him.

As she started down the stairs she made a quick decision to do part of her changing routine in the women's rest room. It was so uncomfortable driving while padded with towels. They raised her several inches higher, the steering wheel felt as if it was in the wrong place. Furthermore, they itched and the girdle pinched. Jason wasn't going anywhere soon. He was physically, spiritually and emotionally attached to that microscope.

The hall was empty. She darted into the rest room, got gratefully out of her padding and into an entirely different set of clothes—trim black trousers, a gray turtleneck sweater, her short black coat. She supposed

Jason thought it was work that made her briefcase bulge on the days she went to these supposed doctor's appointments.

She wasted several minutes worrying. Where could she even begin if she decided to tell him the truth?

Upstairs, Jason suddenly felt lonely and disoriented. He'd been fine while Charity was there alongside him. He wondered if she'd ever consider working for a small-town vet instead of doing research.

Of course not. It was a dumb thought. He got up and paced around the lab for a few minutes, looked in on the dogs, then paced around the reception area for a while. He ate a cookie from the tin. Chocolate chip, and better than any chocolate chip cookie he'd ever tasted. He glanced out the window, walked over to it and looked down at the snow-covered campus. The maintenance staff had cleared the sidewalks, and down one of these sidewalks stepped a tall, stunning woman, rail thin even in her layers of winter clothes. Her stride was long and graceful as she made her way to the parking lot. She moved with confidence in her beauty.

Probably another of the models on campus to do that thing for that magazine. Jason chewed the last bite of cookie. Charity could look every bit as good as that woman if she had half the confidence in herself. He moved away from the window and went back to the lab, but it wasn't the same without her.

THE NEXT MORNING Charity cut down from three bath towels to two and lightened her scar a little bit, thinking it was probably time to show some improvement. Her eyebrows and eyelashes were growing in all by themselves. It wouldn't be long before she looked fairly attractive again.

That was the idea, after all. Although it would really be nice if Jason became attracted to her while she looked this way. Occasionally, when he said one of those nice things he was always saying, when he looked at her a certain way, she wondered if he might be feeling at least a twinge of what she was feeling obsessively.

While she worked, Rags, as usual, put his head on her lap, but when she reached down to pet him, he took the attention listlessly. She touched his nose. It felt warm and dry.

"Rags, baby, you don't feel good?"

He looked up at her. His eyes were bleary and sad looking.

Forgetting all about her appearance, she slid off the dressing table stool to put her arms around him. "Let's look you over," she said gently. "Does your tummy hurt? Did you step on something sharp?"

She couldn't pinpoint anything that might be causing his obvious misery. He needed tests. He needed a real doctor. She wouldn't be able to reach her vet in Antioch this early. She couldn't leave him here all day getting worse. She couldn't skip work, either.

"My dog is sick" was not one of Hope's approved reasons for taking a day off.

Chewing her lower lip, she stared off into the distance for a moment. She'd take Rags to Jason. He'd know what to do.

She explained the situation to the rest of her menagerie and made a bed for Rags in the back seat of the Jeep. Bringing babies to work was also not on Hope's approved-behavior list, but Hope was far, far away and would never know.

JASON WAS ENGAGED in a struggle with his conscience. Sooner or later he was going to have to look at Charity's take on his purification procedure and see if she might be right. It was a galling thought, that Charity might be right, but this way, he wasn't getting anywhere. As he always did when he was deep in thought, he went across the reception area to stare out the window.

The last thing he expected to see out there was Charity struggling her way up to the building, half carrying an enormous Rottweiler who could hardly walk.

He didn't even put on a coat. He just ran downstairs and outside to help her.

"He's sick," she said. Tears were starting to stream down her face. "Can you help him?"

Jason already had his arms under the dog to lift him up into his arms. Charity put a gloved hand up to wipe the tears away, seemed to think better of it and instead, patted at them in a way he'd seen her do before.

Jason started off with the dog. Even he was staggering under the weight. He didn't know how she'd gotten as far as she had. Tenderness filled his heart that she'd even tried, but he was careful to give no indication of it.

When they'd reached the suite, he took the dog into his lab and lowered him gently onto the closest empty surface. He paused a minute to get his breath back, then began a thorough examination. Charity, still in her coat, stood watching.

"What's his name?" he said after a while.

"Rags."

"He's yours?"

She hesitated. "I'm keeping him for someone."

"Well, Rags," Jason said gently, "I'm going to have to take some samples and do some tests. That okay with you?"

"What do you think is wrong with him?" Her eyes were wide and frightened. They begged him to tell her everything would be fine, just like the eyes of any owner of a sick pet.

"I don't know yet," he told her, speaking just as gently as he'd spoken to Rags. "But I'm going to find it and fix it. Sit down and entertain Rags while I get my stuff together. Want some coffee?"

"Just take care of Rags," she moaned.

He wondered who she was keeping Rags for. Oscar?

It wasn't important at the moment. Nor was his vaccine, or the struggle with his conscience. He had a patient to take care of.

He took the samples and did the tests in record time. "You're not going to believe this," he said when he returned to Charity and Rags.

"Is it bad?" She'd composed herself. She was hugging the dog with one arm, and he noticed with some alarm that she was holding one hand to her left cheek.

"Does your scar hurt?" he said, putting aside everything else, even Rags's condition.

"Forget the scar," she snapped at him. "What's wrong with Rags?"

"He has worms."

"What!"

"Worms. *Ancylostoma caninum.* I'll start treating him right now. In a few days he'll…"

"Hookworms? This dog has hookworms?"

Uninterested in his soothing dogside manner, she stared at him, one hand still clapped over her scar. He gazed back. She seemed to be struck speechless. Something glittered in her eyes. More tears, probably.

"Is this one of those things we're going to laugh about someday?" she said at long last. "That a parasitologist has a dog with worms?"

"It's a possibility," he told her, and decided it was probably safe to smile.

THAT HAD BEEN a close one. Not Rags. Rags would be fine. But the choice she'd had to make between sticking by her sick dog or fixing the scar her tears had melted—that had been the close one.

She'd stuck by Rags, of course. He mattered more than Jason finding out her scar was a fake, that she was a fake. But now that Rags was snuggled down into a makeshift bed in her workspace and Jason had gone back to his real job, she was sure as heck going to the rest room for emergency repairs.

She got there, looked into the mirror and gasped. She'd forgotten to put the gray streaks in her hair.

8

─────────

SNOW FELL LIGHTLY on the windshield as Charity set off on the long drive from Chicago, where she'd modeled in a breakfast show. She'd changed back into "Dr. Sumner" in the rest room of the country club where the fashion show had been staged, then bought a large coffee and felt as relaxed as she was able to feel at this complicated stage in her life.

As she left the posh club in her wonderful Indescribable Brown coat, her Grandmother Gray suit and her beloved maroon blouse she'd enjoyed the odd looks she'd gotten.

No odder, though, than the look Jason had given her yesterday afternoon when he finally noticed her hair.

"I've started coloring it a little," she told him. "Does it look all right? Natural enough?"

As usual, his answer had added to the list of things she had to feel guilty about. He'd told her it looked very nice, but that it had also looked very nice with gray streaks. And hadn't she lost some weight?

He was so kind to people and animals who needed

a little kindness. She didn't deserve him, but she couldn't let him get away, either.

The snow was very pretty along the back roads she took when she had time, and she hummed as she drove along, listening to a book on tape, a romance novel by a popular author in which she knew everything would turn out all right eventually, although it seemed impossible at the moment. Her life, she reminded herself, wasn't a romance novel. Wasn't even a romance.

Not yet. But she had plans.

The snow fell thicker and faster with each passing mile. It began to seem less pretty and more threatening. She should have taken the freeway. She no longer had time to dawdle. She began to wonder why, if she were as intelligent as she'd always claimed to be, she'd gotten herself into a situation that involved an hour's drive north to the lab, and an hour's drive south to modeling assignments in Chicago, and therefore the occasional two-hour trip like this one. If the snow got any worse, it was going to take longer.

Her thoughts went to Faith in sunny California, then to Hope in New York, where she could walk or take a subway anywhere she needed to go. But Charity had had to stay close to home. Right. Very intelligent.

She turned the tape off and caught the last words of the weatherman on the local station. "...blizzard conditions in the Chicago to Madison corridor, increasing in intensity throughout the day and into the night. Three to four feet of snow expected.''

A blizzard. And there was nothing she could do about it at the moment but turn on her lights.

SOMETHING ABOUT Charity and the sick Rottweiler, the way she wouldn't leave him even to take care of her scar when it was obviously bothering her, made Jason decide that the big moment had come. With Charity gone from the lab all morning, he had a half day to find out what she thought was wrong with the gels.

He came to work unusually early. It looked like snow, and he was glad he had four-wheel drive. After the trip through the morning darkness, he was relieved to reach the familiar comfort of his workplace with its bright lights, the smell of brewing coffee and the occasional bark of a beagle.

He was so deeply absorbed in his work, in examining the gels that had worried Charity, that when he looked up at last, he was surprised to see that it was still dark and seriously snowing. She would be out there on the road somewhere. He switched on the radio and with a sinking heart, got the news about the unexpected blizzard. He grabbed her personnel file, dialed her phone number and got an answering machine.

"Charity, it's Jason. If you get this message, don't try coming in to the lab. Everything's fine here, the graduate students will be here, you just take the day off.''

It was all he could do. She used a cell phone to make private calls, but she'd never given him the number and he'd been reluctant to ask. Doggedly he went back to the pictures on the screen.

CHARITY WAS FINALLY forced to admit she was scared. The snow blew in drifts across the two-lane road, obliterating the lanes, and to her right and left the fields were wastelands of white. It was as dark as early evening. The lovers in her book on tape had sex for the first time, and she didn't even care.

She suddenly saw it as significant that she hadn't seen another car in ages. Significant and ominous.

She turned the windshield wipers up to full speed. Still she had to lean forward and peer through the glass for a glimpse of the road. There wasn't time for coffee, for sharing the lovers' afterglow, quickly dispelled by a new crisis in their relationship. All the energy she possessed went into going forward.

Where ''forward'' was, precisely, was the problem. In her case, forward led onto the icy shoulder and from there, directly into a ditch.

For a moment she just sat at the wheel of the car, stunned and shaken. It took her several more minutes to determine that she was okay, that everything looked slanted not because she'd suffered brain damage, but because the car was on a slant. The engine

was still running. This was a good sign. All she had
to do was back up out of the ditch onto the road.

This was the impossible part, which she proved by
drilling her tires even more deeply into the snow and
the mud that lay beneath it.

"Charlotte," said the hero in her book on tape,
"it's you I want, not your beauty but your intelligence, your warm heart, your—"

Charity switched off the tape. She needed to think
about how to get herself out of the ditch, not about
the virtues of intelligence over beauty. Something she
knew for sure was that when you couldn't get yourself
out of a ditch, AAA could, and you paid good money
every year to give yourself a feeling of confidence
while traveling through your occasional blizzard. She
reached into her handbag for her cell phone and dialed the number.

Being on hold wasn't much, but it was a connection
to the outside world and the recorded voice had a
comforting timbre.

Charity yawned, then propped her eyes open. That
was when you knew you were freezing to death, when
you couldn't keep your eyes open. It was also a symp-
tom of concussion. It was also an indication that
you'd stayed up late working and gotten up early to
make it to Chicago on time.

"Due to…volume…calls, your wait…be ap-
prox…twenty-four minutes. Please don't… Your call
is impor…to us."

Static drowned out most of the recording. Charity gave the phone a shake, as if that would help, and began to feel panic. She'd better try to call Jason at the lab. She was not only going to be late, she might not make it at all.

She thought about her family's sorrow, her poor orphaned pets, her recuperating Rags, and a tear ran down the ridge of her scar as she hung up on AAA and dialed the lab.

BETWEEN FRANTIC CALLS to Charity's house—utterly futile, but he couldn't help himself—Jason had examined his gels over and over and could only come to one conclusion. Charity was right and he was wrong.

It was a blow to his ego, but it was a blow he'd take like a man. This wasn't about him. It was about a vaccine that would make life happier for the canine species. All he wanted was for it to work. He thanked his lucky stars Charity had walked into his life—into his lab, rather—in time to save him from making a costly mistake.

All he wanted to know now was that she was safe somewhere, that she'd walk back into his life—lab—on Monday when the storm was over and the roads were clear. When the phone rang, he snatched it up.

"Charity!" Even over the static he recognized her voice. "Where are you?"

"In. A. Ditch," she said distinctly, one word at a time. "Can. You. Hear. Me?"

No time for expressions of concern. No time to tell her she was smarter than he was. "Yes!" he shouted. "Where. Is. The. Ditch?"

"Highway 227," she yelled back.

"Highway Two-two-seven," he repeated. "Where on…"

"Just north of Round Hill. Will you…AAA for me and…them to…"

There was also no time to argue with her. He shouted out a few instructions, hoping she could at least hear part of what he was telling her. "Run the engine at fifteen minute intervals and leave your lights and emergency blinkers on! Stay warm! You may have to wait awhile!"

The phone went dead. "Ed!" he shouted. "Oh, sorry," he said when he found Ed just behind him, staring at him. Jason leaped up and was already putting his arms into his coat while he said the few things that mattered. "Can you and Tyler spend the night here with the dogs so they'll be sure to have somebody with them tomorrow?" When Ed nodded, Jason said, "First thing I want you to do is call AAA. Here's where Charity is."

His hand shook as he pressed the notes he'd written into Ed's hand, then left at a run.

CHARITY FELT BETTER just having heard Jason's scratchy voice. She kept the engine running as he'd suggested, turned on the emergency blinkers, switched the tape back on, grateful that it was unabridged and stretched out on the seat of the Jeep. Because of the pitch, she was practically standing up, but she took a sip of coffee and told herself this was about as cozy as it could get.

She closed her eyes and waited.

"CHARITY! Wake up!"

The shout came through the Jeep window directly into her left ear. She leaped straight forward, hitting her towel-padded hip on the steering wheel and her head on the roof. "Jason!" she said, whirling around to peer out the window. "What are you doing here?"

"Roll down your window."

He'd let himself down into the ditch and was stuck between the car and the embankment. When she'd dazedly rolled down the window, watching a small avalanche of snow fall into the driver's seat, he stuck both arms through the window and put them around her. "Are you all right?"

She knew he was just showing concern, but it felt so nice to have his arms around her that she wanted to say no, just to see what he'd do next. "I'm fine," she said shakily. "I guess I fell asleep."

"Thank God." For a moment he just rested his chin on her hair. "I've been so worried. I left a dozen messages at your home number telling you not to try to come to the lab, but you'd already left for your doctor's appointment and I didn't know where to call next.''

She'd never given him her cell phone number, too afraid he'd catch her on a modeling gig and the sounds in the background would give her away. ''I'm sorry,'' she said, letting herself nuzzle into his chest. Then it hit her. ''You came to get me yourself.''

''Of course I did.''

''Who's taking care of the dogs?''

''Ed and Tyler are sleeping over. They'll do the stats, give the guys some company.''

''What about the Jeep?''

''To hell with the Jeep. Ed's calling AAA and they'll tow it in sometime. Come on. Let's see if we can get you out through this window.''

He was still yelling, making himself heard over the roar of the wind as the snow blew in sheets across the field ahead of them. Charity looked down at her padded hips and wondered if now would be the time to shimmy out of her towel-stuffed girdle and surprise Jason.

No, this really wasn't the time. He'd been through enough. He'd come to rescue her himself. The thought kept humming through her brain, warming her heart and awakening all sorts of feelings she'd been struggling to suppress.

''Wish I'd been dieting a little longer,'' she yelled

back, and handed her briefcase and a gigantic handbag through the window to him.

No need to tell Jason to be careful with the briefcase. "Hang on a minute," he mouthed, then hauled himself up the embankment. She heard a door slam. He'd put the briefcase safely away before getting her out of the car. She liked his priorities.

By the time he dropped down the embankment again, she'd made a stab at getting out the door. Failing, she'd crammed herself through the window almost to the waist, coat and book on tape clutched in her arms. There she hung, the window frame making dents in her padding, the snow falling hard on her red-and-green striped stocking cap. Remembering her scar, she tucked her chin into her chest to protect it.

"Uh-oh. What are we going to do here?" Jason shouted as he nearly fell on her head. She could tell he was trying to be gentle, which wasn't easy to do while shouting. He hesitated a minute, sizing up the situation while snow frosted his eyelashes and his sandy hair. "I'm going to have to get personal," he warned her, and dug his gloved fingertips into the nonexistent space between her hips and the window frame. It would have felt really good if she could have felt anything through all her padding. She wondered how she felt to him. Squashy, probably.

She wiggled. He tugged. She popped out, knocking him backward against the embankment, and for a moment he just held her there.

SHE FELT LIGHTER than he'd expected. Warmer, too. He just wanted to stand there holding her until—until they both froze to death. "All right?" he shouted into her ear. She felt a little shaky in his arms, but maybe she was just starting to feel the cold.

He felt more than a little shaky himself. He'd been through the epiphany of seeing how she'd arrived at her scientific conclusions, and on top of that he'd had the worry about what might be happening to her, and on top of that the most unnerving and endless drive of his life to reach her. He had a right to be shaky.

To keep from yelling, he spoke right into her ear, one of those small, shell-like ears he'd admired more often than he cared to admit. "So far so good," he said. "I'm taking you home."

He hauled her up the embankment and helped her into the warm SUV with all the tenderness he felt in his heart.

And a minute later he felt like opening the door and shoving her back out again. What she said was, "If I couldn't get down this road, what makes you think you can?"

It was an arrogantly feminist statement, showing a total lack of gratitude for his gallant rescue. It didn't sound at all like the Charity Sumner he'd developed such an odd fondness for. He clamped down on his tongue to keep from biting her head off. "Well, Charity," he said, "it's not that I'm so sure I can. It's just that I'm your only option." He took his eyes off the road to glare at her. If his voice went up a little at the end, that was just too bad. He made himself take off slowly. He would have loved using his right foot to express his annoyance.

She reacted with gratifying humility. "I'm sorry. I didn't mean that the way it sounded. I'm so grateful to you for coming to get me." She put her hand on his arm, and even beneath his heavy coat he could feel the warmth of that small, graceful hand. "It's my truck I'm mad at. I spent a big chunk of my ill-gotten gains on that Jeep, and look where it landed me, so I wondered if your SUV…"

"Ill-gotten gains?" Her small, graceful hand forgotten, he took his eyes off the road long enough to examine her closely. Had she spent those two lost years—gambling? Selling her body? Not bloody likely.

"The, uh, the insurance money." She said it fast, as if she'd rather say almost anything than the words *insurance money*.

Maybe this was his chance to find out about the accident that had changed her life. She had to be in a state of high emotional tension. She'd driven through a blizzard, gone into a ditch, waited almost two hours for him, not knowing anyone was coming. Maybe this was the moment she'd feel like telling him the whole story.

"From your accident?" he asked.

Her answer wasn't the cathartic flow of words he'd

hoped for. "I don't like to talk about the accident," she said.

"I understand," he murmured, thwarted again.

For a time they crept along in silence. "Don't hesitate to be a back-seat driver," he said at one point. "I can't see much of anything."

"I'm watching the road," she said, "what I can see of it. We need to turn left pretty soon, but I have no idea when."

"Just let me know."

"Can't be far, but it all looks alike under the snow."

"If we miss the turn, we'll just keep going until we find someplace we can stop until this lets up."

"But I have to get home." All of a sudden she sounded panicked. "I have, you know, Rags to look after."

"Try not to worry," he said, smiling at her as comfortingly as he could. "Just keep watching for the turn."

"There it is."

Jason pressed on the brakes and looked left to see a road that was blocked by a state patrol barrier. A Road Closed sign swung crazily in the wind. He brought the car to a stop.

"I have to get there," Charity said, almost in a moan. "They'll be frantic."

Jason set his teeth together, let up on the brake and went around the barrier. "They" were Rags and Oscar at the very least. Rags was a dog. It was Oscar who worried him. But if they mattered this much to her, he'd get her home or die trying. Now they were plunging through several feet of drifted snow. Where the road actually was was a moot point. Until they fell into something, he'd keep going.

"Stop the car," Charity said in an urgent tone.

In Jason's limited experience, when a woman asked you to stop the car, you stopped the car. Heeding her warning, Jason ground his disc brakes to a halt, then waited nervously for further instructions.

"Look," she said. "That poor dog."

The dog came toward them across the snowy field. He was trying to lope toward them, looked as if he were trying to catch up with them, but his feet sank into the snow with each step.

"We have to help him," Charity said. She already had her door open and was unbuckling her seat belt.

"Well, if that's what you want to do," Jason said gruffly from the road on the other side of the car. He'd beaten her getting out. By the time he circled the car, she'd tumbled out onto the road, too.

"Come on, boy," Charity called. Jason noted that her voice had taken on the musical tone it sometimes had. He also noticed that her eyes filled with tears as she watched the dog's struggling progress, just the way they had when she'd brought Rags into the lab.

"I'd better go get him," Jason said. When Charity turned to him with pure worship in her eyes, he added, "Best way to get him over this barbed-wire fence is to lift him."

While Charity held the fence down as far as she could with her foot, Jason carefully crossed it. The dog didn't protest when he leaned down to pick him up. He was a hundred pounds of brown dog. A hundred pounds of grateful dog. His second giant dog requiring lifting in as many days.

"It's okay, fella," Jason murmured, quietly, so Charity wouldn't hear how sappy he sounded. "We're going to take care of you." He grunted as he curved both arms under the dog's massive body and played like a weight lifter, grunting as he dumped the dog more unceremoniously than he'd intended to on the other side of the fence.

It was all right, though. Charity had her arms around the dog at once, fearless, apparently, and the dog snuggled up against her. He, or perhaps she, matched the brown of Charity's coat. When she opened the back door of the truck, the dog jumped in as if it belonged.

"You don't mind, do you?" she asked him.

"No. Where do you want to take him?" He'd take the dog home with him, of course.

"I'm taking him home with me, of course. If he already has a home, I'll find it this weekend." She stretched out her seat belt to turn around and massage the dog's feet, to rub the cold from his body. "You're going to be fine,'' she informed him. ''Wait until you meet—''

When she stopped in midsentence, Jason wondered what surprise lay ahead for him in the mystery of Charity's house. He realized with a sickening feeling of certainty that if she lived with someone, if she already had a man to love and take care of her, he'd have to deal with deep feelings of disappointment.

You might even call it heartbreak.

''Jason, I don't know if you've thought ahead.'' Her voice was soft, tentative.

Yes, believe it or not—to that country vet's practice, that house in the country, marriage, children...

''If we make it to my house you'll have to stay. You can't go back out in this storm.''

9

SHE WAS THE ONE who hadn't thought ahead.

As Charity cuddled the dog, trying to let it know everything was all right now, she wondered how she was going to handle having Jason in her house for the night.

She had a place for him, of course—one of the two little guest rooms. She also had an elegant French beef stew by some other name braising slowly in the Crock-Pot. It wasn't that she couldn't show him the finest hospitality.

She also couldn't show him her array of makeup, her closet full of slim, trendy clothes, and she was somewhat reluctant to show him her—

"I think we're slipping off the edge over here," she murmured.

"Thanks," Jason said, and carefully corrected the trajectory of the car. "You sure Amos here's not going to be too much trouble for you?"

"His name is Amos?"

"It is now."

"I'll hardly know he's there," she said sincerely. She was reluctant to show him her menagerie of abandoned dogs and cats. Kindness to the lab animals was one thing. Keeping a Rottweiler for someone, which actually was what she was doing, was understandable. But collecting animals like other women collected diamonds, letting them sit all over her furniture and sleep all over her bed, talking to them—on the phone, for heaven's sake—was quite another. It was conceivable, she realized, that her house…smelled. She suspected she'd given herself away yesterday with Rags. Jason had probably figured out she wasn't as cool and pragmatic as Dr. Sumner pretended to be, but when he saw the whole picture, he might decide she was deranged.

He would soon meet Oscar, and she'd have to admit she'd lied to him.

"We're going to make it, Jason," she said when they'd passed Four Corners, a landmark distinguished only by the fact that two farm roads intersected there. "If we have a problem, we can walk from here."

"Thank God."

She glanced at him to find him gripping the steering wheel with white knuckles. "I'm so grateful to you," she said quietly. "For coming to rescue me, for stopping the car to rescue Amos."

As if he didn't dare take his hands off the wheel, he did an "it's nothing" thing with his nose and mouth that she found utterly charming. Even if he wasn't quite as intelligent as she was, he was so wonderful to look at that she really didn't care.

"I…I have a confession to make," she said.

"Me, too."

It surprised her. "Well, me first," she said. "When we get to my house I won't have much choice. There it is. Over there beside that stand of pines."

"It looks like an oasis in the desert." Jason said. She could hear his relief. "You sure you're not hallucinating?"

"Not positive, no." When he swiveled his head toward her, she said, "Just kidding." She turned to the dog. "Here we are, Amos. We're home."

JASON HEARD BARKING. More like a barking chorus, complete with sopranos, altos, tenors and basses. Had to be loud; he could hear it over the wind. Slogging along through the deep snow between him and Charity, Amos shivered.

As they drew closer to the back door of the cottage, he saw a curtain flicker, then a pair of slanted, glowing eyes. It reminded him of Mrs. Appleby pretending she wasn't watching for him through her kitchen curtains. Feeling under surveillance, Jason followed Charity up the stoop and into a small mudroom. The door to the kitchen was closed. As he pulled off his snow-drenched parka and boots, he could feel the presence of someone, something, many someones or somethings, behind that closed mudroom door. Charity, talking softly to Amos, didn't seem to fear the demons that lay in wait.

He was tired, wrung out from the responsibility of

getting them both to this house of possible horror. He was imagining things.

"Come on in," she said at last. "Confession time." *Now* she seemed nervous.

First she spoke through the door. "We have company, guys. It's okay, I invited them, so act nice, okay?" She opened the door, and Jason was hit by a wall of doghood that licked him in the face or scrabbled at his knees, depending on size. A much more active Rags led the bunch. As he fell over backward, he could have sworn a cat's tail flashed across his line of vision.

"They like you," Charity said. She sounded delighted.

"What would have happened," Jason said, sitting up and picking dog hair off his mouth, "if they hadn't liked me?" Now they were climbing onto his lap, and several of the supposed dogs had turned out to be cats.

"They would have held their tails high and stalked away."

There was a certain disadvantage to being liked, as he saw it. "Is this your confession, that you house a thousand dogs and even more cats?" He managed to get up off the floor and they made their way into the kitchen.

"It's not that many." She looked distressed. "I have either six or seven cats—I've never managed to count them properly. And only nine dogs. Well, ten with Amos. Six of them are quite small," she said, and her distress deepened into anxiety. "You know Rags, of course, and this," she said, "is Oscar." She stepped over to the kitchen table and scratched the ears of the small, fierce-looking Border terrier who eyed him suspiciously.

"Oscar? Oh, Oscar!" The supposed nephew she'd been talking to on the telephone, the one he'd been afraid would turn out to be a male friend, a lover. That had been his first clue that what he'd begun to feel for her ran deeper than her lab skills. He took another look at Oscar, and Oscar stared back. "That's your confession? That you lied to me about Oscar?"

A strange look crossed her face. "I felt silly about talking to a dog on the answering machine," she said, not really answering his question. She put Oscar on the floor with an extra stroke down the length of his wiry-haired back. "Oscar's the Alpha dog around here, and if he feels okay, everybody feels okay."

"I can understand that," Jason murmured. "Now my confession." If talking to a dog on the telephone was the worst thing Charity had to confess, wait until she heard what he had to tell her.

"Later," she said, "after dinner. If you'll excuse me for a minute, I'd like to freshen up and explain to Oscar about Amos. Then after I feed everybody and give Rags his medicine we'll have a restorative drink. There's another bathroom if you'd like…"

He would like. When she spun on one heel and walked away with Oscar and Amos following, as if they'd understood exactly what she'd said, he started in the direction she'd pointed. But he paused in the kitchen, taking his first unimpeded look at Charity's life.

His first thought was that like Amos, he was home. Not home in his parents' comfortable house with its newly remodeled but infrequently used kitchen, but home somewhere in his heart. It was clear she spent a lot of time here. While the house looked small from the outside, this room was spacious. On one side, the latest in appliances were interspersed with old-fashioned cupboards. There was a delicious smell of something simmering in the Crock-Pot that sat on a white-painted countertop.

Dinner. There would be something for dinner. The idea cheered him all out of proportion. He hadn't realized how much time had passed. Most of the afternoon had gone by in the struggle to get to Charity and then to bring them here.

They might have perished today. What was he doing thinking about something as mundane as dinner? Because it was sitting right there on the counter, staring him in the face and stirring up his appetite. Charity cooked. He already knew she cooked, but at this particular moment, he couldn't think of a more appealing quality in a human being.

The table sat in the center, and there was still plenty of space on this side of the room for a comfortable-looking sofa and two easy chairs on a large oval braided rug that lay in front of a red-enameled woodstove. Pictures covered the walls, dried flower arrangements, books and geegaws, dog beds, water bowls and food troughs sat around everywhere, but the place didn't look cluttered. It looked clean. It looked interesting. Again he thought that what it looked like was a home.

He wanted to light the fire that was neatly laid, collapse on that sofa and stay there for the rest of his life.

Since the sofa was presently covered in dogs and cats, he made his way back to an equally interesting bathroom that connected two tiny, charming bedrooms. There, he splashed a lot of cold water on his face.

In addition to walls covered in botanical prints and stacks of fluffy white towels, the bathroom was stocked with everything a visitor might need. He took a new toothbrush out of its packaging, opened a new tube of toothpaste and brushed his teeth. While he brushed, he stared out the window. If anything, the blizzard was picking up steam. He'd be spending the night here for sure, isolated with a woman he'd developed an unaccountable affection for.

Could he behave himself? He felt less sure every second he spent in Charity's company.

She took in stray dogs and cats. She talked to them on the telephone. Who would have thought it?

He went back to the kitchen to find her in the process of feeding the animals. It was a lengthy and complicated ritual, and while she distributed lots of pats along with dry food and minced chicken, talking to the animals all the while, he watched her move around in her thick black tights, surprisingly graceful for a woman her size.

She'd lost weight. Not that it made any difference in the feelings that were growing inside him, but he'd known all along that the weight didn't belong there, not with those small hands, her slender wrists and ankles. He sat back on the newly vacated sofa and simply watched, wondering what he should say first. "You were right," or "I love you, exactly as you are."

"WHAT WOULD YOU like to drink? I have wine and everything else."

"Red wine. Whatever's open."

"Coming right up. But please," she implored him, "don't let Supercat anywhere close to your glass."

"Supercat's an alcoholic?"

"Recovering. Three months clean and sober."

"Good for him."

"It hasn't been easy." She whisked across the kitchen to present him with a small tray of bruschetta and a glass of red wine. Carrying her own glass, she pushed two of the smaller dogs aside, arranged Amos in front of the sofa and sank down on the cushions beside Jason. She whooshed when she sat down. He supposed it was actually the sofa that whooshed. "Wow. I feel like I've launched a major offensive without losing a soldier."

"So do I."

"But you actually did. That's the difference."

When he turned toward her, she smiled at him.

So far she felt that everything was going fine. He hadn't seemed too upset about her animal kingdom. In fact, something about Oscar had brought a relieved expression to his face.

She'd freshened up her makeup and hidden everything except "Dr. Sumner's" heavy foundation and pale lip gloss. Then she'd shoved her "thin" clothes down to the far ends of her old-fashioned closet and draped towels over them as if they were summer clothes in storage.

She'd done it just in case. She had no intention of inviting Jason into her bedroom yet. If she could make it gracefully through this night, she'd speed up her imaginary diet and laser treatments. The next time she had Jason Segal as her captive, she'd be ready for him.

"I used a toothbrush," he was telling her. "I'll replace it."

"Oh, heavens no," Charity said. "Use whatever you need. I have to keep the bathroom stocked for Faith's visits. She always forgets something, and it's never the same thing twice. She packs huge suitcases and brings along things like clothes steamers and single-cup coffeemakers, then forgets to bring her comb. Hope packs from a computerized list. If her plane got highjacked and she had to spend six weeks in a Third World prison, she'd survive just fine. Out of one carry-on rolling bag and a briefcase." She sighed. "How's the wine?"

"Excellent."

"There seems to be a little hair there on the rim...."

"Supercat checked it out."

"Oh." Supercat had stretched his nineteen pounds across the back of the sofa where he purred deafeningly.

"What am I smelling?"

Just as she'd feared. Her house smelled! She ducked her head. "Oh, wet dogs and—"

He laughed. "No, that wonderful smell. Something cinnamon."

"Oh, thank goodness. I've always worried about... Well, anyway, that's a frozen homemade apple pie I put in the oven. It'll be out in ten minutes or so, and we'll eat while it cools off a little. Want to help me make a salad? What's your attitude toward anchovies? If you like them, we can have a Caesar."

DID HE LIKE anchovies? He loved anchovies. He loved Caesar salad. He loved apple pie. He was going to love whatever was in that Crock-Pot. Outside the wind howled, the snow blew hard across the flat landscape, but inside this house was more contentment than he could ever remember feeling.

"Do you cook like this for yourself all the time?"

"Or did I plan this blizzard?" She turned away from dropping pasta in the shape of bowties into a pot of boiling water to give him a look that was almost impish. "Yes and no. If you hadn't come along, I wouldn't have put the pie in the oven. I might not even have made pasta." She got a huge plastic bag of washed Romaine lettuce out of the refrigerator and began to tear the leaves into a large wooden bowl.

"What can I do?"

"Grate the Parmesan." She put a chunk of cheese and a grater in front of him.

"Better wash my hands first."

"Good idea. I'll change the tablecloth. Don't get up on the table again until after dinner."

He was startled until he saw she was talking to Oscar. "Where did you get all these guys? Were they strays?"

"Some were. Oscar's owner died, and her kids were afraid of him."

Jason's eyes drifted toward the small dog who, deprived of the kitchen table, had taken control of an armchair. "Border terriers can be…"

"Stubborn," she said. "But so sweet when you understand them. The Jack Russell over there, too. His owner had a nervous breakdown, and Rags's owner is in jail. I'm just keeping him until the guy gets probation, but it may be a while. Supercat's owner, of course—" she lowered her lashes "—is in a rehabilitation center. The Antioch vet calls me when he knows about a pet that needs a home, and I keep an eye on the local pound. Several of them were lab animals. What will happen to the beagles when you've finished your work?'' Her voice was very even, but Jason had a feeling a lot depended on his answer.

He'd wanted to take the whole bunch home with him, but that was impractical. He cleared his throat. ''Ed's taking two,'' he said. ''In fact, a lot of the grad students have put in a bid. Especially the students whose grade point averages are shaky.'' He smiled a little so she'd be sure to realize he wasn't serious. ''I, uh, I thought I might take Lionel and Candida myself.''

''Jason Segal. Just as I suspected. You're an old softy.'' She was looking directly at him, and her dull brown eyes were shining.

''You're a great one to call somebody a softy,'' he retorted. ''But Charity...''

''Later,'' she said. ''Everything's ready. Let's have dinner.''

She dumped the pasta into a strainer, whipped the pie out of the oven, took the lid off the Crock-Pot with a dramatic flourish—

And the lights went out.

10

FOR A MOMENT Jason just stood there in the darkness, feeling animal bodies press against his legs. It seemed like a sign, a sign that he should take Charity into his arms. Forget dinner. His hunger was moving out into other parts of his body that would not be appeased by apple pie.

"I know I paid the light bill," she said in a timid voice.

"It's the storm," he said, getting himself under control. "Do you have candles?"

"Oh, yes. If I can find them in the dark. That's the thing about lighting candles because the lights have gone out. First you have to find the candles and the holders—oh, here they are, just where they're supposed to be."

She sounded nervous. He wondered if she knew what had just passed through his mind. He wondered if—hoped that—the same thing had crossed her mind. In a moment, the flicker of a candle illuminated her face and the worried faces of several of the dogs. "I don't know how to explain power outages to them," she said.

"Oscar does," Jason said. He knelt down and held Oscar's face gently between his hands. The wiry little dog looked up at him, just as if he were waiting for instructions. "Oscar," he said, "we're having dinner by candlelight. It's done in all the best places. You'll enjoy it and so will we, especially since the food was already cooked. Dr. Jason wouldn't be half as happy if it hadn't been. Pass the word along to the troops."

Behind him he heard Charity giggle. It was a nice sound, as warming as the candlelight, as the fire flickering through the glass door of the woodstove.

"Oscar says fine, but he wants more candles," Jason told her as he stood up.

"That sounds like a reasonable request," she said. "Would you light them while I dish up dinner?"

He'd eaten in the fine restaurants of a dozen American and European cities when his work took him there, but he'd never enjoyed a meal more. The ragout was dark and richly flavored. She served feather-light baguettes, homemade, to sop up the sauce. The apple pie was what apple pie was supposed to be and rarely was. In his mind's eye, a scientist's mind's eye, he realized, he saw her picking the apples, rendering pork fat into lard for the crust. When he imagined her grinding wheat into flour, he knew he was losing sight of reality.

"How could this be any better?" he said, forking up the last bite of pie with a last dribble of ice cream.

"Well," she said, looking thoughtful, "the stove

heats the whole house, so we're fine there. But water's sort of basic. I'm not on the city system. I've got my own well and pump, electric, naturally. So when the electricity goes, so does the water. Fortunately, I've got gallons of it stored up in the basement, so the dogs will be fine, but don't even think about taking a shower. Coffee in front of the fire?'' she suggested.

"How can you make coffee with no electricity?" *Really romantic, Jason. Good work.*

It was fortunate, he supposed, that she was a scientist, too. "The stove is gas," she said. "I can light it with a match and boil water on it. I have a cone and a carafe to put the cone on top of. I keep a packet of ground coffee for—"

"Charity," he interrupted, "I'm sorry I doubted your ability to produce coffee. I'm sorry I doubted—"

"What?" she said.

"Anything," he said. He felt helpless. Clueless was more like it. It was increasingly clear to him that by some incredible accident of time, place and need he'd found the woman who could complete his lonely life. And he wanted to make everything right between them.

Just as he was about to launch into his speech about his being wrong about the gels, she started looking scared. "I'll make the coffee," she said, and spun away from him.

He was going to have to grip her face between his hands and speak directly into it in order to apologize to her. He'd never had to do that to a woman, but it had worked well with Oscar. His inner tension built as he let her make the coffee, and by the time she brought the tray, he was primed.

"Charit—"

"Have a cookie. I made some fresh peanut butter ones last night."

Put thee behind me, peanut butter cookie! "You're right about the gels."

She grew absolutely still. Those were brave thoughts he had a minute ago about gripping her face between his hands. Now he was afraid to look at her.

"I am?" She sounded so bemused that he let himself sneak a peek at her. She was staring at him and otherwise appeared to have gone numb all over.

"Yes. I checked it out over and over and you're absolutely right. I owe you an apology." He sighed. "I've slowed down the project by being too stubborn to pay attention to you."

He held out both arms in supplication and found the courage to look directly at her. "I was always 'the brain,' remember? Just like you. I guess I started thinking I would always be 'the brain' of any operation. That I'd never find anybody smarter. Now I have. You."

He'd imagined all the ways she might react, but he hadn't expected the stricken expression she was wearing now. Nor could he possibly have predicted what she'd say next. "Was that all they ever said about you?" she said slowly. "You mean nobody ever told you you were absolutely gorgeous?"

IT WASN'T WHAT she'd intended to say. She should have said, "Why, thank you, Jason, but my discovery had nothing to do with being smarter. You were just a little too close to it. I was able to look at it more objectively." Something like that. Some nice acceptance of his apology.

Instead, she'd blurted out what was in her heart.

His green eyes widened. In the candlelight they glowed like cat's eyes, but without a cat's sly mischief. "No," he said, and moved almost imperceptibly closer to her on the sofa. "I don't think anybody ever has. Has anyone ever told you you were beautiful?"

This was her chance to blurt out the rest of what was in her heart, that she'd deceived him and she was sorry. "Yes," she said softly. "Jason—"

"You still are." He moved closer. "Even after the accident. Every day we've spent together I've thought you were more beautiful, because you're so beautiful inside."

His mouth came down to hers. At the first shock of electricity she knew how long, how intensely she'd wanted this kiss. Desire quickened inside her when her lips met the sweetness of his, when his arms slid sinuously around her, pressing her breasts into his hard, muscled chest. She felt affection in that caress, but also passion held carefully in control.

He wanted her just as she was. Didn't that make her deception worth everything it might cost her? His mouth slid across her cheek. "Stop me any time," he whispered. His mouth tasted of apples, spicy with cinnamon. Stop him? How could she bear to stop him when she ached for him in every part of her body, when the floodgates at last had opened to rivers of need that raced through her?

"I shouldn't do this," he continued, still blowing soft kisses against her cheek with each word. "We work together. It's not right. But I give you my promise. This kiss has nothing to do with keeping your job."

"Yes, it does," she breathed.

He drew back a little. "No—"

"If you don't shut up and kiss me again, I'm resigning."

"Oh, Charity." His arms tightened and his mouth made its way swiftly back to hers. He deepened his kiss, giving her the velvet of his tongue as he searched the heat of her mouth. She gave back to him, everything she had to give. Her breasts swelled against his chest, the nipples hard and aching. The ache between her thighs was driving her wild, demanding and not being satisfied with mere kissing. It had been a long, long time. The smallest taste and her appetite was spiraling out of control.

He kissed her mouth, her eyes, her throat. When he nuzzled her ear she shuddered, a deep, hard shudder that intensified the ache until it was unbearable.

He moved his hand up between them to undo one button of her dreadful maroon blouse. His fingers slipped inside, his knuckles against her skin as he freed the second button. His silk-and-sand hair brushed down her throat as he bent to her breasts, pulling down the lace of her bra to kiss the swell above. When he tugged her nipple into his mouth and let his teeth close on it lightly, she moaned with pleasure, stretched out further on the sofa, trying to give him access to more of her, more and more and more...

His hands were at the waistband of her gray skirt, tugging the maroon blouse from its moorings. It wouldn't come free. She wanted it to come free, wanted his hands to roam her waistline, her rib cage, slide up and down her sides until—

She sat bolt upright. If he'd been kissing her on the mouth, she would have knocked him out. She had just realized there were many reasons, many, many reasons she couldn't let Jason run his hands up and down her body, and most of them were made of terry cloth.

"I'm sorry," he said. His voice was hoarse with desire, and in the candlelight she could see his swollen mouth, his heavy-lidded eyes as he tried to pull himself back. "I scared you. We'll stop right now."

"No. No." She was breathless, could barely get the words out. "I don't want you to stop. I just…"

She stopped because he was holding his hand up to the flickering light, gazing at the smear of dark makeup she used to fashion the scar on her cheek. Her heartbeat slowed to a dull thud.

I have to tell him now. Tell him everything, even if it brings an end to this glorious moment. It's better this way. I'll be happier this way. Every act of kindness he'd shown her had made her feel worse. "Jason, I—"

He leaned forward and kissed the scar lightly. "You don't have to use this heavy makeup. Not for me, not for anybody. How can I make you believe me when I tell you how lovely you are? Your intelligence, your sweetness—" his arms closed around her again, holding her close, stroking her back with a seductive rhythm "—your *honesty* are the things that make you beautiful," he murmured into her ear. "You're the woman I've been looking for all my life."

Her *honesty.* She almost drew away from him, made him listen to just how *honest* she was. Once again, guilt battled against desire, but the passion she felt for him was too powerful to be driven back. She wanted him. She realized all at once that she loved him, knew he was the man she'd been looking for all her life. There had to be a way to have him now and forever after, and that way was to change back into herself slowly. Never tell him, until years and years from now when—when they could both laugh about it.

She rose from the sofa and held out both hands to him. The look in his eyes made her doubt her judgment again. He loved her, too. He deserved the truth from her. But she had to have this night with him first. She tugged him toward her, held him close, felt the pounding of his heart against her breasts, and knew there was no going back.

His lips seared hers with their fire as she led him to her bedroom. A single candle flickered there, like the single flame that burned inside her for him.

"Charity…"

"Shh," she whispered. "Get into bed. I'll be there in a minute."

"The bed is full of dogs," Jason whispered back.

"Oh. Well, give me a minute. Okay, you guys," she said, "off the bed." Trying for her usual disciplinary tone, kind but firm, she found she could barely speak, that her voice shook, but one by one the dogs obeyed. She herded them out of the room and closed the door, leaving Jason inside and herself outside. She knelt on the floor and said, "It's okay. Charity needs a little privacy tonight, that's all. Let me explain," she continued, deciding she needed to go a little further to allay their anxiety and not leave them with any lingering trauma at having been replaced by some stranger. "Sometimes a man and a woman meet and begin to have a special kind of feeling toward each other—"

Behind her the bedroom door opened, a hand closed on the collar of her maroon blouse and Jason pulled her back inside the bedroom.

"...tell you more about it in the morning," were the last words she was able to speak before his mouth closed over hers again.

"You must think I'm crazy," she moaned.

"And I love you for it."

The words were out and he couldn't take them back. He felt a small jolt of surprise from her and wondered if he'd made a fool of himself. A second later, plundering her mouth, drinking in its sweetness, he didn't think he cared. When her arms slid around his neck, her fingers tangled with his hair and her breasts crushed against his chest, he knew he didn't care.

He longed to undress her slowly, peel her shirt away from her breasts, slide her skirt down her hips an inch at a time, kissing his way down her body until she was wild with passion. But when she slipped away from him, taking the candle with her, he didn't protest.

Maybe she had a better plan. Maybe she'd come back to him in something black and lacy he could peel off, or naked with a couple of fans strategically placed. He wasn't sure why, since there wasn't a ray of light in the room, no streetlamps casting a seductive glow through the white curtains, no moonlight to cast a spell. But he knew women had their fantasies, and whatever Charity's fantasy was, he wanted to live it with her.

So he shucked off his clothes, put the packet of condoms he never traveled without on the night table and slid between the sheets of her bed. It was a warm, soft bed. She was a warm, soft woman. His body throbbed with his need for her, his heart with love for her.

He felt he'd stepped several hundred years back in time. He might be a sultan waiting in his tent for the latest delicious tidbit in his harem to be brought to him by her handmaidens, perfumed with sweet oils, draped in a single scarf. Or Henry VIII waiting for his current bride Anne Boleyn to come to him in his kingly canopied four-poster.

He couldn't imagine Henry VIII having the patience to wait this long. At last he heard the soft pad of bare feet, felt the covers being lifted back, felt her slide in beside him. He put a hand on her shoulder, expecting silky skin and finding—flannel, it felt like. He slid his hand down her arm. Flannel to the wrist. Down her sides. Flannel. She was wearing a head-to-toe flannel nightgown.

"I hope you don't mind," she whispered. "It will make me feel less self-conscious about my body."

She nuzzled her mouth into his throat in a way he found promising. It was not a flannel-nightgown thing to do.

"No," he said hoarsely, not in the mood for conversation, "but you don't need to be self-conscious about your body, and it's too dark for me to see you anyway."

"The lights could come back on at any time." While she made this practical observation she put her flannel arm across his chest and trailed kisses from his throat to his earlobe, which she teased with the tip of her tongue.

He wanted to shout, "Okay! Fine! Whatever!" but that would certainly break the mood. "Mmm," he said instead, his fingertips already examining the gown, looking for a point of entry in a seemingly impenetrable fortress. He wanted to cry out with the pure joy of his discovery when he found buttons. Down the front. Now if only she wasn't—and he wouldn't put it past her—wearing a chastity belt.

At the moment, he was sure he could break the lock with his teeth.

11

THE WORST WAS OVER, and the best was just beginning. When Charity felt Jason's fingertips working the buttons of her nightgown free, she felt herself bursting free, too. Her mind cleared of everything except awareness of his touch, his heat. He pulled her gown apart to bare her breasts, just as if he could see them. She felt him moving over her, felt his hair tickle her chin as he took her nipple between his lips to tease it with his tongue.

Sparks of electricity shot through her veins, down to her toes, out to her fingertips, and she moaned. She seized his head in her hands, raking her fingers through his hair. She let one hand run down his back, felt the tension in his muscles, slid it farther down to his buttocks, felt the urgency in his kisses.

His mouth was traveling again, blazing a trail down to her navel, down her stomach, down to her very center.

She writhed against him, mindless, nothing more than a flood of pure sensation that pooled heavily at the apex of her thighs. As his hands stroked a path down her rib cage to her hips, only one stray thought went fleetingly through her dazed mind. Would he notice that the hips he caressed weren't as heavy as they had been a few minutes ago, the waistline not as thick? But the thought fled at once, because she knew Jason wasn't thinking at all. And neither could she when the spasms began and she gave herself up to the shudders of exquisite pleasure.

His energy, his urgency, inflamed her. She needed more of him for herself, needed to give him the same incredible sensations he'd just given her. She slid onto his sweat-slicked body, molding her still-throbbing center to his engorged manhood, and wrapped her legs around him. He seized her, tugged her down to him, clutched her bottom to bring her closer. And she wanted to be closer, wanted to be a part of him, one with him.

She felt his hesitation, heard the slight sounds, knew he was protecting her and himself, and then, in a single gentle thrust, he joined them together. It was so easy, felt so right. Tears came to her eyes as she rocked against him, feeling the sensations build again, higher and higher. When she felt she couldn't bear any more, he slowed, stroked her back with feather-light caresses, kissed her breasts, then engaged her again in the age-old dance of giving and taking, bringing her to new, undreamed-of heights.

Until at last nothing could bring her down from the high peak of her desire. She toppled over and soared, weightless, into a magical universe where Jason awaited her with outstretched arms, and there was nothing between them but a pure and perfect love.

It was a night of splendors and delights. A night of heat and frenzy, of passion and pleasure, of tenderness and joy. It was a night to remember all her life. She had a lifetime of nights like this to look forward to.

All she had to do was wake up before Jason did.

JASON SLEPT LITTLE, but deeply. Still half-adrift in sleep, memories of the night racked his senses, reawakened his desire. She'd felt slimmer to his touch than she looked in her clumsy clothes. There was no clumsiness to the woman he'd made such exquisite love with, just sensuous, sinuous grace in the way she writhed against his body.

The room seemed less dark than it had in the night. In the dimness, he turned to gaze at Charity, who lay sprawled beside him in a pose that was somehow graceful and appealing, even in a flannel nightgown. She was facing him, lying on her right cheek. Her skin looked smooth and beautiful. He admired the straight line of her small nose, the slight curve, almost a smile, of her full lips. Just as he leaned down to brush a kiss over those lips, the lights went on.

Bedside lamps, the bathroom light, a radio, the television set in the kitchen, everything went into action at once. Charity's eyelids flew open and her face zoomed right past his as she sat straight up in bed.

She moaned something unintelligible, still dreaming, Jason imagined, of him, he hoped, and he looked up at her, intending to pull her back down to the pillows and another delicious hour of pleasure.

Her scar was gone.

It was a jolting sight. He blinked. She stared at him with something like horror, as if she couldn't imagine what he was doing in her bed. He felt as if he should introduce himself. He felt as if she should introduce herself!

Disoriented, he looked away from her, looked to her side of the bed, reassuring himself that the night had really happened, and a dull pain replaced the heated pleasure he'd felt a moment earlier.

Her scar wasn't gone. It was right there, on her pillow, smudges of dark brown, of red.

He stared back at her face. It looked pale and frightened. He put out his hands and ran them down her sides from her armpits to her hips. She was as slender as she'd felt in the night, small-boned and lithe beneath the flannel gown.

Her dark, silky hair swam around her narrow shoulders. Her eyes weren't two shades of brown. They were the most extraordinary blue, the blue of violets. She was beautiful, the most beautiful woman he'd ever come across, and there was just one problem. She wasn't the woman he'd made love with the night before.

"Why?" It was all he could think of to say.

The words came slowly through lips that suddenly looked tight. "I wanted the job. I'd been interviewing for jobs for two years. Nobody would hire me. I just don't look like a serious scholar."

"I can understand that. I also understand it was something you could have explained to me the first day you came in to work." He felt cold all over and knew he sounded the same way. But he didn't care. She'd lied to him, deceived him, played on his sympathy, on his soft heart—yes, damn it, he did have a soft heart, and he didn't care who knew it.

"I still wasn't sure you'd take me seriously." Her voice was small and mournful.

"There was no accident."

"No."

"Where have you been going when I thought you were having laser treatments?" Laser treatments. He'd been a complete fool.

"Finishing up my modeling jobs. The ones I'd already accepted when—"

"Modeling jobs!"

"That's what I did to earn a living while I tried to get a job in parasitology."

It explained that crazy scene in the restaurant when she'd tried to hide from Celine behind her dessert menu. And then, Jason thought bitterly, he'd made a fool of himself again by launching into one of his pedantic self-esteem lectures. He was pathetic. Really stupid to have fallen for a fake scar. Made him happy to be working with animals. They didn't try to pull things like that on you.

He didn't know who she was anymore. He didn't know if he loved her or not.

He dragged a blanket off the bed as he got up, wrapped himself in it, then stalked over to the closet and flung open her door. He recognized the clothes she'd been wearing. He saw at once the clothes shoved down to the end of the closet and pulled them back into view. Short, narrow skirts. Skinny black pants. Sleeveless tops and dresses. Lots of Lycra. He was a scientist. He knew Lycra.

He whirled on her. She was still sitting up in bed, but she'd buried her face in her knees. He stormed on to the bathroom, opened a cupboard door and found not only linens but a collection of stage makeup. And a spray can that said, "Temporary Streaks. Steel Gray," under the brand name. In the very back was a large black girdle and a heap of wrinkled towels.

Twenty pounds of fake Charity.

He gathered up his clothes and took them to the guest bedroom where he'd intended to spend the night, where he should have spent the night, where he now wished fervently he'd spent the night. If he'd done that, she'd still be the woman he knew and loved and he wouldn't have to deal with the fact that he'd fallen in love with a woman who didn't really exist.

"Brilliant Young Scientist Jason Segal Falls For

Imaginary Woman.'' How had anybody ever gotten the idea he was brilliant?

CHARITY STOOD at the bedroom window surrounded by dogs and cats, crying as she watched Jason shoveling her driveway. Each time he pitched a heavy shovelful of snow off to the side, she knew he was imagining her in that shovel. His anger showed in the clenched muscles of his face, his taut stance, the way he plunged the shovel into the snow. When he'd cleared a path, he got into his car and left.

He would never come back here again. He would never share her bed again. She wouldn't be his assistant when he became a country vet, and they wouldn't cuddle up by the fire and talk about worms.

She could hardly bear the loss of a dream she'd only just begun to believe could come true.

The phone rang and she snatched it up. "AAA," said the voice. "Where do you want us to bring this Jeep?"

Charity was sorely tempted to tell the voice exactly what it could do with her Jeep.

THE SNOW HAD STOPPED, leaving disaster in its wake. Slow-moving equipment was even now trying to clear off the highways. As he ploughed a dangerous path into Madison, Jason talked to himself. It had been important for him to leave at once. It was one thing for the Charity Sumner he knew to have seen something in him besides his brain, to have shown him she wanted his body as well. It was quite another to discover that a woman as beautiful as that stranger he'd just run away from had thought he was—how had she put it? "Absolutely gorgeous."

It was too much for him. He couldn't handle it.

If he'd stayed in her house one more hour he would have run the risk of falling in love with this new Charity Sumner, the beautiful one. It was important for him to remember her as a woman who'd deceived him, who'd lied to him as skillfully as a professional con artist.

He had to stoke his anger, keep it hot. It was the only thing holding him together.

That, and the need to produce his vaccine, and do it right this time. Her way. Gritting his teeth, he went straight to the lab.

CHARITY'S WHOLE LIFE had changed. Over the course of one weekend she'd reached the heights, then hit rock bottom. She'd found a man she could love forever and lost him, just like that, with no one to blame but herself.

Late Sunday afternoon, tears ran down her face as she packed away the props of her deception—the Grandmother-Gray suit, the Burnt Toast trousers, the maroon blouse, the sweaters that matched one eye or the other. She put the box in the back of the Jeep.

She'd drop it off at the thrift shop in Antioch, the sooner the better.

Work. She had to go back to the lab tomorrow, face Jason. She couldn't imagine how to handle it.

JASON SPENT the weekend at the lab, snatching a few hours of sleep on the reception room sofa when his fatigue threatened his project. Early Monday morning he went home, showered and changed, and endured a full English breakfast cooked at length by Mrs. Appleby.

When he got back to the lab, a tin of cookies sat on the desk in the reception area just as it always did. Not always. Just since Charity. Jason made himself ignore them. He heard happy sounds coming from the beagles, so he cautiously made his way back to the kennel and peeked in. Charity was petting two of them at once, moving around the room, saying good morning to each dog, receiving kisses graciously.

Don't trust her! She's a fraud! he wanted to warn them, but of course they could trust her. She'd never do anything to hurt them. Just him.

As this thought went through his mind, she straightened up, turned and saw him. Her expression as she gazed at him was one of uncertainty. Her dark hair was pulled back and fastened at her nape. She wore no makeup that he could see. Maybe something on her mouth that made her lips a pale glossy pink, but that was all. Her skin was smooth and pale as ivory, and her eyes were such a vivid blue that they dominated her face. A fringe of thick, dark lashes floated down, then back up again. She wore flat shoes, skinny black trousers like the ones he'd discovered in her closet and a ribbed black sweater that outlined her narrow shape. Her clothes were peppered with dog hair.

He gave himself three seconds to drink her in, then said, "Good morning," as coldly as he could.

"Hello, Jason." Her voice quavered.

"In another few days I'll have the vaccine ready to inoculate the test group and start the trials." He spun on one heel and went to his lab. He didn't dare look at her a second longer.

The day went by, then another day, while he stayed calm and cold on the outside and inside his frustration built to the boiling point. Charity came to work and simply stayed, taking cat naps in odd places and doing the work of two people. He was the second person whose work she was doing. When she was close by, he couldn't think, made stupid mistakes.

He finally couldn't stand it any more. "Shouldn't you go home and take care of your own animals?" he said, but he glared at her when he said it. He didn't want her accusing him of being a softy again.

"I hired a baby-sitter," she told him. "Ed put me on to somebody. She's a Ph.D. student in parasitology who'll keep a close eye on Rags. She's working on her dissertation, she brought a laptop and a hundred pounds of research materials with her, she needs the money and she won't leave until I tell her to.''

He was pretty damned tired of Charity being on top of everything—except him. He drove that thought out of his mind and rephrased his complaint. He was tired of watching Charity do the right thing for everybody except him.

Wednesday morning he ran across the schedule she'd handed him—it seemed like a lifetime ago— and noticed she'd be out that afternoon. Now, of course, he knew the poor thing wasn't going in for a laser treatment. She was fulfilling one of her prior commitments to her modeling agency. It seemed like a blessing. He'd have the lab to himself and pull his own weight, work with the concentration he'd found so easy all weekend. *Easy* wasn't the right word. It had been his salvation.

He was looking at a slide under the microscope, but for a moment he closed his eyes and tried to imagine Charity as a model. She was more than beautiful enough, more than thin enough, but try as he might, he couldn't imagine her in heavy makeup and over-painted eyes. He couldn't imagine her—posing. He couldn't imagine her without dog hair all over her clothes and the dog itself somewhere nearby. There was more to Charity than her looks.

With great determination he opened his eyes and returned his attention to his slide. He couldn't have thoughts like those. It meant he was taking a step toward understanding why she'd disguised herself, to give him a chance to see what lay inside her beautiful body, behind her beautiful face, and he had no intention—ever!—of understanding the way she'd deceived him.

He heard the outer door close quietly and knew she'd left. With a muttered expletive, he gave up on the slide and began to pace. He paced past the cookie tin and saw that the vet students had made enough inroads on the cookies that she'd never know if he ate one. Oatmeal raisin. His favorite.

He paced past the window, where something caught his eye. Charity was moving down the sidewalk toward the parking lot, tall, slim and graceful in a long, belted black wool coat and a stylish hat with her ponytail tucked up under it. A pain in his heart reminded him of the day he'd watched a beautiful woman on her way to the parking lot without recognizing her as the Charity he'd already begun to love.

And now had stopped loving. Definitely. It was over, over, over!

12

So THAT WAS how it was going to be. Cold and clinical from here on out. She'd do her work. He'd do his. The vaccine would be a success, but their relationship was a complete and total failure.

That, she supposed, was why you shouldn't fall in love with your boss. If everything went well, what could be more convenient for a work-driven person? When it didn't go well, you messed up two parts of your life at the same time.

With a dull ache of sorrow and regret in her heart, Charity arrived at the location of her modeling assignment—The Art Institute, of all places, where she, Celine and two male models would assume kooky positions amid the wonderful Red Grooms assemblages that were part of the museum's collection. The spread would be in the magazine that came with the Sunday newspaper. At least it was different from her usual assignment. But where she wanted to be was back in the lab, working on those last crucial steps toward getting the vaccine ready for the trials.

She arrived to find that area of the museum closed to the public while the photographer and several assistants set up their equipment for the session. The other models were already milling around. "We've got to stop meeting like this," she told Mark, who was also on hand and setting up a makeshift dressing table, then made her way over to Celine.

"You look a heck of a lot better," Celine commented, her long, beautiful nose just a smidgen up in the air.

Charity had never liked Celine much, but at the moment, she felt indebted to her. "I haven't really thanked you properly," she said, "for not giving me away that day in the restaurant."

Celine waved a long, perfectly manicured hand, managing somehow to look it over critically while she spoke. "I figured you were just doing something you had to do," she said offhandedly. "He sure is a gorgeous guy."

"Was," said Charity. "I mean, he still is, but I managed to give myself away. The relationship, such as it was, is over." She managed to sound calm, but felt her eyes filling with tears.

"What a shame," Celine said. "I do hope it wasn't something I said?"

Something in her voice made Charity eye her with suspicion. Even though Celine was a bit out of focus through the impending tears, Charity could see what was going through her mind. "No, it was nothing you said. It was something I did."

"Life is tough," Celine said. "Ah, what did you say his name is?"

Charity gritted her teeth. "Jason Segal," she said distinctly.

"And he's a vet?"

"Yes."

"They make a lot of money, don't they?"

Celine was as transparent as her gauzy white blouse. "Some do," Charity said. "Jason probably won't."

"Why not?"

Her tone had sharpened, which pleased Charity. Her spirits lifted. "Worms aren't a high-ticket item," she informed Celine, gratified to see the model's creamy skin take on that familiar, attractive green shade.

"They aren't?" Celine said in a strangled voice.

"No, but Jason doesn't care about money, only about worms. It's all he can talk about, over dinner, even in…" Charity paused delicately, then went on without finishing the sentence. "Oh, Celine, you wouldn't believe the endless variety of worms that can get inside dogs and eat away at their poor little intestines until—"

"Charity!" It was the photographer. "Call your agency. They want to talk to you right now."

"Excuse me," Charity murmured to Celine, who was sitting down, slumped on an upturned equipment crate and resting her head on a camera dolly. "We'll talk more about worms later. It's *so* exciting to find someone who's interested.''

''Guess what! I've got news for you that'll knock your panty hose off. It'll sure get you off this crazy, 'I'm a scientist!' kick you're on.'' The gravelly voice with its sarcastic bite belonged to the head of the agency Charity had signed on with when it became clear she wasn't going to become an acting parasitologist any time soon.

''The Emir of Shamirizbad has asked for my hand in marriage,'' Charity said.

''Who? What? No. Try cover of *Vogue*.''

''Saundra,'' Charity said patiently, ''you know I've closed out my contract. No shoots after I finish the last one I'd already scheduled.'' She hesitated. ''What did you say? The cover of *Vogue*?''

''Oh. Wonderful. The word *Vogue* brought you down from your ivory tower.''

''It got my attention,'' Charity had to admit. Not that she wanted the cover of *Vogue*. All she wanted was something to lift her out of the depression she'd been in since she drove Jason away through her own stupidity.

Wait a minute. Stupidity? Wasn't she the ''Beauty with a Brain?'' Where had the ''brain'' part gone?

Into loving Jason.

Didn't mean she'd lost her intelligence altogether. If she returned to modeling, she could walk away from the lab, from Jason, from the pain she was living with. In due time she could start interviewing universities, laboratories and drug companies again, and somebody, somewhere, some day, would hire her.

While she wondered what to do, Saundra filled in the details. A Chicago-based model on the cover of *Vogue* was a major victory for Saundra's agency. It was a giant step toward supermodel status for Charity. There was money in it, lots of money.

"I have to think about it," she told Saundra.

There was a lot of gravelly squawking at the other end of the line. The gist of it was, "I offer you the cover of *Vogue* and you have to *think* about it?"

"YOU LOOK AWFUL."

"Thank you." Jason clipped the words. "Excuse me, Mrs. A, but I have work to do."

"Stay right where you are, young man!" Jason halted on the first step. "You're not going anywhere until you tell me what's wrong with you."

He sighed, slumping his shoulders. "Woman trouble."

"What woman?"

"The woman who works with me at the lab. We had a little thing going, and now it's over." He took another step up the stairs.

"Halt!" He halted. "You had a thing and it's over and I never even met her? I would have had her over for dinner." He'd hurt Mrs. Appleby's feelings badly.

"And you never will meet her." Now he'd added

shock to the hurt on her face. "What I mean is..." Jason gave up, turned around and came back down the two steps. "The woman I fell in love with never really existed."

After a long silence, Mrs. Appleby said brightly, "How about a nice cup of hot tea?"

"I'm not insane, Mrs. A, it's just a crazy story."

"All I asked was if you wanted a cup of hot tea?" She used the reasonable voice of a nurse speaking to a dangerous psychotic.

"Please." He hated hot tea. A cup of hot tea was just what he deserved.

"You need to talk to somebody," Mrs. Appleby said when Jason had finished his story—leaving out the good parts—his tea and a slice of the most amazingly awful cake he'd ever tasted. She called it Hummingbird Cake, but he had a feeling she'd actually put in the birds.

"I just did."

"I'm an old woman. What do I know? You have family you could talk to?"

Could he talk to his brothers? Charity often mentioned having just talked to her sisters. He'd never told his brothers anything about his love life. He just let them tease him about not having one.

Maybe he'd do it. Call Ken the playboy golf pro first, then talk to Mike, who'd been dating the same girl since high school and really ought to be thinking about marriage sometime soon. Two different perspectives. It was a good plan.

Well, it had seemed like a good plan at the time. "Hey, Little Bit," Ken said, "I think you're overreacting here. It's not like you're going to marry her, know what I mean? So she's a little sneaky. Thing is, is she good in the sack?"

"Ken, there's something else I'd like to run past you," Jason said. "You may be older, but I've been taller than you since I hit the eighth grade. Don't you think it's about time you stopped calling me Little Bit?"

He hung up before Ken could riposte with one of those things men say to each other, like, "Doesn't have anything to do with your height," and dialed his younger brother Mike.

Mike was plenty smart. He just needed time to think things over. Jason told Mike about Charity, then fidgeted while Mike thought it over. Eventually Mike said, "Let me see if I've got this straight. You fell in love with her when she wasn't beautiful, and now that she is beautiful, you don't want to be in love with her anymore."

"That's not the point," Jason argued. "She lied to me, over and over."

But once started, Mike gained momentum. "Heck, man," he said. He'd been watching his language since he started coaching high-school football, setting a good example for his players. "If Shelley woke me up one morning and told me she was really J.Lo, I sure wouldn't throw her out of my bed for lying to me."

He paused. "Forget what I said, okay? About going to bed with Shelley? Got to set a good example for the boys, y'know."

"Mike," Jason said, "I think the rumors would fly faster if anybody thought you'd been going steady with Shelley for ten years without going to bed with her. Hey, thanks. Great talking to you."

He didn't think he could make anybody understand that what he loved—make that *had* loved—about Charity was her honesty, her intelligence. Except maybe Charity. He was starting to wonder if that was what she'd had in mind all along.

Seeing Mrs. Appleby and remembering the zing of the horseradish in her heart-shaped Cardinal Salad got him thinking that Valentine's Day was coming up soon, next week, in fact. He'd have to look at a calendar to see exactly what day it was, but he'd make that his deadline for figuring out what Charity was—and could be—to him.

AT LONG LAST the vaccine met each of Jason's exacting tests. With a combination of hope and anxiety, he inoculated the test group. He and Charity, assisted by the vet students, began testing the beagles for antibodies five days later, and so far, the results were promising. He started sleeping at home, leaving his work-study students in charge of the night patrol. Charity went home, too, so apparently she'd dismissed her sitter.

Jason's mind was filled with just two thoughts, Charity and the vaccine. He'd be thinking hard about the vaccine, and suddenly realize Charity had sneaked in at the edges of his mind.

He needed a distraction, a third thing to think about.

"Dr. Segal?" Ed hovered behind him.

Jason looked up from his microscope and frowned.

"We've got fleas."

It was a long, long journey from the memory of Charity in his arms to the concept of fleas on the beagles. Jason finally made it to the end. He hopped off the lab stool. "I said I needed a distraction," he growled. "I didn't mean *fleas.*

Too late, he realized he hadn't said anything to Ed about needing a distraction. He'd only been thinking it. The heat in his face told him he was blushing, the curse of those unlucky enough to be born blond. He scowled more ferociously to make up for it. They couldn't use a systemic flea killer in the lab. It would interfere with the effects of the vaccine. There was only one way to deal with the situation. "Call Dr. Sumner," he said. "It's bathtime," and his face flamed even hotter.

Some time later, Charity had assembled a host of work study students and volunteers from the veterinary program. Solemnly they leashed the beagles and led them down to the basement, where they would be bathed in a nontoxic pesticide while their runs were disinfected.

"It's a parade," another resident of the building murmured as the dogs marched by.

"I'll stay tonight and be sure everything goes right," Charity said.

"No need to." Jason maintained his cool tone. "We have vet students to take charge." He paused. "How did you get all those volunteers?"

"I promised them a round of beer in the Student Union Rathskeller after the dogs were back in the kennel. My treat."

"I'll take care of it," Jason said gruffly. "Go on home."

Her face lost the glow it had had earlier when she'd been organizing the beagle parade. He told himself he didn't care.

She must have come in to work early the next morning, because when he got there he found her in the kennel, and she wasn't happy.

"This isn't Candida," she said flatly, scratching the imposter behind the ears.

Jason knelt beside Candida's run, careful not to touch Charity, hurting simply from being so close to her. "What makes you think it's not Candida?" he said. "She's in Candida's run and wearing Candida's collar." But as he tilted the dog's head up to look her in the eyes, he had a terrible feeling Charity was right.

"She doesn't look like Candida," Charity said.

Exasperated and tense, Jason looked out over the sea of beagles and snapped, "How can you say that? They all look alike."

Her air of stretched-out patience was even more annoying. "Not when you get to know them. However," she said, "I base my observation on more tangible evidence."

"Which is…"

"She didn't come when I called her," Charity said, "but dogs sometimes play that little game with you, so I didn't think anything of it at first. But when I got her attention and started playing with her, she didn't respond the way Candida does, and then came the clincher."

He could hardly wait to hear what the clincher was.

"Lionel won't have anything to do with her."

This got Jason's attention. He glanced over at Lionel, who was usually close to the barrier that separated his run from Candida's, ogling her. Today he was lying down in an attitude of despair with his back to Candida's run.

"Lionel, come on," he said to the dog. "Speak to Candida."

Lionel got up on his short legs, tossed his ears and stepped haughtily into his cage.

"She must have made him mad," Jason said.

"Maybe she flirted with Skip over here on her other side."

"Do you realize how silly you sound, *Doctor?*"

"Yes," Jason said tightly. "Ed?"

The young man came around from the other side of the room. He looked worried.

"Have any idea how another dog might have gotten into Candida's run?"

"Last night when we were dipping them, well, we had to take off their collars, of course, and I guess, ah, maybe…"

Jason groaned. He stood, already feeling tired, even though the day had barely begun. Mixing up the dogs could compromise the experiment. They'd have to start over. He couldn't bear to think about the delays.

"The first thing we have to do," he said, "is determine whether this is or is not Candida."

"You know she isn't." Charity spoke up quietly.

He turned on her. "Then find the real Candida," he said through clenched teeth, and stalked away to hide in his lab, wait for his chance to interrogate the work-study students who'd messed things up the night before, and establish a procedure for assessing the damage.

One small mistake, and the whole study could be screwed up. He might end up as a country vet sooner than he'd planned to, and he would have wasted two full years of his life.

Just as Charity felt she had. Everything seemed to be falling into place—the wrong place.

CHARITY FOUND Candida almost at once. There was no doubt in her mind when she found a female beagle looking anxious, as if she knew she wasn't where she was supposed to be. And when Charity called her name, the little dog responded at once, running up to her and panting ferociously.

Unfortunately, Charity found Candida in the control group of dogs that had not been inoculated instead of in the test group she was a part of. She knew what this meant—Candida could no longer participate in the study. Neither could the dog who'd been in Candida's run, although it was too much to hope they'd simply been switched.

She moved both dogs into quarantine cages. Then, with Ed at her side, looking as anxious as Candida, she moved from run to run, talking to the dogs, playing with them and looking for additional problems. The news worsened as she went along. Based on nothing more than her intuition and her knowledge of the dogs, she was pretty sure that Mojo wasn't really Mojo, either. And her heart sank when she found Jeremy, a test-group dog who was unmistakable due to a heart-shaped white spot on one ear, in the control group.

Four dogs at least, two males and two females, could no longer participate in the program.

"Oh, hell," Ed said when she showed him Jeremy's ear.

"Language," Charity reproved him.

He gave her a look that was a lot like the look Jason might give her in the same circumstances.

Looking pale and cold, Jason emerged from his lab with a plan of action. Each dog would have to be tested to determine its true identity.

"I'll stay here day and night to get the testing done," he said.

"You take the days and I'll take the nights," Charity said. "I insist on it."

"We'll talk about it," he said, not looking at her.

"I'll take the rejects home with me," Ed said, gesturing toward the quarantine cages. "I'll have to move, but that's okay. I'll call my dad and see if he'll help out a little on the rent. I'll look for a new apartment tonight. No, I guess it had better be a house. With a fenced-in yard." He chewed on his knuckles.

"No need to do that, Ed," Charity said. "I'll take them home with me."

Jason's look told her she was crazy. "They'll go with me," he said distantly. "I'd always planned to take Candida anyway, and Mrs. Appleby will be thrilled."

With a weak little laugh that had no heart in it, Charity said, "At last. Somebody else to eat Mrs. Appleby's dinners."

He glared at her. "Not on your life. It's bad enough

that I have to eat them.'' Unexpectedly he asked, ''How's Amos doing? And Rags?''

While she explained that Rags was doing better every day, and that Amos's frantic owners had arrived in tears at her house to pick up their lost dog, she gazed at him, trying to hide the longing she knew must be showing in her eyes. The man she'd always dreamed of finding was right there in front of her, and he was as inaccessible as the planet Jupiter.

13

CHARITY FOLDED her arms across her chest. "I'm not going home," she said. "I called the sitter and she's already at my house, one of the students brought me a pizza...with anchovies," she added, giving Jason a hard look, "and I'm staying here tonight."

"This is ridiculous," he said. "You'll be exhausted and no good to anybody."

"I'll have one bad night," she retorted. "I'll sleep tomorrow and by tomorrow night I'll be established on the new schedule."

"I insist on having the one bad night."

"I demand that you go home and leave me to my work."

It startled him. He didn't go home immediately. Eventually he left, she thought, just to get away from her.

She worked with the dogs for a couple of hours, and when she went back to her lab for a slice of rather chilly pizza, she discovered she'd missed a call on her cell phone. When she retrieved the call, it was from Faith, who sounded a lot like a two-year-old.

"I'm in my own bed at Mom and Dad's house,"

Faith said tearfully, "and I'm never getting out of it. Call me, okay?"

Chewing pizza and fearing the worst, Charity called.

"Hi, honey," her mother said, and at the sound of the familiar, comforting voice, Charity almost burst into tears herself.

"Faith called," she said. "What happened? Did she get fired again?"

"Much worse," Maggie Sumner said. "Just a minute. I'll put her on."

It was a struggle to follow the story, but it seemed that Faith, like Charity, was suffering from a broken heart. Charity could only listen, finish the pizza slice and make appropriate clucking sounds of sympathy.

"How are you?" Faith said at last, at which point Charity finally did burst into tears.

After they'd cried awhile, Charity said between sobs, "Where did we go wrong, Faith? It all seemed to happen so easily for Hope."

"Hope went through a rough spot with Sam," Faith reminded her.

"This is more than a rough spot," Charity said. "My relationship with Jason is over." Her voice broke.

"So is my relationship with Cabot, if you could even call it a relationship," Faith said, sniffing. "It helps to talk with Mom, but—"

"It helps to talk to the dogs, too," Charity said, realizing she needed to get back to her job, "but—"

"Yeah," Faith said. "But see, I can think of things you could do to make your relationship all right again."

"What? Should I take notes?"

"Thursday's Valentine's Day," Faith said. "Drown him in valentines. Leave them around everywhere. Buy him candy. Send him flowers. Write love notes on everything."

Charity drummed her fingernails on the lab counter. "Why don't *you* do that?"

"Oh, I couldn't possibly! Cabot is so cold and distant I'd feel like a fool!"

"Uh-huh," Charity said. "Like I wouldn't?"

When Faith finally ran down, it occurred to Charity that it wouldn't hurt to have Hope's practical take on the situation. Calls to Hope always went quickly. The dogs could wait another minute.

"The two of you should sit down with a counselor and negotiate. Put your deception right out there on the table, discuss fully and openly your reasons for doing what you did and—"

"This is love," Charity said, "not a hostile takeover!" She didn't merely end the call, she turned off the phone. It was clear that she needed to talk to her mother.

Too exhausted to do anything but sleep through Tuesday, she went to her parents' house Wednesday morning on her way home from the lab. To her surprise, Faith had gone home.

"She's feeling much better about Cabot," Maggie told her. "She's going back to her job to try to forgive and forget."

"And not get fired," Charity said.

"That too." Maggie smiled. "And I think with those two there's always the possibility of 'someday.'"

"I'm so h-h-happy to hear that," Charity said, and gave her mother her own sad story.

"I thought we'd be just like *Syngamus trachea,*" she sobbed. "The worm I did my dissertation on, remember? They mate for life. The male *fuses* himself onto the female's body. Doesn't that sound wonderful, to have a man fused to you?"

"I don't know," Hank said. Charity's father had come downstairs for coffee by then, and was hunkering over his mug like a man who desperately wished he'd gone out for breakfast. Perhaps slid down a rope from the second story of the house to avoid the kitchen scene altogether. At least he hadn't turned green.

"Maybe Jason just needs a little time to get used to the new you," Maggie said, hugging Charity and stroking her hair.

"Stupid fool," Hank muttered.

"That's putting it a little strongly, Hank," Maggie said, eyeing her husband with affection.

"And wrongly. He's a smart fool," Charity said glumly.

"Is he?"

"Oh, yes. And if I had it to do over, I'd go back to being the beauty and just let him be the brain and everything would have turned out p-p-perfectly." She ended in a wail.

"Now, now," Maggie soothed her.

"Well, Mom," Charity said, realizing that she didn't sound any more mature at the moment than Faith had on the telephone, "I was the one who was stupid."

"Then I guess you'll have to be the one to fix it," Maggie informed her.

"There's no way to fix it. It's broken forever."

Hank snorted, and Charity took time out from weeping to give him an indignant look.

"Let's think for a minute," Maggie said.

"Can you think and toast an English muffin at the same time?" Hank wanted to know.

Although in Charity's opinion almost anyone was capable of toasting an English muffin, even her father, Maggie got up and began forking a muffin apart. "I was thinking about you girls," Maggie said, "about the day you showed up at our front door." She smiled reminiscently. "You three were all scared to death, poor darlings, and wondering if we'd accept you. And you. You were like a porcelain doll in your white dress, with your beautiful black hair that Faith had brushed and brushed so you'd make a good impression. The baby of the family, the one Faith and Hope had decided was the beauty of the family, but in your eyes I could already see you were the brightest.'' She paused as if she were looking for the words to express her feelings. ''Already, at that age, you'd begun to question yourself and what you wanted to do with your life.''

Charity felt startled—because it was true. She remembered. She hadn't wanted to show up at the Sumners' house with perfectly brushed hair. She'd wanted to stand on the stoop and do her seven times table.

''And you're still doing it,'' Hank spoke up.

''So maybe it's time to give yourself some answers,'' Maggie said.

''This is getting sort of heavy,'' Charity moaned. ''Is now the time to decide if what I really want to be is the beauty instead of the brain?''

''Sounds like it,'' Hank said. ''You want to settle down to a vet's life with this Jason imbecile or be on the cover of whatever it was?''

''I told you already, he's not an imbecile!''

''Anybody who hurts you girls is an imbecile in your father's eyes,'' Maggie said. Her own eyes were twinkling.

''Well, what do I actually *do?*'' Charity grumbled.

''First, decide whether you want to be a supermodel and resign from the lab. Then you can just put

Jason out of your mind and time will heal your wounds.''

Her mother's complacent tone fired the opposite reaction in Charity. She realized all at once that she didn't have to think about it. She knew. She picked up the kitchen phone, dialed the agency and informed Saundra that she was turning down her big chance.

Saundra was squawking away when Charity had a sudden thought. Maybe it was time she lived up to her name, showed a little Charity. ''Saundra,'' she said between squawks, ''you represent Celine, too. She's the obvious choice for a *Vogue* cover.''

The squawks diminished in volume as Saundra pictured Celine on the cover of *Vogue*. It sounded as if she liked the picture. When Charity hung up, she felt better already. ''Now Jason,'' she said. ''What do I do about him?''

Maggie did some more thinking. The kitchen was quiet except for Hank crunching on his muffin. ''Right now he's looking at your weaknesses. Am I right?''

''I guess you could say that. He thinks I'm a lying, deceitful—''

''So you need to point out your strengths.''

''I don't have any.''

''You certainly have!'' Maggie exclaimed.

''I can cook,'' Charity said sullenly.

''That's a start,'' Maggie said.

''I like animals.''

"Even better."

"I look my best in red."

"Come on, Charity, you're deliberately—" Hank began, but Maggie's voice rose above his.

"Fine. See what you can do with those three things."

"That's it?" Charity leaped up from the kitchen table.

"No."

She sat back down again.

"You'll have to figure out what Jason's needs are, too. If you can coordinate your strengths with his needs, you'll win him back. I'm sure of it."

Charity looked at her with narrowed eyes. "What advice did you give Faith?"

"She told her," Hank said, "that maybe Cabot wasn't quite as much of an imbecile as I thought he was."

SHE'D DRIVEN all the way to her parents' house in Oak Park, and now she had to drive all the way back up to Antioch, just to hear that nonsense about strengths and weaknesses. What a waste of time. She should have been at home sleeping.

But she wasn't, and she had a long drive ahead of her. What did she have to think about besides strengths and weaknesses?

Jason liked to eat and she liked to cook. While this

was a pleasant coincidence, it did not a romance make.

Jason was a vet and she was a parasitologist who cared about animals. She supposed she could turn that into something—as long as the two of them were so constantly surrounded by animals that they wouldn't have time to communicate with each other. That would be romantic, all right.

Jason was a "brain" who…

…who'd said, "Do you ever wish they'd see that there's more to you than brain?" Was that Jason's real need, simply to be loved for himself?

By the time she got home she'd come up with an idea. Sleep would have to wait.

"COULDN'T HANDLE another pizza," Charity told Jason when they slid gingerly past each other that night and he couldn't help staring pointedly at the cooler she carried with her. Her tone was frigid, as it always was these days. Unless she was talking to the beagles.

Did she discuss him with them, he wondered? The way he'd discussed her with them after just one meeting with her?

It would be simply wonderful, he thought, if she was gone when he came back in the morning. It was painful to see her. She seemed more beautiful to him every day, beautiful, kind and tender with the beagles and a stickler for perfect work. Each time he stepped past her he had to run down the list of her lies and deceptions just to keep from throwing himself at her feet and begging her forgiveness.

He especially didn't want to see her in the morning because tomorrow was Valentine's Day, the deadline he'd given himself to decide whether to focus on the things he'd come to love about her or on the list of lies and deceptions, which he'd pretty much memorized.

But she'd still be there, he knew. She wouldn't leave until he arrived to take charge. They'd straightened out the dogs, Jason had taken all four of the rejects home with him and Mrs. Appleby was in hog heaven making homemade dog biscuits. The crisis was over, but he'd decided not to let another one happen.

The vaccine would be a success. It was far too early to announce it to the world, but he knew he had it right. All because of Charity.

Who had also— He ran quickly through the list of lies and deceptions.

The night went by, and he still hadn't made a decision. He needed sleep and wasn't getting any. Feeling grumpy, sleepy, frustrated, sad, mad and every other negative emotion he could imagine, he dragged himself into the lab.

There was no sign of Charity. He took off his coat, then went back to the kennel. He opened the door. He blinked.

Every beagle was wearing a bright-red ribbon

around its neck. God, he was such a sap. He felt something opening up inside him, felt a desperate need to list those lies and deceptions again, because he could think of only one person who would have put red ribbons on the dogs for Valentine's Day. But she wasn't in the kennel, either. Only Ed was there, giving him a sheepish smile.

When he went back through the reception area on the way to his lab, a cake of some sort sat on the desk where the cookie tin was supposed to be. She was determined to celebrate, apparently. What, he couldn't imagine. He would ignore the cake, at least until he could be sure she wasn't anywhere around.

So he walked past it and into his lab, and then walked right back out. The spicy scent emanating from the cake was irresistible. He'd also noticed a sign sticking out of it. You should never, he'd always thought, pass a sign without reading it.

The sign had been done on a computer. It said, "Jason Segal" and below that, "Doctor of Veterinary Medicine," and below that, "Patients of All Sizes Welcome."

He stared at it. It was stuck to a peppermint stick that rose out of the cake, which was a heart-shaped gingerbread, he thought, frosted and decorated with...

He squinted. If you approached it from the right angle, it looked like the outline of a cottage with crooked windows and a dangerously tilted chimney.

A cottage like Charity's cottage. A cottage for a

country doctor. His heartbeat quickened. He tried to summon up the litany of Charity's lies and deceits and couldn't.

He became aware of a presence in the room with him. He looked up to see Charity standing not far away, wearing a short, bright-red dress with very high heels. Her mouth was red, too. Her black hair shone as it swirled around her shoulders, and her eyes, her beautiful eyes the color of violets, were watchful.

"I'm not very artistic, I'm afraid," she said in the soft, musical voice he loved so much.

"You did fine. I'm not sure that chimney's going to draw, though." He was afraid to say any more, because he didn't have the words for what he wanted to say.

"Read your valentine."

He saw the corner of an envelope sticking out from under the cake. He pulled it out, half longing, half dreading to open it. But he did. Slowly.

It was a fairly typical valentine, hearts and flowers, a sentiment that wasn't too gushy, but she'd written a personal note under the message.

"To the sexiest man in the world. With my brains and your beauty, we could reach the stars."

He looked at her, and the only stars he could see were the ones in her eyes. She loved him. All of him. She didn't even think all that highly of his brain! Wasn't that what he'd wished for, longed for in a woman?

And look how much more she had to give him.

He knew what to do next. He opened his arms and gathered her in.

"I TOLD YOU I was taking you to the best restaurant between Madison and Chicago," she told him several hours later.

"And you did." He tucked her head under his chin and gazed into the flickering flames of the woodstove, the eyes of the many dogs and cats that surrounded them, and felt so contented it almost scared him. "When did you do all that cooking?"

"Last weekend. When I was depressed."

"You don't cook *just* when you're depressed, I hope. Because I can see a real downside to spending my life trying to depress you."

He felt her smile against his throat. "Think Ed and your sitter are doing okay with the dogs?" he said next.

"And with each other, maybe," Charity said. "I know the dogs will be fine. I'm glad we brought your beagles with us. They seem to fit in just fine. With blended families, you never know." She yawned. "I have to tell you, when I was daydreaming about the life we could have together, I imagined us sitting on this sofa talking about worms. I don't feel a bit like talking about worms."

He hugged her closer. "Last thing on my mind, frankly. Oh. One thing I'd like to do before bedtime.

Where's that flannel nightgown, the one with the buttons down the front?''

She drew back and gave him an oddly suspicious look. "Well, I suppose I washed it and hung it up in the closet."

He rolled up off the sofa, found the nightgown he could only remember with his fingertips and brought it back with him. Her eyes widened when he lifted the lid of the woodstove and dropped it in.

"Jason, what are you doing? That's my favorite…that's the gown I wore when…"

"That night didn't end well," he said quietly, settling in beside her and taking her back into his arms. "The rest of our nights will be a different story."

"A never-ending story," Charity murmured, and kissed him.

Epilogue

"WE SURVIVED," Maggie Sumner said as she sank down on the sofa beside Hank.

"Raising three daughters? Just barely." He put his arm around Maggie.

"I meant three weddings," Maggie said reprovingly. "Wasn't it just like them to insist on separate weddings and receptions?"

"They've never done anything the easy way," Hank grumbled.

"But weren't they beautiful brides?" Maggie sighed. "All three of them. So beautiful, so smart."

"So incorrigible."

"Hank!" A second later, Maggie said, "Hank!" again, but this time she gripped his arm.

"What!"

"I just realized," she said, "we're going to have grandchildren!"

"Ah," Hank moaned, sinking back into the pillows with his hand clasped to his forehead. "Ahhh..."

"Oh, Hank, don't be so dramatic."

"We're selling the house," Hank announced, his voice muffled by the sofa cushions he was attempting to hide beneath. "Moving to an efficiency apartment. Getting an unlisted number."

"Now, come on, Hank. It will be such fun. It's not as if they'll all come at once the way our girls did. Hank. For heaven's sake. Stop it this instant, do you hear me?"

Even as she scolded him, she smiled. Grandchildren! She could hardly wait.

Meet the Randall brothers...four sexy bachelor brothers
who are about to find four beautiful brides!

WYOMING WINTER

by bestselling author

Judy Christenberry

In preparation for the long, cold Wyoming winter, the
eldest Randall brother seeks to find wives for his four
single rancher brothers...and the resulting matchmaking is
full of surprises! Containing the first two full-length novels
in Judy's famous *4 Brides for 4 Brothers* miniseries,
this collection will bring you into the lives, and loves,
of the delightfully engaging Randall family.

Look for WYOMING WINTER in March 2002.

And in May 2002 look for SUMMER SKIES,
containing the last two Randall stories.

HARLEQUIN®
Makes any time special ®

Visit us at www.eHarlequin.com

PHWW

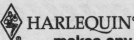

TRUEBLOOD, TEXAS

Coming in March 2002...

THE SHERIFF GETS HIS LADY

by

Dani Sinclair

Lost:

The joy of motherhood. Needing to convince herself that she made the right decision, Skylar Diamond hires Finders Keepers to find the baby girl she gave up for adoption all those years ago.

Found:

A grown-up daughter and an overprotective father. Sheriff Noah Beaufort doesn't like it when he discovers a high-society type watching his daughter, Lauren. But in spite of himself, he takes a fancy to the mysterious Skylar....

Do Skylar and Noah stand a chance together once he discovers her "secret"?

Finders Keepers: bringing families together

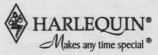